It was the *desire* that rose between them now, pushing back at Katie until she jerked herself free.

No. *Not free.* Hunger still washed over her skin, leaving a flood of warmth and fluttering sensation in its wake. It left her in thrall, aware of every whisper of air across her skin, every tingle of sensation. Maks lay heavy against her, leaving her aware of the soft flannel of his shirt, the muscle beneath, the breadth of his shoulders.

He was so big. He was *tiger.* What had she even been thinking, to haul him into her lap for healing?

What had she been thinking, to linger and to explore the whispering fugue of confusion clinging around him?

What the *hell* was she thinking, to look down into those green eyes and lower her mouth to his?

Books by Doranna Durgin

Harlequin Nocturne

**Sentinels: Jaguar Night* #64
**Sentinels: Lion Heart* #70
**Sentinels: Wolf Hunt* #80
**Sentinels: Tiger Bound* #142

**The Sentinels

DORANNA DURGIN

spent her childhood filling notebooks first with stories and art, and then with novels. After obtaining a degree in wildlife illustration and environmental education, she spent a number of years deep in the Appalachian Mountains. When she emerged, it was as a writer who found herself irrevocably tied to the natural world and its creatures—and with a new touchstone to the rugged spirit that helped settle the area and which she instills in her characters.

Doranna's first fantasy novel received the 1995 Compton Crook/Stephen Tall Award for best first book in the fantasy, science-fiction and horror genres; she now has fifteen novels of eclectic genres, including paranormal romance, on the shelves. When she's not writing, Doranna builds webpages, enjoys photography and works with horses and dogs. You can find a complete list of her titles at www.doranna.net.

SENTINELS: TIGER BOUND

DORANNA DURGIN

HARLEQUIN®

entertain, enrich, inspire™

Recycling programs
for this product may
not exist in your area.

ISBN-13: 978-0-373-88552-7

SENTINELS: TIGER BOUND

Copyright © 2012 by Doranna Durgin

Dear Reader,

To some extent, we're born who we are. We're formed and refined by our environment and experience, and if we're smart, we never stop growing.

Maks Altán and Katie Rae Maddox know what I'm talking about. Both are Sentinels, humans born with an alter ego tied deeply to their souls—an alter ego that eventually expresses itself in shape-shifting. Circumstances led Maks to change early and often; he and his Siberian tiger are much more deeply integrated than most. Circumstances drove Katie to a heightened sensitivity of her Chinese water deer nature—a rare prey shifter that makes her way too vulnerable in the midst of a warrior-like Sentinel society.

They knew who they were, right from the start. The question is, what can this deer and her tiger become—together? And can they overcome not only their beginnings and their natures, but their shared enemy plans for them?

Stop by my Facebook page or blog, and let me know what you think! www.dorannadurgin.com.

Doranna

To all the Wild Things.

Chapter 1

Maks clawed back to himself, hand braced against old brick, the quiet engine of a shuttle bus in the background... small-town street traffic passing nearby. Mortar crumbled beneath his fingers.

Not getting better.

Getting worse.

Not that he hadn't known it when he'd talked his way back into Sentinel field status—even if no one else had guessed.

"Mommy, look at that man!" said a young voice, bright and curious. "Is he going to throw up?"

"You never know." Brisk retreating footsteps drove the tight voice. "Let's leave him alone."

Maks opened his eyes, knowing it was too soon. Knowing that the red brick of the shuttle bus depot would strobe with his accelerated heartbeat, in and out of double vision, in and out of reality. He caught the merest glimpse of a little boy trotting away—pulled along a little too fast for comfort, casting a look over his shoulder, stumbling—

Maks growled. Softly, but a growl nonetheless—fighting the protective urge to pluck the boy up and away.

Control, Maks.

Not much of that lately.

Just as well that he could do no more than roll his shoulders against summer-warmed brick and focus on where he was and what he was doing here.

Katie Maddox. That's why he was here.

Katie Maddox, nominal field Sentinel…nominal visionary, plagued by uncertain portents. She'd wanted the Sentinel's Brevis Southwest region to look into it; she'd wanted brevis to watch her back. And the brevis consul— Nick Carter—had sent Maks.

Maks closed his eyes, breathing in the scent of hot pine and astringent air…turning his head to the breeze as it fingered his hair.

Home.

"Maks? Are you…Maks?"

Damn. He stiffened, knowing from the doubt in her voice that the fugue still showed on him. Probably *in* him, and to judge by the dossier he'd studied between Tucson and this little high-altitude forest town, she could well see it.

Then see to it that it's gone.

He played to the tiger within—a big cat in full stretch exuding lazy confidence and lurking strength. When he opened his eyes, there was a prowl behind them.

She recoiled a step. Light of foot, long of leg, perfect in balance—if she ran, she'd go far and she'd go fast. Her eyes widened, cinnamon brown, pupils big…straight brown hair with that same cinnamon tint spilling out of her doubled ponytail.

Yes. Katie Maddox knew he wasn't right—quicker than anyone at brevis, she'd picked up on the growing threat from within him. And she knew, too, that he'd just seen the same in her—that she wasn't the usual Sentinel. Wasn't a hunter, a power-leashed protector…a predator.

No. Katie Maddox was prey.

Katie Maddox, hold your ground.

She'd had years of practice. Years of growing up the only Southwest Sentinel who didn't take the form of something big and fierce and powerful, armed with fang and claw. Years of being bullied, pushed around…dismissed and ignored. Until she'd retreated from the Sentinels, moving out to this tiny, high-country timber town to start her own small business and live life on her own terms.

Until now.

She'd known he would be tiger. But she hadn't known it would shine through from him to her unpredictable seer's eyes—more than just chestnut hair with subtle black chunks nearly hidden in the shaggy nature of it, she could detect the hint of white at his temples that could well be mistaken for gray. More, too, than the size of him.

It was the intent in him. So completely quiet, and yet written there for the world to see.

Or just me?

She never knew.

But Katie didn't run, no matter the impulse of the deer. Her legs might tremble faintly with the restraint and her nostrils might flare with the effort, but she held her ground.

Because Maks Altán, Brevis Southwest field Sentinel, was the only help she was going to get.

She took a step forward, held out her hand, and smiled just enough to show the faint reflection of her own *other*—faintly elongated canines rested against her lower lip.

Full-blooded field Sentinel, no less than he.

Just *different*.

"Katie Maddox," he said, and his voice came from his chest, faintly rumbly and unexpectedly gentle, softened at the edges. Leaning against the wall with his head tipped back, he was bigger than she'd thought at first glance— mainly because he wasn't beefy, wasn't exaggerated or barrel-chested or overly built. Long legs, broad shoulders, the muscle all to proportion.

Tiger.

Don't think about it.

"I'm sorry I'm late," she said, glancing around Pine Bluff's shuttle bus depot. It was already empty of the few others who had disembarked with him in this high country cow town gone to vacation industry, smack in the middle of Sitgreaves National Forest. With fir and pine every- where and more vacation cottages than homes, the entire town stretched along one winding road and a few offshoot clusters. They rated a big box store and a Dairy Queen, but not a bus route...just a shuttle winding its way down to the valley and back. Here, Katie provided therapeutic massage and physical therapy to sick and injured animals from the entire region. It was a modest living, but she *did* make a living. It didn't hurt that she was a healer in truth, even if she was limited by the need to go unnoticed.

This man would never go unnoticed. Not for long. It was another reason she'd been surprised to learn he was com- ing in on the shuttle. "I can't believe brevis HQ couldn't spare you a car."

His glance sharpened, full of wild green. "The shuttle gives me time to think."

"To read about me, I imagine," she said, arms crossed in challenge before she thought better of it—and then couldn't believe herself. *This* conversation was where she wanted to go with their first meeting? This man she wanted on her side? The man she'd quickly assessed as being so close to his tiger, and a Sentinel with enough field experience to dress in the all-natural clothing that would take the change with him, simply as a matter of course.

And still she challenged him—because she had to know where she stood with this man. "Brevis must have given you my file—what did you think after reading my history? A marginal seer having the vapors over vague portents? Just like always?"

She braced herself for the response—and got only a mild frown. He lifted his chin briefly, eyes narrowing—and she saw, then, the strength of the tiger in him. Could see in her mind's eye the image of a big cat, making that vaguely impatient acknowledgment to something in its world.

"Whatever's going on, brevis sent me to keep it from being a problem for you," he told her.

Right. He probably didn't believe her, but he had a job to do and he'd do it. Not as good as she'd hoped. Not as bad as she'd feared.

Except there was something else…lingering in the air, tickling at her healer's instincts. Subtle and unfamiliar. She resisted the urge to shift a restless leg. So many little gestures, so many natural expressions, repressed in a world of Sentinel predators.

"My house has a little studio over the garage," she said, expert in the art of obscuring her own instinctive responses. "I thought we'd put you up there."

Maybe not so expert as all that, to judge from the look he gave her. Not so much challenge or annoyance as simply…*knowing.* That she was faking her aplomb, for one. That she'd found herself unexpectedly affected by his presence as a man as well as a tiger.

But she'd read up on him, too. He had no empathy, no special skills or connections. He was simply what he was—a big man with a tiger's speed and strength at his disposal. So it wasn't true *knowing*, that look. It couldn't be.

It was only *guessing*.

He didn't respond to her suggestion; he merely reached down and hefted, with absurd ease, the battered black leather duffel sitting beside him.

At least, until he faltered.

It was only an instant—a hesitation, his eyes closed and a sharp breath drawn—and then he straightened, so casually that only her modest healer's skills allowed her to discern it at all.

The wave of unfocused energy washed through him and faded out again.

"Are you—?" She stopped at his glance.

Not a man of many words. And not one who was going to talk about the moment. But she understood, now, as she imagined he understood, too. Why brevis had sent him here. A damaged Sentinel to help an inadequate and overreacting seer.

The Southwest Brevis consul no doubt figured they deserved each other.

"Be still." Jet ran her hands down Nick Carter's back as he leaned against his broad office desk. Her fingers searched out the cramping knots of muscle. She found the scar tissue deep within, almost-fatal wounds taking their time to heal.

Sentinels, she thought, weren't as invincible as they supposed themselves to be. Even the Southwest Brevis consul—their regional leader and her love—wasn't.

The night of *Core D'oiche* had taken much from them all. Fabron Gausto, the local Core *drozhar*, had escalated his enmity beyond the perpetual cold war against the Sentinels, striking a deep blow against the Southwest Sentinels. He'd used Jet to do it, ripping her from her natural gray wolf form.

He'd ravaged her pack.

"All of this pain," she said, her thumb holding muscle until the problem trigger point began to relax and thinking not just of Nick, but of her pack, of his wounded Sentinels, "because too many years ago, a certain woman had two husbands." Her voice slipped into recitation mode of the details she was still learning. "One was Roman, and one was a druid. And they had no TV."

Nick stiffened against a laugh. "No, that they did not."

She stroked practiced fingers along the length of muscle, easing it. "And the druid's son could use the earth to make things happen, and the Roman's son didn't like it."

"Lower," Nick murmured, which Jet took for agreement.

"So the Roman's son learned how to take powers from other things and store them in amulets."

Nick looked over his shoulder, surprised. His features were still sharp-cut in the wake of recovery; his hoarfrost hair had a sprinkling of actual gray at the temples. "Who—?"

"Marlee told me that," Jet informed him. She slipped away to pace along Nick's office window; Tucson's Old Town spread out before her. "She's sad."

He turned to sit against the desk and watch her, his expression implacable.

"She's sorry," Jet offered. Thinking of the young Sentinel woman who had been so deceived by the Core…and who had betrayed the Sentinels in turn.

But not to the end. Because of Marlee Cerrosa, Jet lived. Because Marlee, Core mole, turned on her makers, Nick lived.

"Jet," Nick said, and rubbed the side of his nose, wincing a little. "We can't trust her. And we can't spare the time to address her situation right now. She's safe; we're safe."

And a prisoner, right here in this building.

But Jet saw the look on Nick's face—the one that meant Nick's responsibilities to this giant pack called *Sentinels* weighed heavily on him—and she let that detail pass. She said instead, "So the Roman's son started the Atrum Core, and said it was to protect everyone from the druid's pack, even though the druid's pack hadn't done anything wrong yet. Just because they *might*."

"That's the story," Nick said. "But I doubt the Sentinels were perfect then, either."

"And the druid's pack said they would protect the land from the Roman's son, and they did."

"All these years," Nick said, looking out the window himself…visibly feeling the weight of *Core D'oíche*. Feeling the particular weight of…

"Maks," she said out loud, if not very loudly. "You're thinking of Maks."

He closed his eyes, took a breath. "By everything we know, he's ready." And then, because he wouldn't lie to her and she knew it, Nick added, "He's ready for *that* job."

"He still isn't right," she pointed out, as if Nick didn't realize the region's best bodyguard still hadn't fully recovered after the Flagstaff ambush prior to *Core D'oíche*— and after the six-week coma.

Nick turned away and headed back to the desk. Gleaming wood desk, thick carpet, bright windows and plants everywhere—this was the office of the man who commanded the entire region of the druid's modern sons and daughters. "He can handle this job."

Jet might have been the only one to hear the strain in his voice—or to know it for what it was. The weight of recent losses, recent injuries, recent betrayals. The weight of the decision he'd made about a friend.

Nick turned abruptly, his gaze the same sharp, pale green that had first sought hers in the Tucson desert—first *caught* her there. "That area is where we found Maks," he told her, maybe a little too fiercely. "That area is *home* to him. He's the best man for the job. And—just maybe—going home will help finish his healing."

Jet didn't know how. Not when she'd seen Maks's closed expression, the body language of a wounded predator trying to hide his weakness.

But because she'd also seen that look on Nick's face—heard that strain in his voice—she didn't say the words that came to mind.

What if you're wrong?

Chapter 2

Maks stood back in the bus shuttle parking area, giving Katie space to absorb what she'd so obviously understood. Her dismay shone clearly in those expressive healer's eyes—clearly enough for him to read. Brevis had sent her a wounded tiger, and thought it response enough.

But her attention quickly shifted beyond him, out to the small parking lot where the dark asphalt wavered in the sharp heat of the sun. Maks moved to her side, turning to face the parking lot.

He spotted a man and his dogs.

Not the classic Atrum Core minion, nattily dressed and tending toward swarthiness, easily passing for dark Mediterranean. And not one of Sentinel blood—that, Maks would have seen.

Just a man, one such as any Sentinel could readily handle—Chinese water deer or no. But still Katie had held her breath that quick instant, and still the man looked as though he thought he had some upper hand.

As if it pleased him.

At his side, two large Malinois leaned against their short leather leads, panting—their big upright ears swiveling, their bodies tense and alert. The man didn't seem to pay them much attention—and yet he wielded their presence like a weapon. "Katie Maddox," he said. "Have you got a new pet project?"

He meant Maks; he meant to be insulting. But Katie's response was steadier than Maks thought it might be. "As long as you're training dogs, Akins," she said, "I'll have plenty of *projects*."

"People are going to figure it out sooner or later," he said, as if she hadn't spoken. "The way you lie. The things you do. You'll pay the price."

Maks threw off the remnants of the recent fugue; he stood just a little bit straighter.

But Katie didn't need him. "People are going to figure it out sooner or later," she said, flinging the words right back at this man. "The way you abuse dogs—the harm you do. You'll definitely pay the price." The quick flicker of contempt on her face startled Maks—he hadn't imagined seeing it there, on features so open and thoughtful.

Anger darkened the man's face. "As if a fraud like you could tell an injury from an attitude problem. You've got nothing on me!"

"I will." Katie's voice held determination and promise. She turned abruptly to Maks, gesturing sharply at several cars lined up to face the little shuttle depot. Her face held an expression he wasn't inclined to disregard even if he'd had reason.

Akins might not have seen it, or he might not have cared. He took a sudden step toward Katie, hand outstretched to grab an arm, dogs triggered from alert to aggressive—their gazes locking on Katie, their tails gone stiff and quivery. "Don't you turn away from—"

Maks stifled the rumble in his own chest, but he didn't stifle the rest of it—one step forward, his head tipped to a warning angle, his eyes narrowing.

Akins snorted. "You and what army?" he asked Maks. "Do you really think these dogs are just for show?"

Maks didn't spare the animals a glance. He made of himself a physical shield, as he always did; he could stop the dogs if they went for Katie.

But they wouldn't.

Because the dogs were 100 percent smarter than their handler, and they'd seen in Maks what the handler had failed to see. One whined in sudden anxiety, licking his lips; the other flicked its ears back and forward and back again, alert but no longer aggressive. Submissive, both of them—no longer looking directly at Maks or Katie at all.

Akins felt it through the leads; he looked down and transferred his scowl to the dogs, shifting his grip on the leather to give it a good jerk—

"Don't," Maks said, quiet in the promise of it.

Akins opened his mouth, a snarl in the making and turned to Katie.

"Don't," Maks said.

The moment stretched out. Maks stood in it, absorbing the unremarkable features, sturdy build and bristling presence of the man. Katie's hand slipped around his elbow; the tremble of it betrayed her.

Akins's mouth tightened in frustration; he looked past Maks to Katie. "He won't always be with you."

"I think," Maks said, his very self-control a threat of sorts, "maybe I will."

Akins sneered by way of comeback and turned away, jerking the dogs to heel.

Maks eyed the man's hard stride, his stiff shoulders. "Whatever is between you," he told Katie, "that man will be back."

"He's the least of my problems." Katie's voice was as hard as the man's anger. "And he's not why you're here. I can handle him."

He shifted just enough to glance at her while keeping Akins in his peripheral vision. "You can," he said, no doubt in the words. "But while I'm here, you won't have to."

She took a deep breath, blowing it out in a soft gust. "Right," she said. "Of course. Just don't let the prospect of a good fight distract you from why I contacted brevis in the first place."

Akins headed toward the pine-lined curve of the entry to this small, offset strip of shops that would take him out of sight—but he hesitated there, glancing over his shoulder. Maks watched him, even as he gave the greater part of his attention to the woman beside him. "Katie Maddox," he said, "if I had *wanted* to fight that man, then I would be fighting." A hint of rueful honesty won out. "Not that he would have been a *good* fight."

"Uh-huh." She sounded far from convinced, already heading for the parked cars, cinnamon-touched hair bouncing with her step.

"Wait," he said softly, as Akins glanced into the spreading juniper bushes at the base of the trees then back at Katie, his dogs straining at their leads.

He'd put no command in his voice, and maybe that's why she responded, retracing her steps with her brow faintly drawn, her mouth impatient—and her gaze following his.

Akins said something harsh and low to one of the dogs. It sprang into the bushes in a sudden flurry of caterwauling and clouding dust; the second dog roared frustration, lunging against its short lead.

Akins regained control, hauling the first dog from the bushes, but by then Katie had breathed "Oh, *no*," before breaking into a run—quick, long strides, flashing legs, graceful arms—easily out-running Maks. The alarm of it bristled right up Maks's back as he hit his own speed and headed right for Akins and the dogs.

By the time he got there, Akins stood aside with an expression both smug and self-satisfied. Katie knelt at the curb, pale with horror. "That was a monstrous thing to do, Roger Akins! And why? Just to upset me? That's even worse!"

"Brago took me by surprise." Akins shrugged. "A powerful dog like this? It happens."

"You *made* it happen!" Distress choked her voice as she reached beneath the spreading bush. "You think I don't *know?*" Maks came to a stop between them, pushing Akins back by dint of his presence even as he saw what Katie cradled.

Rumpled black fur, soaked with saliva and blood, body twisted, eyes glazing and lip lifted in a lopsided sneer, exposing tongue and teeth in a gaping mouth; the little chest pumped in short, shallow breaths.

"It's just a *cat*," Katie said, full of dismay. "Does it really make you feel big to let your dog do this?"

"I've already said it was an accident." The words sounded bored. "Besides, you know as well as I do that it would have gone to the coyotes sooner or later."

"You *pig*," she said. "You horrible, horrible *pig*."

Akins only smiled, a tight and impenetrable expression, and Maks found himself wary, aware that Akins seemed to be waiting for something—and that they didn't want to be part of it. "We need to go," he told Katie. "We can take the cat."

"I'll only be a moment." She touched the animal between the eyes, lightly stroking short, shiny fur. She seemed oblivious to the small crowd gathering just across the parking lot, pointing and murmuring and upset—and obviously not willing to come any closer to the dogs. "You poor baby."

"Surely you want to get the cat to help," Akins said, his voice pitched loudly enough to include the crowd.

"You know damned well it's too late for that." Katie closed her eyes, took a deep and peculiar kind of breath—touching the cat between the eyes, her other hand resting so lightly on its broken body that she might not have been touching it at all.

The cat, too, took a deep and peculiar breath. And then it…didn't.

Katie didn't move, not for a long moment. Akins shifted as though he might come closer; Maks tipped his head in warning.

Katie wiped her hands on denim-clad thighs, and stood in a single fluid motion, one that held the same grace as her swift running stride. The glare she sent at Akins should have sent the man for cover.

"You *killed* it?" he said, his voice loud and his surprise unconvincing. "Just like that dog?"

She faltered, her flushed face gone pale and her body stiff, as if she saw the blow coming and couldn't do anything about it. *"That dog,"* she said, strain showing in her voice, "was terribly ill."

His sneer was back. "And it died on your table, under your hands. Just like the dog the month before, and before that it was, what…some sort of pet pig?"

Her struggle to stay above the moment showed on her face; her chin gave a single, betraying quiver. "You're a monster, Roger Akins, and you don't deserve those beautiful dogs of yours for one moment."

She turned on her heel and walked away, leaving the handful of onlookers big-eared and big-eyed on the sidewalk—and leaving Maks one step behind again. He looked at the cat; he looked at Akins. The man shrugged, all innocence, and Maks wanted to snarl at him.

But sometimes the quieter warnings were the better ones. He took a single step closer, a silent step—a meaningful step, in the face of Akins's sudden uncertainty—and then Katie Maddox was too far ahead of him to linger any longer.

He caught up with her as she outpaced the few onlookers who thought they might speak to her—calling her name, hastening to reach her. She headed past the car to the garden at the outside edge of the complex, sitting on the ornate wooden bench set in rock. Her followers might not have taken the hint at that, but when Maks glanced at them, it was enough; they fell back.

Maks joined her on the bench, quietly enough to hear it creak faintly under his weight—not responding to the single glare from behind her wet-lashed eyes and thinking, to his surprise, that they had something very much in common. In her own way, she was as much a protector as he was.

He pondered that, pushing away the lingering dissonance from the recent spell—feeling again the sting of the circumstances. The tiger who wasn't whole, coming to help the deer who hid from herself. *Marginal seer having the vapors over vague portents,* she had said, her tone faintly bitter.

And so her file had said. But Nick Carter had been plain enough. *She knows more than she thinks she does—and we can't afford trouble right now. You know the area. You're the best man I can send for this job. Go see what's happening.*

Of course, in the wake of *Core D'oíche,* Nick had few field agents to choose from. He'd been, Maks thought, not so much the best man as the *only* man.

Katie shifted suddenly, drawing Maks's gaze from its constant sweep of the area. Her expression, eyes still bright and cheeks still flushed, had shifted to annoyance. "I can deal with Roger Akins," she said. "He's certainly not why I called brevis." And she stood, unfolding with graceful ease to head back for her car.

"Katie," Maks said, without following—she stopped, turning back to him. "Why *did* you contact brevis?"

She closed her eyes, an acknowledgment of the question she didn't look quite ready to answer. "Please," she said. "Let's just go home. We can talk there."

"You want time to figure out how to deal with me." Still honest. Always honest…or else silent.

She offered the smallest of smiles as she reached a sporty-but-sensible little vehicle. She flipped open the back hatch, and stood aside so Maks could toss in his duffel.

It wasn't so much a polite move as it was wary. All in undertones, as if she didn't even realize it—always a certain buffer of distance between them; always a certain balance of readiness.

This particular car model no doubt worked just fine for a slender body that folded with limber ease. His own? Not so much. Maks leaned over and pushed the seat all the way back, giving the resulting leg room a dubious look before he eased himself into the available space. He groped for the seatbelt before he closed the door, knowing there'd be no room to find it afterward. His knees bumped the dash.

"Well," Katie said, and bit her lip. "We can check with brevis about renting something while you're here." She reached behind him, stretching—the rustle of clothing, the sweet scent of woman and prey combined, brushing up against him and—

"Here," she said, and maybe she'd already repeated it once or twice, nudging his hand with the seat belt buckle. Maks clamped down on it with such abrupt reflex that her breath caught—right there in his ear—and he swallowed hard. *So close. So sweet. So...*

What was he even thinking?

She sat back behind the wheel, her hands quiet in her lap. Not reaching for her own seat belt at all. "Maybe," she said, "this was a mistake."

He turned on her with more ferocity than he'd intended, then desperately swallowed it down.

Because it didn't matter if she carried the faint scent of something he might well hunt, and it didn't matter that her movement mesmerized him. Maks had grown up protecting the weak, the small, the injured...he had made it his life. Before he'd even spoken fluent English, he'd conquered his instinctive responses to such factors. So it *shouldn't* matter.

He managed to gather his thoughts. "It's not a mistake to ask for help. Or to give it."

She sat a moment longer, hair spilling free of the careless waterfall at her nape, a ponytail running through elastic and then half again, the ends spraying free in cinnamon undertones that matched her freckles and brows and eyes. Searching eyes, large and dark-lashed, irises rimmed with chocolate. She finally reached for her own seat belt. "I don't think it's going to be that simple."

Maks couldn't argue that.

He barely watched the road as they drove the mile to the first turn—but then, he never watched the road. Oh, he could drive and he could navigate. But it had never been natural...never been a part of who he was. They'd been too late in finding him for that.

Pine Bluff was a small town with a single wide, meandering main street; one turn took them onto narrow asphalt, another onto dirt. They passed a house set far back in the woods, then another; after a third, they came to a straight quiet stretch and Maks rolled his window down to take in the scents of the place. All the green, all the fir and pine, all the sharp, dry dust and a thick overlay of dried needles breaking down black over silty soil.

Not a tiger's native land...unless that tiger happened to be Maks.

The dirt road ended without fanfare, turning into the stumpy driveway for a well-worn log cabin tucked in among the trees. It was old enough to precede the existence of manufactured log homes; old enough for the trees to crowd it, ponderosa pines looming tall.

She cut the little car's engine, and they sat in silence for a moment.

Maks breathed.

Maybe for the first time in a long time.

"I need to do some fire clearing," Katie said finally.

Maks pulled himself from *being* to thinking—to applying himself to Katie's situation. Unlike many Sentinels, he had little in the way of additional talent. He could handle shields; he could create faint boundaries, and knew when those were crossed. He couldn't heal, or see and manipulate wards, or sense subtle amulets. He had no clear mind-voice—only a few words conveyed with much effort, and the habit of sending impressions and concepts that didn't always make an impact on the intended recipient.

Of course, there was the silence. A gift from his early years, born of necessity and seldom used. But not even the best tracker—using Sentinel gifts or Atrum Core amulets—would discern his psychic scent if he went silent.

It wasn't likely to be of any use in the protection of Katie Maddox. His mouth twitched; he returned his full attention to her, finding her paused and waiting, fully aware of his wandering thoughts.

She pointed through the windshield. "This is where I started. The road turns into a trail…cuts through to the forest land. Bikers, hikers, horseback riders…it's a trickle this time of year. You never know when someone might toss a cigarette, so I cleared out the deadfall—but the stuff near the house…" She shrugged, shoulders eloquent. "That job has always been bigger than I am."

"But you've worked on it," he said, seeing the signs. Areas where the smaller trees had been thinned, the space between them cleaned of the ladder fuels that would leap-frog a fire straight to the house.

"I love this place," she said simply, looking down at hands that, indeed, bore calluses; she probably didn't even know about the smile curving her mouth, or the way it brushed light into her eyes. "After the Chediski-Rodeo fire pushed right up against this town…" She brushed her hands off. "Well, I may not be able to do it all, but I'd be a fool not to try."

"Is that what you thought when you contacted brevis for help?" Maks asked. "Only that you would be a fool not to try?"

She'd reached for her door latch. Now she let the door finish its opening arc, but made no move to get out of the car. Her face had stilled. No smile, no light. And no flinching. She studied his face a moment, and then nodded. "Yes," she said. "Because I couldn't not try. No matter what I expect."

Maks had never learned the art of layered conversation; it wasn't in his nature or his nurture. Not when survival meant clear action and clear communication. "I don't know what you *expect*," he said. "But you asked for help. I'm here to give it."

She laughed, short but light. "Your cleared field profile is a study in contradictions and things unsaid. But it doesn't make me think you're the right one to deal with this. With *me*."

He tried not to feel the sting of that—the accusation.

Or the truth of it.

Although maybe not for the reasons she thought it.

She must have seen it anyway. She bit her lip, a single canine briefly peeking out, and looked down at her hands, fingers brushing over the calluses. "I'm sorry. But you must see it. You're a *tiger*. And me, I'm…" She shrugged, hands tightening around each other as she looked out her side window. "I'm a deer. A Chinese water deer. I'm what you might eat for lunch, if I wasn't—"

She didn't have to say the words; he knew what she was. *Sentinel. Borderline seer. Most times human.*

Her mouth took on a tight set. "I told myself I wouldn't get my hopes up. I knew they wouldn't take me seriously—and they didn't. They sent a man who's barely off medical. Who's going to spend all his effort fighting the instincts we all have."

He made a noise of protest, wanting to say that he was off medical and that he'd gotten his instincts well tamed long ago—

Except he'd already come to the same conclusion about his assignment here and he knew better about his field status.

She didn't notice the protest, too wound up in her own words. "Instincts I've had my fill of already, or I wouldn't be way out here trying not to get visions and using my healing on people's *dogs!*"

Deer. Small, dog-size deer, at that. What had it been like for her, growing up among young predators? Jostling her, crowding her, making comments and insinuations...

Maks couldn't guess. He hadn't had the chance to be among them at all.

"Katie," he said, trying again—and earned a sharp glance for invoking her name. "Maybe you're right." That slowed her down, all right. "Maybe I'm all they had to send. Things are bad there since—"

Core D'oíche. The night that death and destruction had unfolded throughout the Southwest region at the hands of the Atrum Core—only a month ago at that. Maks had been barely recovered enough from the earlier Flagstaff attack to do his part.

And Katie, gentle healer with seer's eyes, had been so spared by that night that she didn't truly understand. Had she even dreamed it, marginal seer that she was?

He shook his head. He took a breath. "I'm all they could spare," he repeated firmly. "But it doesn't matter."

She narrowed her eyes at him, darkening the cinnamon with shadow.

"I know this area. I *know* it, in ways you can't—" He stopped, closed his eyes. Drew breath—the pines, the cedar, the blur of time and memory. Tried again. "This is my place, these woods. I can keep you safe while you figure out the things you've seen."

She watched him with eyes that remained unconvinced. She watched him as a creature on the edge of flight—emotional, if not literal. Far too aware that he skirted the edge of things that mattered deeply, but unable to interpret his emotions. And not knowing, after all, how seldom he came to such truths with others.

Maks grumbled—disgruntled, wordless again. It often happened that way; always had. He'd spent too much of his life without words at all.

A flicker of movement reflected in the passenger side-view mirror—Maks focused on it, found a man in a garish orange-and-lime shirt hesitating behind them on the road, one leg bracing his mountain bike. Found him, and reacted to him.

Just as Katie reacted to Maks, recognizing instantly that his inner timbre had changed—moving away from him and up against her door. "I told you…people use this road."

Maks kept his gaze on the mirror. "Do you know this man?"

She shrugged. "Lots of people ride here. My neighbor—Williams—he comes this way all the time."

He glanced away from the man just long enough to find her gaze—the faint annoyance there, the fears. He felt his own annoyance rise to meet it.

"I don't have any special side talents," he told her, patience thinning. He returned his attention to the man, who had peeled off into the woods onto what must be a rough deer track. "I do one thing—I'm a protector. And I do that well."

She hesitated. "I didn't mean to insult you. I—"

"You just want me to do this your way."

Her hands closed over the calluses again. "I just…" She shook her head. "I just want to believe. I want to know that someone hears me."

He turned on her, a surge of frustration and ferocity, held back until it came through only his expression, a blow he didn't pull when she caught her breath. "That's why I've *come*. That's what I *do*."

The man on the bike disappeared from sight, his outrageously flashy shirt no longer peeking between the trees.

Maybe just a man with attitude, triggering Maks's innate response. Maybe related to Katie's vision, maybe not.

One way or the other, Maks would find out.

That's why I've come. That's what I do.

Katie took a deep breath as she slipped one foot out the open car door and onto solid ground. *Don't antagonize the tiger.*

And, just as sensibly, don't antagonize the man who's here to help you.

Maybe he was right. It didn't matter exactly what he believed of her. He had his own reasons for working with her.

An object thudded lightly against the bumper, moving up the back hatch window in a blur of motion followed by tiny skittering sounds on the roof.

Maks reached for his door handle in response; a touch on his arm stopped him. She nodded at the windshield, where the marmalade yard cat stalked to the bottom of the windshield and plunked down, curling his tail around his body to offer them a unique perspective. "Maks," she said, more than relieved for the change of focus. "Meet my cat's ass."

Maks gave the cat's ass an unreadable look.

"Used to be a tom, when I moved into his yard," she said. "Still pretends he is." A glance. "You're not going to squirm, right?"

His growl was as eloquent as any glib word. She laughed.

And stopped short as she recognized just how quickly she'd dropped her guard.

The realization froze her breath in her chest. She'd been living here away from Sentinels too long, and she'd forgotten how to protect herself from them—and now the most Sentinel of them all was *right here.*

Maks turned green eyes on her, hampered by the way

he filled the seat, his legs cramped in the foot well. There was no sign of what she'd seen at the shuttle bus depot—the hesitation, the faint confusion…the faltering. It changed his face entirely, bringing out the strength of eye and brow and jaw.

"Katie," he said, as directly as was his wont. "I said… you are safe with me."

And he took her hand.

It seemed an absent gesture. It didn't stay that way. Not with her hand cradled in his, his thumb brushing the calluses, his fingers warm and—

A deep groan, a sharp breath, warmth and scent and swirl of feeling—

Katie stiffened. *No, no, not—*

A touch at her waist, a hand gripping the curve of her hip, fingers brushing sensitive skin and heat skirling down through her body—

A cry. Rough and masculine, wrung from a body in both pain and ecstasy.

Fingers clamped down on hers. Katie jerked away with a gasp—freeing her hand, freeing her mind from this predator, so much more powerful than she—his pupils gone big and his body clenched. Understanding flooded his expression—of that unexpected invasion, of their fleeting connection…

Of the astonishing and unexpected intimacy.

Katie, Chinese water deer, long of limb and quick in flight, could only gape back at him—the tiger, roused and filling her small car. She couldn't find words.

But it was Maks who ran.

Chapter 3

Maks didn't go far. Not with the log cabin before him and the surrounding woods beckoning of *home*. He stood there, caught up by it—breathing it in, feeling the very ground press up against his feet as if to claim him.

Katie approached him from the side, stopping some distance away and dropping his massive duffel there in a studied attempt to remain casual in spite of the moments in the car. "You do love this place, don't you?"

Maks glanced at her. Only a smoldering undertone remained of what had passed between them in the car. "Whatever I am," he said, "these woods made me."

And the Core. The Core, too, had made him, whether they'd meant to or not.

Katie laughed, short and rueful. "Whatever I am," she said, "the Sentinels made me. Whether they want what they got, I couldn't say." She brushed non-existent dirt from the front of her lightweight hoodie and, before he could find a response to her comment, asked in a completely different tone, "Are you hungry? I've got some steaks."

It took a moment, but he suddenly got it. She was, in her own quiet way, apologizing for his reception. He gave her a slow smile. "Thank you."

He wouldn't mention how recently he'd learned to eat his meat cooked.

He stopped just short of her porch. The cat stalked on ahead with its tail straight in the air and a dignified air that proclaimed the utter coincidence of their mutual destination. "Why did you call brevis, Katie?"

She gestured vaguely beside her head, frustration evident. "No real specifics yet. No details. Just this feeling that things aren't right." She met his gaze head-on for the first time since the bus shuttle station. "But, Maks...they *really* aren't right."

"Not Akins?"

She waved a dismissive hand, the gesture graceful. "That's personal. I recently told a second client that her dog had shoulder and neck injuries from rough handling. I didn't know it was him either time. In fact, the first time, I thought it was the owner." Her expression grew darker. "Worse, I'm certain he's using strays to bait his dogs— just like that cat. Reporting him without evidence would just make me look petty—but I *know*." She gave him a defensive glance.

"Did you help them, then?"

"Did I—" She stopped, uncertain—as if orienting herself to the conversation they were having and not the one she'd thought they'd be having. "Over time. I probably could have done more, been faster, but then..." She gave her hands a rueful look. They were strong hands, with long fingers and blunt, strong nails. "Then people would notice."

"They come here? Your clients?"

"I have an appointment this afternoon—a surgical recovery, and he's doing great." Her face had shed its inhibitions, its tight concerns—her eyes now full of spark, her mouth expressive. "I'm really excited about that one—I think I can make a real difference to his recovery time. At least, if he stops eating things that no dog should eat, which is why he had surgery in the first place. And," she made a face, "the second."

He did it without even thinking—reached out to touch her, a brief brush of his hand over her arm, drawn by that spark in her eye.

She stopped short, startled, and before he could apologize, she shook her head. "You," she said. "One moment you're standing there in classic John McClane pose, the next you're…you're…" She shook her head, fingertips lingering on her lip.

And Maks could only say, "John McClane?"

She sent a skeptical look his way. *"Die Hard,"* she said. "Lone man stands against overwhelming odds. Looks heroic a lot."

He could only shrug.

She shook her head. "You had a long trip," she said. "Let's eat, and I'll try to explain my whole vision thing." Her mouth compressed, no less the beautiful for its determination. "However little brevis thinks of it, *I* know there's something brewing." She took the porch steps with the quiet squeak of tired wood under a soft tread, and reached for the screen door handle.

The cat at her feet gave a sudden little spit, flattened its ears and ran off. Maks would have remarked on it, had Katie's hand not faltered before reaching the door, had her face not paled, her gaze gone wide, her pupils rushing to huge.

A faint electrical tingle skittered across the back of

Maks's neck, raising the hair on his arms. He leaped for her, wrapping his arms around her to swap places, shoving her away from the door—all the things he should have done those months ago in Flagstaff to protect his team from the attack that ravaged them. "Katie!" he said, and when she showed no awareness of him, adding a little shake. "Katie!"

She blinked, and saw him again; her pupils closed down against the bright high-altitude day and its impossibly blue sky. She went wide-eyed at the sight of his arms around her, the alarm on his face. "Maks? What—?"

"You're all right," he said, and couldn't quite bring himself to step back from her, his mind still reverberating with memory. *His hand reaching for the hotel door in Flagstaff...the agony of the Core ambush...the darkness and the lingering fugue...*

"Oh," she said, and a healer's understanding crossed her face. "Oh," she said again. "You *do* still need to heal."

He managed to pull away. "Brevis medics have done what they can."

"Except maybe to give you time." She said it with some asperity, her annoyance aimed at brevis again—but only briefly, as uncertainty took over. "You know...maybe I can help."

He couldn't help but send her a startled look, still reacting to what he'd seen—and to what he remembered.

"It's what I *do*," she said with some asperity, her words an obvious echo of his response to her in the car. "You know—healer?"

He didn't even think—he stepped back, his body language defensive, his eyes alarmed. As if he would ever let her be so vulnerable, when he had no idea what was happening within himself—and when whatever had just happened at the doorway still lingered in the air.

"Never mind," she said, just a little too quickly. She

looked away, biting her lip so a faintly pointed incisor peeked out as she reached for the door again.

Not just yet. "What," he said, and put a growl to it, "was that?" He stepped between her and the door, nodding at the handle she'd touched before.

For a moment, she stared blankly at him, as if she'd simply forgotten all about her pale little frozen spell at the door. Then she said, "Oh. *That.*" She made a little face, nose wrinkling dismissively even as her eyes held hurt. "That's as close as I get to having a true seeing. No real details, just…feelings. Something waiting to happen." She shivered, buffing her arms in the cool overhang of the porch.

"Here?" He lifted his head, eyes narrowed—raking the brightly sunny edge of the woods with his gaze.

"Close enough," she said. "I never see things at a distance. And, Maks…" She shivered again, and said the words reluctantly, as if bracing herself for the blow of disbelief. "It tastes like old iron…it smells like death. And it scares the hell out of me."

Katie waited for the usual dismissive response—to her fear, to her vague portents.

Maks only looked back out to the woods. His was a still and predatory strength; the breeze plucked at his flannel shirt with the sleeves rolled up tightly over his biceps, stirred his hair to show the black streaks within dark chestnut. Katie didn't let his half-lidded eyes fool her; she knew the sight of a big cat in utter concentration. She knew, too, when he came back to the here and now, could all but hear the deep rasping huff of a tiger's released breath. Whatever he'd been looking for, he hadn't found it.

She pulled herself together, feeling the sting of his skepticism—but her response went unvoiced as they both re-

acted to the wayward clink of clay pottery, barely audible at
the back of her log house. *Unmistakable and invasive.* Her
ears strained to flick back; her foot lifted from the ground
in an instinctive, nervous gesture—her body's way of telling her to flee and check the situation from a safe distance.

Maks had different instincts. He acted on them in an
instant, ignoring the steps to vault over the porch rail, jar-
ring Katie to scramble after him. He was faster than she'd
expected, but no match for her own swift legs—she would
have overtaken him at the corner had he not thrust out an
arm to prevent it, stopping short with an agility she'd an-
ticipated no more than his speed.

He peered around the corner, blocking her view. She felt
the disgruntled rumble in his chest more than she heard it,
and only then realized she had pressed against him—trying to see what he saw, heedless of his warm and predatory presence.

On her tiptoes, she could just see over his shoulder to
the man fussing at her window. Dressed in camo below,
black T-shirt above, he looked uneasy and nervous, looking over his shoulder to check the woods behind him. And
he had the hard features, dark olive skin tone and flashing
silver earring that marked him as Atrum Core.

Even as Katie understood, stunned, that this man had
come in from the trail, that he had clearly and clandestinely
targeted her very own home, the man quite suddenly realized he was no longer alone. He fumbled a small, heavy
object, and it fell into the tufty grama grass as he jerked
away from the window to face Maks.

Maks didn't react at all. Just…watched.

A shiver of recognition tightened Katie's chest. *Tiger.*
Waiting for the prey to make a mistake.

The prey bolted.

He stumbled a little, grabbing at one of the many pockets in his fatigues, but he still hit a full-speed sprint for the edge of the woods.

Maks didn't seem to hurry. He didn't *seem* to move at all. And yet suddenly there he was, flowing forward—one moment the man, then a bright silvery flicker and swirl of his change—synthetic shoes left behind, all-natural jeans and shirt carried along with the shifting energies.

The tiger on the run. In her yard. Huge. *Immense.*

And so very fast.

He sprang forward in twenty-foot bounds that took him swiftly through the thin trees to his quarry. One massive paw swatted the man into a tumble and roll, and the tiger doubled back to pounce, slamming a heavy blow down on the man's thigh with claws unsheathed just enough to prick.

Katie fought the impulse to take the deer and flee—dog-size and rabbit-fast, her tusks no more than a sharp-edged hint but enough to take some humans aback. *Not with a tiger in the yard.* What had she even been thinking, to follow Maks so closely?

The man squirmed beneath that paw; the tiger's lips lifted in a silent snarl of warning. He lifted his head to look at Katie—directly at Katie—and she felt an unexpected trickle of comprehension.

He wanted her to do the talking. To be the human.

She took a deep breath, hunting for the mantle of implacability she'd cultivated so assiduously during her training years. *You don't frighten me. This situation doesn't frighten me.*

She stepped out into the scattered pines and high prairie grasses.

But she'd taken only that single step when daylight flared into a sickly green light, a soundless explosion of corrupted Core amulet energy. She cried out, covering her eyes—ducking, as if it could do any good. Or as if it mat-

tered at all at this distance—close enough to hear the tiger
grunt, flinging itself aside to land crumpled, stunned—
and human.

Amulet ambush. Just like the one in Flagstaff that had
wounded Maks's team, had sent him so deeply into a coma
for so many weeks—

Please, let it not be that bad.

The intruder scrambled away, tossing aside the used
amulet and jerking out a small gun from concealed carry—
pointing it straight at Maks and pulling the trigger without hesitation in a sharp, short report. Maks's body gave
a little jerk.

Katie gasped—and then she was running, her legs
swifter than she'd ever meant them to be, bringing her so
close, so fast—close enough to see the startled expression
on the man's face, to see the gun as he brought it to bear
on her. She froze, staring back, forgetting to breathe entirely—seeing his body tense, seeing his intent, his finger
on the trigger.

But the man didn't shoot her. He cursed, looking from
her to Maks, and then he snarled in frustration—right before he bolted for the woods, his gait hampered by a new
and definite limp.

He didn't shoot me.

He didn't—

Katie shook herself free from the shock of it and ran
to Maks's twisted form. She laid a tentative hand on his
shoulder—feeling instant relief at the life throbbing beneath her healer's hand. The Core working hadn't been
profound—the lingering stench of its energies told her
that much—and the bullet hadn't been instantly mortal.
And that meant, given a Sentinel's amazing constitution,
it likely wouldn't be.

Or so she thought, until she saw the steady pulse of arterial blood soaking the flannel shirt above his elbow. *It shouldn't be this way.* Not with a Sentinel's body, normally so fast to address such critical injuries.

But when she reached to stanch the wound, Maks snatched her hand in mid-reach. He rumbled deeply in a tiger's warning, the snarl turning handsome features harsh, his gaze never focusing on her at all—nothing but wounded instinct, defensive and striking out. Her hand twisted back most cruelly in his grip; she bit her lip on a cry of pain.

Prey knew better than to make a sound of the wounded while in a predator's grip.

After a frozen moment still punctuated by that tiger's warning, she used the warm slickness of his own blood against him, twisting within his grip until her hand popped free.

He rolled over, hands clutching at his head, the rumble turned to nothing more than a man's low groan.

"Ohh, no," she breathed. "Get back here." Even a Sentinel would fail to recover from bleeding out. But the amulet injury, no matter how mild, came first. *Had* to, with this man who was still recovering from the last ambush, or she could lose him before she even started. To judge by his vague and distant gaze, she had little time indeed.

Katie pulled his hands away from his head—oh, his blood everywhere—and replaced them with her own, fingers threading into the hair above his ears. "Maks," she said, her voice low and barely quavering at all, her resentments and disappointments forgotten. "Look at me."

Not that he could, with his focus dazed and shifting, a wrenching panic creeping in behind the wild green. The flutter of it bloomed to life between them, a stab in Katie's own chest—his confusion, his instinctive urge to fling himself into the tiger and run from this threat. And then his fear when that, too, slipped away from him.

But Katie held him tightly. She slipped into the lightest of trances, grounding herself with his gaze—sliding into the same state from which she worked every day and then further, drawing on the healing potential that lived mostly untapped within her. Beyond the comfort for easing muscle, for generating the subtle knit of flesh that a vet might mistake for an exceptionally successful rehab. A deeper connection, reaching beyond body to soul.

The energy of it came through her in gentle waves, insinuating itself into the rhythm of her breathing.

Maks jerked away from her—or tried. He twisted uneasily; he closed his eyes and turned his head aside—or tried. But she held onto him with a strength well beyond the physical.

Breathing. Touching. Connecting...

His rumbled warnings faded, his breathing quite suddenly synched to hers.

Touching. Connecting. Understanding...

Wanting.

He blinked a few times, hard and fast, his eyes widening—and then he was looking at her again. Looking *back* at her.

The lingering buzz of connection should have faded instantly away; it didn't. She floundered, decided to fake it... and when she smiled at him, he frowned in such befuddlement that she couldn't help but laugh just a little. "There," she said. "You're back. Now just lie still a moment."

He had no intention of it; she saw it in his eyes, and caught him just in time—a firm hand on his shoulder when he would have come upright. "You've been hurt," she told him, a commanding, if understanding, tone. "And you're not healing properly. *Lie still.*"

For the merest instant, he allowed it. And then alarm—the full awareness of where they were and what had happened—crossed his features. He rolled away from Katie, lightning quick—coming to his knees to search for the intruder, full of fierce and fury.

"He's gone, but—"

Katie bit off her words as another kind of surprise passed over Maks's face, waiting in both resignation and impatience. His eyes rolled back, his body went limp...he folded back to the ground with a boneless grace.

She glared down at his unconscious form and finished what she'd started. "*But* you've lost a lot of blood, so you'd better just...lie...*still*."

Maks opened his eyes to an ultra-blue sky overhead, the upper branches from the wide-spread pines just barely intruding on his peripheral vision. His head rang with a strange and distant ache, his arm hurt like hell and an unfamiliar, comforting presence lingered in his mind, echoing through his body like an intimate touch.

Katie sat cross-legged beside him, matter-of-factly wiping her hands on a red-blotched towel. A rusty stain brushed one cheek, and her doubled-up ponytail ends had largely escaped to cascade over her shoulder, shiny and straight and in complete disarray. She dropped the bloody towel into a metal mixing bowl and picked up several others to toss in on top of it. Only when she leaned over Maks to reach for some wayward item did he clear his throat.

She jumped, snatching up yet another soaked towel as she jerked away.

"What?" he asked, although it didn't come out very clearly.

She didn't have any trouble understanding him. "A Core soldier," she said. "He had an energy-blast amulet. It hit you pretty hard, but you're okay now. And when were you going to tell me that you don't heal like a Sentinel should? I mean, yes, more than *human* normal, which is why you're still in my backyard and your bullet is in my mixing bowl." She lifted a smaller metal bowl, shifting it so the bullet rolled. "But not enough to stop that arterial bleed on its own. Enough to recover from the blood loss, I hope, because getting you a transfusion would be a bitch."

Maks closed his eyes, considering the circumstances—remembering what he could of recent moments. *A blast of energy, painful and bright, insinuating itself into the very fissures of a damaged soul. The sense of retreat—the despair of familiar wounds.*

And then…*breathing.*

Breathing, imposed over his…calm and anchoring… intimate. Healing. Bringing him back.

Some sense of it still lurked within him. Some sense of her.

He absorbed it all in silence, and then let out a deep breath to admit, "I didn't know. Not about the healing." When she frowned, her elbow on her knee and her gaze steady on his, he added, "No one thought to shoot me and see."

She scoffed, flicking a hand out to lightly smack his shoulder—and then, looking a bit startled at herself, said, "Well, the bullet's out, and I've protected you from infection, but…we need to keep an eye on how fast you heal. We need to know what you're dealing with."

Had they known? The Sentinel medics? Had they even suspected?

Then again, Maks had been well on his way to being perfectly recovered on the day they cut him loose. Only afterward had the fugues crept back in.

"Maks," she said, a little too patiently—by which he knew his thoughts were still wandering and unfocused. "It's important. Tell me you're going to cooperate on this."

He said, "Yes. The healing. I'll let you know."

She snorted, a feminine sound. "I think I'd best keep an eye on it myself."

A complete contradiction, Katie Maddox. One moment timid, the next bursting out with matter-of-fact confidence. And even on the heels of the thought, she startled him again, frowning. "He didn't shoot me," she said, as if it puzzled her.

Shoot her? The Core agent? But Maks had left her in a safe place—at the house, at a distance. He sat up—if slowly, leaning hard on his good arm; the lingering weakness didn't soften his voice. "What do you mean, *shoot you?*"

She flushed, wiping her hands against the sparse and stemmy grass. "I wasn't thinking," she said. "When he triggered that amulet, I ran in to—well, I don't know what I was going to do. But I was here—and he *wanted* to shoot me, he really did. But he didn't do it."

Maks had no words for that. For what she'd done—for his horror at it. But she saw it on his face, clear enough.

"I wasn't *thinking,*" she repeated, defensiveness creeping into her voice. "And I'm okay. I just—it seemed strange. Why *not* pull the trigger? And what was he doing here in the first place?"

That, indeed, was a most excellent question. "We'll find out," he told her, and untangled his legs to stand.

"Oh—hold on…" Katie reached back to grope at the ground, impossibly graceful in that awkward position. When she straightened, she'd retrieved a scarf—a decorative thing, long and narrow and awash with artfully smeary green. "You'll want a sling, I think—at least until we can see how fast you'll heal."

And broadcast the weakness? He shook his head. "I'll be careful."

Her hand tightened around the scarf, knuckles just white enough to give away her frustration. "Maks," she said, and the next words seemed to get stuck for a moment. But not forever, though she had to look away from him. "I thought I was going to lose you. Just so you know."

He drew in the sweet scent of her, tasting the sharp lingering edge of her fear—and he wanted to say, *I'll protect you, Katie Maddox,* even though it made no sense inside this conversation at all.

So, instead, he simply rose to his feet, a sharp grunt escaping him at the fiery pain twisting down his arm.

"Oh," Katie said, so casually. "Didn't I mention? I'm pretty sure the median nerve took some damage. Probably lots of inflammation there. A sling might help, though." She let the scarf dangle from her hand. "You know…like this one?"

Maks stared at her a moment, and then gave a snort of helpless laughter. No, Katie the deer wasn't nearly as timid as she thought she was. He tucked his thumb into his waistband to keep the arm still, and held out the other to pull her to her feet.

She reached for it, gave him a knowing flash of a glance, and changed her mind to stand smoothly on her own.

He knew it then—she, too, had felt all of that which had passed between them. And she was either more frightened by it than Maks…or else she was smarter.

Probably both.

Chapter 4

Didn't he just look like hell, Katie thought as she gathered her impromptu surgical supplies with sharp movements. She tucked the little medical field kit under her arm, pretending she wasn't affected by Maks's pale, strained face—or that she wasn't wondering how brevis could even send her this man so clearly still wounded from his previous battle.

But maybe she didn't pretend all that well. Because he hesitated, jaw tensed, and he looked away from her before he managed to say, "Don't tell them."

"Don't—?" she said, stopping short, and not quite understanding.

"Brevis." The words were hard to say, to judge by the strain in his voice. "Don't tell them how it is."

She gave a short laugh. "If I did, would they send someone else?"

He met her gaze with a direct if reluctant look, the turmoil still evident. "Not right away."

Not that she hadn't done that herself—downplaying her ability to discern the visions and what they meant, finding subtle ways to prod people into action if action was necessary—which it rarely was. Distancing herself from the skepticism she'd simply rather not fight.

Then, obviously uneasy, he added, "But it would change things for me."

She got it, quite suddenly—brevis didn't have any idea how affected he was. And if they found out, it *would* change everything for him. They'd call him in from the field, they'd call him back into medical…they'd take the tiger from the wild green—from the freedom and the action.

She'd left them for her solitude; he gambled for the freedom to hunt. Nothing alike, and yet not so very different at all.

Before she could react out loud, he added, "I'll call them. This—" he nodded to the back of the house "—is bigger than anyone thought. But until they do send someone else…I *will* take care of you."

She didn't throw angry words back at him—especially not the all-too-easy *like just now?*

Truth was, he had protected her just fine. That she'd looked down the barrel of a gun was her own fault.

So she let the whole thing go. "But listen to me about that arm, okay? Maybe I'm no Ruger—" Ruger, the ultimate brevis healer—he took the bear, he took care of others and he took care of himself "—but I'm a healer. I've had training, I've worked in the field. I'm here because I choose to be apart from brevis, not because I couldn't pass muster." She made a little face. "I'm a little surprised they didn't call me in after *Core D'oíche*."

He shrugged, a one-shoulder gesture. "Many of those who were untouched…they chose to leave untouched.

Doing their same work. It—" He made an impatient gesture—an encompassing movement, and she had a sudden impression of strength and wholeness.

"Kept us as a foundation?" she guessed.

He looked at her in surprise, as if he hadn't expected her to understand, and nodded.

"I warned them, you know," she told him, unable to hide the tinge of bitterness in her voice. "A month before it happened. But 'the bogeyman is going to get us' isn't much of a starting place. I can still feel that…the darkness from that vision." She buffed her arms in spite of the day's warmth. "But compared to what the field agents have been through—and before that, you and Ruger—"

"And Michael," he said, looking away from her with an expression gone tight. "And Shea. Because I opened that door."

She tried to hide her surprise—that Maks had been with the legendary Ruger when he'd been injured, that Maks considered himself responsible for what had befallen them all. That he'd so quietly taken up such an important role, and so silently borne it. "Your field file is need-to-know about a lot of things like that," she said. "Are…are the others recovered?"

"Still trying," he said. "Like so many of us." He nodded at the house. "Our friend dropped something."

A blatant change of subject. Katie let him have it. She was too busy absorbing the fact that Maks had been on that Flagstaff team. Too busy realizing what it said about his nature—about his place in the Sentinels.

Brevis may have sent her a wounded tiger. But they hadn't sent her just *any* wounded tiger.

And watching him from behind, she saw clearly what he was—*all* of what he was: a big man of perfect proportions, his shirt soaked with blood and his arm tucked to his side, his stride powerful and at the same time not quite steady. His tiger strong and close to the surface—and yet his energies damaged.

Strength in need.

Ohh, Katie. What have you gotten tangled in?

She caught up with him, easy strides that bore little resemblance to her deer's delicate movement. Not for the first time, she wished herself born into a shape of more nobility than a Chinese water deer—an elk, a strong whitetail, even a mule deer. She ran her tongue over her teeth, feeling the sharp bite of those slightly elongated canines. At least her deer had a little token set of tusks.

She overtook him, jamming her first-aid supplies under the rail of the side porch to meet him near the window, moving nimbly among the unused flowerpots that lined the back of the house. The same pots that had, no doubt, tripped up their intruder in the first place. She crouched at the window, poking among the sparse grasses—and recoiling at the sight of something black and oily, a sheen of unearthly metal.

She started to reach out, but Maks moved faster than she'd thought possible and caught her arm, pulling her back. She squeaked a protest—she'd hardly been about to touch the thing. Before she could say as much, he gentled his hold; by the time his fingers left her arm, it felt more like a caress.

"Amulet," she said grimly. Of course, an amulet—what else did the Core do but leave their little missives of evil? Amulets that eavesdropped, or that induced slow, subtle malaise…those that disrupted wards, disrupted talents. But they had to be triggered first…and surely this man hadn't had the time to do that? Not if he was still holding it when they found him? She shook her head. "I haven't seen one of these since training. What—?"

He shook his head. "No idea." He reached for the nearest flowerpot, flipped it upside down in one big hand, and plopped it down right over the metal.

Katie snorted a startled laugh. "Don't tell me that makes it safe."

"No," he said reasonably. "But it will keep your cat from walking on it."

She reached out to almost touch the red clay pot, then let her fingers fall away. She felt as though she should be able to perceive something—some tingle of warning, some miasma of evil. "I wonder what it's meant to do."

He scowled. "It's theirs; that's enough. And it lacks... scent." His jaw briefly hardened. "Like the one in Flagstaff. And those found at Fabron Gausto's workshop."

"You were *there,* too?" It startled her all over again.

His grin took her just as much by surprise—it was fierce and full of memory. "I wasn't cleared for it," he said. "I went. Nick needed us."

Nick Carter, he meant—the Southwest Brevis consul. And *us*—that meant the small team that had infiltrated Gausto's home, the Sentinels who had saved Carter and who had kept *Core D'oíche* from being worse than it might have been.

No. Not just any wounded tiger.

Eduard Forrakes ran his hand over the array of silent amulet blanks on the worktable before him, waiting for one of them to speak to him—the faint warmth that meant it was ready for impression.

Fabron Gausto had once scorned Eduard's insistence that he could discern the ripeness of any given blank. But then, Gausto was dead, wasn't he? Too arrogant to listen to Eduard's advice, even as he took credit for Eduard's accomplishments.

"Yes," he murmured. "It's good to be king." And then smiled at his own faint self-mockery even as he selected an amulet blank.

Once he'd impressed a working upon the amulet, its unadorned leather thong would be knotted so as to identify it; the dull and crudely stamped metal would acquire its own particular sheen. It would become a thing of beauty...and a thing of power. With such a blank, he had once created the working that had located Dolan Treviño in the Sky Islands of southern Arizona; he had penetrated the troublesome Sentinel's wards. He had left a surprise for the nosy Sentinel team in Flagstaff, and still resented the fact that they hadn't been killed outright. He had, for a short time, taken down the man who was now Southwest Brevis consul. He had even created the woman Jet, once known as only wolf.

And he had created the working that changed Fabron Gausto into a creature greater than any Sentinel, more werewolf than wolf—and if Gausto hadn't been so arrogant, Eduard would now be experimenting to perfect the stability of that working, rather than trying to recreate it from scratch. Or to recreate his own personal stash of preservation workings—those that had given him the extended vigor and youth to pursue his craft to such perfection.

A commotion in what passed for a hallway broke his concentration. Suddenly, Eduard again became aware of his crude surroundings: the arching Quonset structure and its permanent underground chill, the always-inadequate lighting, the workspace walls that stopped well short of the high central ceiling.

The prefab nature of the buried building and its contents annoyed him in all ways—always just a little bit flimsy, far too much metal and not nearly enough well-waxed wood. For Eduard was the master of an ancient craft, and it was a craft that deserved the finest circumstances, the best materials—and, by damn, a coffeemaker that didn't come from the dollar store.

He didn't turn around as he finished his thoughts out loud. "It deserves the courtesy of subordinates who *knock*."

Silence followed that statement…perhaps a moment of dawning regret. Eduard turned to see who had intruded on his work. "Guyrasi," he said, turning the name into a disapproving statement.

Guyrasi took a step through the doorway into this, the largest enclosure within the buried Quonset. This was the entire back third of it, in fact, an area that had served as breeding-stock quarters years earlier.

Eduard said softly, "Have you a problem?"

He'd learned that from Gausto—the effectiveness of a soft voice when there was cold cruelty behind it.

Guyrasi made a token attempt to straighten himself. "She was supposed to be detained! That civilian of yours was supposed to keep her away from the house!"

Eduard gave the man a cool stare. "In this posse," he said, "those who wish to survive don't make excuses."

"If I had been given time—" But the man stopped as Eduard dipped a hand into one of the many amulet-filled pockets in his custom black lab coat, and when he spoke again it was with more discretion. "I located the house without difficulty. I was securing the amulet when your target arrived home with a man." He took a deep breath and met Eduard's gaze with, at last, the appropriate aware-ness of his failure and its potential consequences. "The amulet is live, but I was unable to conceal it before they came after me."

"They?" Eduard absorbed the man's disheveled appear-ance, fondling an amulet within his biggest pocket in subtle threat. "The man was another Sentinel."

Guyrasi nodded once, making of it the slightest bow

of acknowledgment. "He took the shape of a tiger—a Siberian."

A Siberian tiger. There had been a Siberian at Gausto's compound raid, too. Eduard didn't recall that he'd done much.

Of course, Eduard had wisely departed before those events had played themselves out. He'd left his work and his home; he'd lost the woman he'd loved. He was here to succeed where Gausto had failed. Regardless of what Gausto's superiors said about laying low in the wake of Gausto's embarrassing failures in the cold war between the Core and the Sentinels.

When Eduard didn't respond directly, the man filled the silence. "I handled him," Guyrasi said, bravado mixed in with his confession. "I stunned and shot him. He's badly hurt, if not dead." Guyrasi shifted uneasily. "Will the amulet work if not placed directly against the house?"

It had been one of Eduard's more subtle workings, and a lovely execution at that—carefully impressed into a blank amulet with the perfect structure to hold it. Had it been properly located, it would have gradually brought Katie Maddox under Eduard's influence. As it was...

"Perhaps," Eduard said. "If it goes undetected. I'll know soon enough." His partnered amulet would tell him what he needed to know. "Now, have yourself tended."

The man drew himself upright, his annoyance turned to determination—and, if he was smart, to gratitude for a potential second chance. By then, Eduard barely saw him.

He saw instead the unsuspecting face of Katie Maddox, working on the stray dog Eduard had taken from the Apache reservation—easing its old injury.

Of course, she'd had no idea who Eduard was, dressed in his cheap tourist's clothes and unflattering glasses, his hair mussed and a subtle, silent working washing out its black color and his robust complexion. She'd had no idea he wanted the dog whole for his experiments. She certainly had no idea what had befallen it upon its return to the Quonset, tucked away so neatly in the old Sitgreaves Forest logging area. In return, *he* had no idea exactly what she'd done to help it—but he knew it had fared the best of any experimental subject so far, and he knew he wanted— he *needed*—to reproduce the effect with his other subjects.

And that meant Katie Maddox would be his.

Chapter 5

Maks emerged from the house—showered and in a clean shirt, his thumb tucked into the worn belt of his jeans to support his raggedly throbbing arm—to find Katie waiting for him on the porch. Whether it was her habit to sit in the old rocking chair tucked into the corner or whether she simply didn't feel quite comfortable sharing her home with him, he wasn't sure.

"I'll call brevis," he said. "If I can use your phone."

She looked at him in surprise. Her eyes had a red-rimmed look to them, but she seemed calm enough. "Don't you have a cell phone?"

He shrugged, hurting and irritable and not in the mood for any of it. "I just don't like them." Among other things, all of which he could use if pressed, and none of which he used when not. Cell phones. Radios. Computers.

Cars.

Impossible to explain, without going places he had no intention of going.

"We barely have reception here, anyway," Katie said, lifting one shoulder in a shrug. "Of course you can use the phone. Do you think they'll…I mean, will they listen? Really listen?"

He heard her unspoken concerns; he understood them. *Will they take it seriously? Will they take me seriously?*

The difference was, he had never truly cared.

But Katie cared. Her eyes said as much. Her fingers, picking at the fray of her shorts, said it too. Maks lost his irritability; he forgot, for the moment, the stabbing pain of his arm. He felt, instead, the sudden wash of impulse to comfort her—to protect her.

Not that it made sense, to have it hit him so hard. This is what he did, what he was, what he'd always been. The one who protected the cast-outs, the runaways, the unwanted, two legs or four—always on the lookout for those who hunted him, and those who had hunted the mother who'd died for his freedom.

The Core.

And so he made his voice matter-of-fact; he protected her from what he didn't understand. "They'll want to know about the amulet," he said. "The Core hasn't been active in this area since—"

No. He wasn't even going to open that door.

"It's been a while." She'd relaxed a little, following his lead.

"I don't think they'll send anyone else here," Maks told her, bluntly enough. "But we should be able to send the amulet to brevis."

She nodded. "I'd like to know what it was supposed to do."

"I'll call them," he said again. And then, because she'd said she had a client coming and he hadn't yet scouted the area, he looked out to the craggy ridge of pines rising around her home.

It must have shown on his face. Not just the need to scout these woods, but the yearning for them. She came to her feet. "Where—?" And then, understanding, shook her head most decisively. "Oh, no. Not yet."

"I won't be long," he said. "You'll only be alone until your client comes."

"I've been alone plenty," she snapped at him, with perhaps more vehemence than she meant, because then she hesitated. "You really need to rest—we need to give your body a chance to build on the healing. Besides, I do my work in a room off the kitchen, and the couch is..." she eyed him up and down "...almost big enough."

He looked out to the woods, breathing of them.

"Maks," she said gently. "You can't use that arm yet, man *or* tiger. And you lost a lot of blood."

Maybe because she said it as though she understood—as though she regretted—he took a step back. But he didn't look away from the pines, or from the forest rising into rugged ridge-and-swale beyond.

She moved up beside him. "Later," she said. "We'll set wards, and you can go." And then, with an understanding that sent warmth through his chest, she said, "You grew up here, you said. It means a lot to you."

"It was..." He shook his head, looked down to her. "Everything." All he'd known. A life lived fast and lean... and *free*.

"Were you born in this area?" she asked. "Do you still have family here?"

Father, unknown. Mother, buried in a shallow, unmarked grave. Birthplace...

Foul. Something to escape.

And he had. So now he said mērely, "It was a long time ago."

She laid a hand on his arm—so lightly, so gently. "Come inside. Let me get you the phone and show you the couch."

He met her gaze, and felt the healing of her. He didn't even think about it—he reached out to touch her hair, her jaw...rested a thumb lightly on her chin. No matter that it quickly fell away; she felt what he did, that swell of something meeting between them. Her eyes widened even as his narrowed.

For that instant, if only in his mind, nothing separated them at all. For that instant, he suddenly had this woman in his arms—and there, in his mind, she responded to him with a fervent enthusiasm. He felt the heat of it, the sweetness of it—and, startlingly, a rising stab of pain, far too easy to ignore for the rest of it.

When the moment passed, they were man and woman on the porch, deer and tiger, watching each other with the complete, stunned awareness of what just hadn't quite happened.

"She needs someone else." Maks's voice reached Nick with an unusual edge, the phone lines between them doing nothing to dull it. "Someone who isn't me."

Nick's response held the weight of responsibility, and the aftermath of *Core D'oiche*. "I know what I'm asking of you," he said. "And of her. But you're the best available agent for the job."

Maks's hesitation meant nothing in particular; the man chose his words carefully, and he chose few of them at all. "Then someone else should become available."

"Let me rephrase that," Nick told him, even as he propped the phone on his shoulder to type a few quick keystrokes into his desktop computer, pulling Maks's file up to sprawl across the luxuriously large monitor. "Because nothing's changed. You know that area. You can protect her. You can do—*there*—what no one else can."

Another hesitation. When Maks spoke, it sounded as if the words cost him. "It might be too soon."

"I'll send someone up for the amulet," Nick said, knowing there wasn't anyone immediately available. His thoughts wandered to Meghan Lawrence, who knew nothing of amulets but who could weave a ward stronger than any Atrum Core working. Or Ian, who had been walking around the AmSpec lab gaunt and obsessed since they'd acquired a cache of the undetectable new "silent" amulets. *Yes...Ian.* "I'll pull Ian out of the lab."

Maks made a disgruntled sound, no doubt aware of just how long that might take. And then his silence became more uncomfortable, until it burst back into words. "This is bigger than you expected me to find—more aggressive. I shouldn't be the one. There's something—"

"Wrong," Nick finished, as gently as he could, eyeing the file contents. "Something wrong with *you.* That's what you haven't been telling us, isn't it?"

It was clear enough, if you read between the lines of Maks's clearance interview—conducted by a medic too reliant on test results and not discerning enough of subtleties.

Then again, Maks could stymie anyone. And when he chose not to talk, why...that was just *Maks.*

After a silence, Maks said, "I thought if I went active, it would help."

Dammit, if Maks was even having this conversation—

Not good. And Nick couldn't afford to lose another field Sentinel. He couldn't afford to lose *Maks,* so often taken for granted because of his silence—a man who blended into any team, and who protected them all with a focus no other could match.

Nick cleared the file from the screen. "If you're in trouble, we'll pull you. Katie can come in for a while."

"She—" Maks didn't finish the sentence. It didn't matter—Nick knew of Katie Maddox and her reluctance to be near other Sentinels, never mind an entire brevis of them. Maks made a noise that Nick couldn't then interpret. "No, we're not in trouble. She just needs better—a whole team."

And Nick knew, with the intuition that had gotten him this far, he *knew* that Maks was lying. "Maks," he said, a warning. "Talk to me."

And Maks said simply, "I'm here." It meant a plethora of things, but Nick understood the most important of them. Maks heard him; Maks chose, for the first time in his active field duty career, to do as so many of these headstrong Sentinels did on a regular basis—to push back. And when he added, "I believe her," Nick knew something else, as well.

Maks, in his silence, had seen something that the rest of them were missing. The little deer had, somehow, gotten through to the tiger.

"Send someone for the amulet," Maks said, and hung up.

Nick found himself giving the dead phone a resigned and contemplative look.

Maks in defiance. And the Core—or at least an individual within the Core—was evidently now targeting a healer of no dramatic talent, a seer of questionable skill.

Or not so questionable. There had been too many signs that Katie Maddox downplayed her abilities. She'd been one of few to tender warnings about *Core D'oiche*, and if she'd had few details, she'd been genuinely distressed that she couldn't offer more—*desperate* to offer more.

"I believe her, too, Maks," he told the dead phone line, and then reached within his mind for the polite ping that would catch Annorah's attention and subsequently let Ian know he was wanted in the consul's office.

But I'm not so sure I believe you.

Chapter 6

Maks dozed more than slept, with one leg propped on the padded couch arm, one leg dragging off the side, a pillow under his shoulders and his fingers curled through his belt to keep his sore arm in place.

He was aware when Katie's client arrived at the front door, speaking of recently missing livestock and a glimpse of something huge in the woods. He absorbed it when that excited tone lowered to talk about Akins and his sly commentary about Katie. "He uses the word *Kevorkian*," she said, nearly whispering. "And *angel of death*."

He was aware, too, when Katie eased through the room with a big dog of quietly goofy nature; he knew when the dog's owner stopped and whispered, in a manner she probably thought to be quiet, "Katie Maddox! What have you got sleeping on your couch, and did you bring enough to share?"

"A friend," Katie had murmured, humor in her voice. "He's helping me clear out a firebreak."

"I could use a firebreak," the woman said, somewhat wistfully. But her voice changed as she said, "Is that—on his shirt, is that *blood?*"

"Oh, dear," Katie said, as if it had all been nothing. "I thought I'd taken care of that. Just a little kick-back branch from the chainsaw. You know how men are. I could hardly get him to stand still long enough to put something on it."

Sentinels were, if nothing else, adept at hiding their other natures. And at making light of even significant injuries, lest their rate of healing become cause for question.

Maks let their voices drift away until they were no more than the occasional lilt of laughter and amused tone. The pain of his arm followed him into deeper sleep, and so did the indistinct murmur of Katie's voice…no, not her voice. Her *presence*. Whatever subtle healing she worked on the dog lapped gently through the house…touching him and skimming along his body like a breeze made of her essence.

He breathed deeply of it, at first relaxing into it—and then reaching for it, leaning into it as he might lean into a touch. Sweet warmth and comfort, scented energies…they caressed him, soaking in. He shifted on the couch, found a new ache coiling deep and yearning. And though the injured arm had ceased its pile-driving throb, the clenching tension spiked a renewed bolt of pain through his body— enough to wake him back to a light doze. Enough to recognize a hard-on even jeans couldn't disguise, as sprawled as he was.

Maks turned toward the couch, constructed the lightest of shields, and fell asleep to regret.

His mother's voice came as remembered words on a sigh. *Maks…my boy…so proud of you…*

He gripped her hand, too young for the words he needed, awash with the need to protect her. To make things all right. To mend her bones and the things broken within her.

Ssh, not your fault...

Of course, it was his fault. His job to protect her from those who seemed ever determined to hurt her; his fault that she'd managed escape just so he would grow up free of them...

Don't let them find you...

The scent of her, her tiger lingering in the air, her human overlaying it, her wounded nature tingeing it all.

Be safe...safe...safe...

Grief was the color of brown dirt and scattered red cinders, the scent of torn roots, the sensation of bruised pads and tired young limbs. It was not breathing and not wanting to breath, of fear and panic and bereft confusion.

It was running, a gangly young tiger not meant for distance or speed, hunger gnawing deeply, ever aware of the hunt—and of fear growing so great, a great big ball of it taking up all the spaces within him and pressing outward... and finding, suddenly, purpose.

Live. For her.

Protect what he could, when he could. For her.

That grief flailed through one reality to another, with the murky darkness closing in around him, flashing shadows and fear. Terrified screams drilled into his awareness, the dreams tangling with then and now and—

A hand landed on his shoulder.

Maks exploded out from the couch, a snarl on his lips and his shirt twisted, his arm a shriek of pain, ready to—

To—

The main room spread out before him, quiet and undisturbed. A woman stood frozen not far away, distressed and frightened and unfamiliar.

Maks slowly straightened, cradling his arm. He could say he'd been having a bad dream; it was true enough. He could make excuses that she'd startled him—also true enough. But excuses only drew attention to the unusual nature of his reaction…and she was the one who had trespassed. He let that truth fill the silence.

She didn't resist that silence long, easing back a step—late thirties, sturdy and plump, her pleasant face now flushed red. "Katie," she said, pointing toward the kitchen, her voice as urgent as her expression. "There's something wrong with Katie. I wondered if you knew…"

"Did you scream?" Maks asked, his sleep-roughened voice abrupt as he looked past her to the undisturbed front door, to what he could see of the kitchen. He straightened, tugging his shirt back around. "Did she?"

Baffled, the woman said, "No, she just—she froze. And she looks…frightened. She never mentioned, but—does she have some kind of weird epilepsy, or—"

But Maks was no longer listening. He didn't question that the screams in his sleep had been real—if not out loud. And he didn't need to ask *where*—the tug of it called to him, and he headed barefoot through the house as if he'd always lived there, into the kitchen and through it to the open door along the south side of the house.

The little room might once have been a pantry or a long, narrow breakfast nook. It held a stack of dog crates at one end; the largest crate was full of amiable dog. And in the other end, a high, padded table stretched lengthwise, with just enough room to move around all four sides.

Katie stood clutching the far end of the table, just as frozen as the woman had described.

The woman moved up behind him now—but not too closely, not this time. "We'd just finished with Rowdy," she said, and the dog waved his plumy tail at his name. "And she made a funny noise, and she…" The woman made an expansive gesture, visible in the corner of Maks's eye. "This. Do you know—?"

"No," he said. "And yes." He closed his eyes, taking a quick scan of power in the room, the house, the yard. Looking not for specifics, but signs of Core intrusion. Finding nothing—not even the amulet he knew to be lurking.

He did what he should have done earlier, placing wards around the house. Not the usual intricate knots and energy labyrinths, but with his hands raised, palms out…a little push of his inner strength outward, he created a circumference through which Core individuals could not pass undetected and Core workings could not pass at all.

The woman made a startled noise. From the porch, the cat yowled and fled, knocking over a crockery flowerpot on the way.

Katie gave no sign at all.

Maks eased past the table, and then between Katie and the wall, closing in behind her.

The woman moved up to the doorway, watching with both concern and no little wariness. "What did you—"

"Ssh," Maks said, paying little attention to the woman, speaking only to Katie. Fine tremors shivered through her frame; the energy of it reached out to touch him, trickling to raise invisible hackles. It invoked his silent snarl—a tiger's gesture of lifted head, just a hint of a lifted lip.

He pushed his way past it, settling his hands at the base of her neck; they curved gently to cup her shoulders, his fingers marking the graceful curve of collarbone. He looked again into the energies surrounding this place— hunting for any sign of attack—and found only that which seemed to resonate from Katie herself.

He had little experience in saving others from themselves.

But if nothing else, he was a creature of instinct. He moved closer to wrap his arms around her, hands resting flat against her slender, toned midriff, damp heat trapped beneath his palms. He pulled her in against his body, ignoring the quick flare of reaction…expecting it. A man's body, doing what it would. He focused instead on the energy remaining deep in the center of himself, that which he had not yet pushed out to protect the house—and he sent that out, too.

Right through her.

She gave a little cry and flung her head back, banging his chin and very nearly his nose, brown and cinnamon hair brushing his face. For an instant, she seemed to push back at the forces he'd sent through her—pushing back at *him,* with glimpses of glinting metal and splashing blood, a blur of startled green eyes, a muted roar and a cry of pain. It rocked him, and he released the faintest undertone of a snarl. Then she gave way, going limp in his grasp—head drooping, legs wobbling.

"Ssh," he told her again, a not-quite usual rendering of the comforting sound he'd heard from his dying mother's lips long before he'd ever heard it in its more customary form. He lowered his head, his cheek against the side of her face. And so he stood, holding her—holding her up, and holding her close.

From the doorway, her friend drew breath to speak, stopped her words on the edge of sound, never quite voicing her concern or question—never quite intruding.

Katie stirred; she put her hands over his at her stomach. "What…?" she asked, lifting her head.

"You saw something," Maks told her, quite simply.

"Katie!" the woman let her words explode on a breath. "I was so worried—what on earth—?"

It was Maks who brushed the loose hair from her face,

one hand scraping it aside even as she realized he was there—right there—and glanced aside at him in surprise, still too dazed to protest. "A nightmare," he told the woman. "A waking memory. Gone now."

Katie's laugh had an edge of tears in it. "A nightmare," she said. "Oh, God, Maks, you were—"

Splashing blood, startled green eyes...

Maks's own eyes.

But Katie was pulling herself together fast, straightening within his grasp, not leaning on him quite as hard. She found her friend. "Marie, I'm sorry," she said. "I was just so relaxed working on Rowdy...it snuck up on me. I didn't mean to frighten you."

"Never mind that," the woman said, dismissing her fears with a wave. "As long as you're all right. You will be all right? Are you getting help with...*this?*"

Katie's response rang with an honesty that surprised Maks, considering the words. "I'm getting help," she agreed. "I just started, in fact."

He understood then. She meant him. Whether or not she truly believed in him or trusted him. It shouldn't have filled him with so much warmth. Or so much relief.

Marie risked a glance at Maks, but persisted. "This... it doesn't have anything to do with what Roger Akins is blathering about, does it? He doesn't really have something on you, does he?"

Roger Akins. Maks's hands tightened against the soft skin of her abdomen; her hands settled on top, light and cool and not nearly large enough to cover his. She shook her head at Marie. "Akins is just looking for a way to dodge the consequences of his own brutality." A shudder ran through her, the energies still fluctuating around them; she tensed with the effort of hiding it, silently nurturing her intent to gather evidence so she could call the local au-

thorities. "It's got me on edge, that's all. Anyway, I guess
we're done for the day—but this one's on the house, Marie."

Marie dismissed that with a wave, too. "It most certainly
is not. Rowdy is clueless, as usual, and I'm perfectly fine.
But don't you worry about it just now. I'll leave a check on
the counter on my way out. You," she said, and she looked
directly at Maks, as if he'd never exploded out of sleep at
her, never showed her his snarl, never pushed a basic shield
right through her. "You take good care of her, then."

"That," said Maks, "is why I'm here."

Katie dimly realized that Marie had left, taking Rowdy
with her; that Maks still held her, letting her recover as
slowly as she needed. She had been so taken by surprise,
the vision so much stronger than expected, so much more
real and immediate...

The healing she'd performed on Rowdy's rock-inflamed
digestive system and surgical repair—deeper than usual,
more personal than usual on this day of fear and danger
and surprises—had somehow left her open.

Vulnerable.

And now she stood with Maks's arms around her, surrounded by the sharp layered scents of man and tiger.

It should have felt threatening. Maybe, in a moment, it
would. For this moment, it came as a comfort. His arms,
his breadth, and his strength.

*Glinting metal and splashing blood, a blur of startled
green eyes, a muted roar and a cry of pain—*

"Oh, be careful!" She cried it aloud, turning in his arms.
"Maks, be careful!"

"Ssh," he said, the word not quite right. "Let go of it,
now."

He didn't understand. He couldn't. She didn't *see* like
this; she never had. As much as her recent intuitions had

driven her to call on brevis, this was so much more than her
usual impressions of activity, her flutters of borrowed emotions and expectations. It was all of that—the sensations
that spoke to her of dread, and of dangers looming large—
but it was full of details that had never been hers to see.

And it had been full of Maks. Subtle hints of a desperate flight, a violent past merging into a violent present...
right through to a violent future. *Maks fighting and Maks
losing*—she was sure of it. Just as she was sure that if she
looked through her notes and her memories, she would
find him tangled in those earlier warnings, too subtle to
pick out until she'd actually seen those green eyes, run her
hands through that dark chestnut hair...felt the warmth
of him against her and rinsed his blood from her fingers.

She framed his face with her hands as though it was
hers to touch, as though it always had been. "Maks," she
said desperately, still adrift in what she'd seen, and deeply
adrift in the flavor of him that had come with it, "there's
something..." *Desperate flight and violence...past tied to
future...*

She searched his expression, found his eyes gone dark,
his mouth grim. She touched his lower lip—a different
Katie Maddox, caught in the grip of the vision's undertow.
Unfettered by the deer's caution, and living in a moment
where she knew this man, had always known him. She
found his mouth soft and firm and serious...and silent as
ever. "There's something you're not telling me."

And there must have been, because those eyes grew
more shuttered, and she felt the familiar flicker of hurt.
But he responded to her touch as though he, like she, had
been caught in the grip of the vision, the thing that made
them strangers no more. His hands tightened on her shoulders as he closed his eyes to breathe deeply of her, leaning into her touch.

"Maks," she whispered again. "There are things you're not telling me..."

But there was plenty he was, right then and there. He dipped his head, touching his forehead to hers; his breath came in a gust against her cheek, his mouth barely open... she could all but feel the touch of it. Her hands roamed—fingers tracing his neck, feeling the planes of his chest, the strapping muscle of his abdomen. They curved around his flanks, fingernails scraping against tough jeans, pulling him against her.

Maks made a desperate noise in his throat, just the hint of a growl. He ducked his head, and his teeth lightly scraped the side of her throat.

Reality flooded her. A thrill of fear tightened the skin on her exposed throat and all the way down her back.

Maks froze. He stopped breathing for that moment—like Katie, jerking back to reality. He stumbled back the few steps he could, looking at her with all the desire still writ large on his face and all the realization of how close to *out of control* they'd gotten. When he opened his mouth, it formed the beginning of one word, and then another, and finally he just closed his eyes and shook his head.

"I—" she said, and found herself no more coherent than he. Every inch of her skin felt exposed; every inch of it ached for the feel of his hands—and still she felt his teeth on her throat, knew herself not brave enough to reach for what she wanted. She slid around the table, freeing them from forced proximity, dragging her focus back to the soothsaying—to what it meant for them all. "I saw—"

What she realized then was that he was in no condition to talk about this, to think about it. That he looked as wild as she felt, and just as inclined to bolt.

She said, "I don't know what I saw. I have to think about

it. I'm…I'm sorry." She retreated all the way to the crates, giving him a clear shot to the exit.

He took it, quickly enough to generate another tiny stab of hurt. At the last moment, he turned in the doorway, caught in such imminence of motion that she caught her breath on it—seeing for once not the predator to be feared, but the magnificence behind that presence. He finally managed, "The woods. I need to know them."

She nodded, recognizing the brevity that seemed to overtake him at times, and was completely unprepared when he turned upon her a gaze of the purest intent and said with no hesitation at all, "I *will* keep you safe."

And left.

Katie stood, stunned, staring after him—and for that brief instant, she first believed that he could.

That he would.

Eduard would have preferred to meet in a private place—a secluded place with no windows, one entrance, and silence around them. Deep night rather than late afternoon.

But there were few such places in this former timber town, and insisting on such a spot would have given Roger Akins cause to wonder.

Also, none of those places had this coffee.

Iced white chocolate latte lingered on Eduard's tongue. He took a bite of his gooey cinnamon bun and wiped his fingers, gazing out the window at the main street of the town.

Akins swung through the shop door twenty minutes late, full of swagger and full of himself; more than one gaze flicked from the day-old Phoenix newspaper that had been left spread companionably across the tables.

But no one bothered to look long. Only the barista, and that particular look wasn't the least bit fond.

Akins pulled a chair out opposite Eduard, flipping it around to straddle it with his arms propped over the curving wood back—his elbows sticking out, his knees sticking out, and altogether proclaiming himself worthy of the excess space he took up. He didn't wait for Eduard to speak, and he made little effort to lower his voice. "I tried, but you didn't give me enough information."

Uncivilized, this man; he'd lacked the Core to mold him. But Eduard wouldn't mention it. Men such as this weren't even to guess at the Core's existence. Nor of the Sentinels, for that matter—for the security of one faction ensured the security of the other. After two thousand years, this man was hardly worth the risk.

So Eduard tolerated him, and Eduard used him. And, if necessary, Eduard would then have him killed.

Akins frowned as Eduard sipped his latte. "You're the one who asked me to come here. Do you want to talk, or what?"

"Simply being thoughtful," Eduard said in a mild tone— the one his men had learned to fear. He set the coffee down and flexed his wrist—the one broken, not so long ago, and still barely healed in spite of his ongoing personal restorative workings. Once, Vasilisa would have seen to his healing needs, but he had fled Gausto's workroom without her, and had since learned of her death at Jet's hands.

He hadn't yet replaced her, not in any of her capacities—but if Katie Maddox was malleable enough, she just might do.

But that meant that this pathetic, mundane civilian had to come through for him, and Eduard was beginning to have his doubts. "I feel the need to mention, Mr. Akins, how many times you assured me you could delay Miss Maddox for some period of time."

Akins had the grace to look disgruntled, but it quickly passed. "I *could* have, too. She's a skittery little bitch most of the time—easy enough to push her buttons. But you didn't mention there'd be a guy with her. I had to improvise."

A guy. Of course. The very Sentinel who had foiled Guyrasi. "Nonetheless," Eduard said, eying Akins's truculence and deciding the man's eventual fate on the spot. "There are many ways to create distraction or delay—unless you found that particular man intimidating."

Akins took quick and righteous offense. "I could have handled him," he assured Eduard. "*If* that's what I'd wanted to do."

"And yet your failure put me in a difficult situation. I'm afraid our association no longer truly benefits me."

"Shit," Akins said. "Can't you ever just come right out and say what you mean, instead of dancing around the words? What are you, gay or something?"

Eduard closed his eyes for a long moment. "Charming," he said. When he looked at Akins again, it was with a little more of his inner Gausto showing. Indeed, Fabron Gausto had taught him much. "Mr. Akins, I was prepared to pay you a reasonable sum for what you so clearly want to do anyway—ruin Katie Maddox. Now, I'm afraid, I must insist that you simply stay out of my way."

Akins scowled; his gaze flicked to Eduard's men—correctly assessing their role here, to judge by the way he subsided. "Look," he said. "That bitch is out to ruin me, and I want her to go down before she can—I want to be part of that. What I don't get is you. You don't live around here, you don't do business here…. What's it to you?"

Finally. An intelligent question. Eduard inclined his

head. "It's very simple, Mr. Akins. I need something from her, and it's something she's not inclined to give me. Therefore, I'll tear down what she has until she's desperate to save what's left. To do that, I need information—which I was attempting to gather when your failure created a significant problem for one of my men." He gave Akins a pointed look. "You had best hope you never meet my operative. He has no kind feelings toward you."

Akins snorted. "Yeah, well," he said, as if that was meaningful. "Still doesn't explain why you need *me*."

"You live here. You know this place and its people. You can accomplish more readily, more effectively, the things we cannot."

Akins sat up straighter. "That's right," he said. "I can. But you have to be more straight with me, you know?"

Eduard took a deliberate sip of the latte and patted his lips with the cheap paper napkin, reminding himself that this was the outcome he'd wanted all along. Intimidate the man, pressure him...but ultimately position him to insist on helping. "I see your point, Mr. Akins."

"So we're good, then?"

Eduard couldn't quite bring himself to respond in the affirmative. "We need to know more about the man from the bus stop. What he's doing here, how long might he be there, and whether his presence is changing her habits."

"You mean, like, is he screwing her?"

"A small matter in the larger scheme of things, but yes, that would be useful information." Eduard eyed him. "The specifics, should you discover them, you may keep to yourself."

Akins snorted. "You sure you're not—"

Eduard's expression went cold. "The details of her skills in that area," he told Akins, equally coldly, "I intend to discover for myself."

Akins stared at him for a short, surprised moment, and then grinned. "Edoo-ard, my man!"

Eduard couldn't help it. He did roll his eyes. And he said, "Use your imagination as to how you proceed—but do it quickly. And if it amuses you to gratuitously harass her in some small ways, you may feel free."

Akins's grin grew wider. "My *man*," he said, by way of enthusiastic affirmative.

Eduard only smiled tightly. *And when she disappears, all who have seen you will know who to blame.*

Maks shed the human to take his tiger at the first opportunity, slipping through the heavy pine woods with relief. These woods—or ones very close to them—had sheltered him at a time when he'd needed a home, and a time when he needed safety. He easily avoided the human footpaths, identifying them from scent, from the behavior of the birds and small creatures in those areas.

He found a high prairie meadow with intruding juniper, slipped through thickets of scrub oak, noted the game trails and human incursions, and let the old habits wash back through him.

Habits instilled young. *Too young,* some had said, doubting that he would ever truly be integrated into a more civilized world.

Maks had never doubted that he could, only if he *would*. His mother had taught him *civilized;* his early years had taught him discipline, and the ways of life and death.

Most of it had been as the tiger.

His foray into the world of Sentinels had suited him, in its way. It gave him the chance to explore what had been his mother's life before she'd fallen captive to the Core. It gave him affiliations and company that the tiger had not even known the human had craved.

He had soaked up an education, troweling in manners; he had learned that silence was as useful in the human existence as it had been for the young tiger and those others under his early protection. He had even learned the ways of men and women, and readily kept himself satisfied in a community where such things were matter-of-fact and where sexual initiation with a Sentinel of power was a carefully planned event—the partners chosen, the resulting maturation of power nurtured and documented.

But in this place, on this day, with the scent of Katie Rae Maddox lingering in his very being, Maks Altán began to suspect he really knew nothing about any of it after all.

::*Maks*.::

He lifted his head in an unconscious gesture as Annorah's soft mind-query plucked at his attention. He sent back no words—his attention and perked ears of response were enough for Annorah, the communications hub for brevis; she'd know he was listening to her spoken thoughts.

She was much changed from the woman who had gone to Flagstaff with his team, in over her head and too busy proving herself to fit in—an attitude that had ultimately contributed to his injury. She was well into the period of extra supervision and training she bore in consequence, but she still felt a certain responsibility to Maks—to all of the team members injured in that single, damaging blow.

In a strange way, they were both survivors of that moment.

He wasn't surprised to hear from her now, or ever—she was one of very few agents who could reach out and tap another Sentinel on the shoulder—wherever they were, wherever she was—even as she juggled central communications there at brevis.

::*Maks*,:: she said. ::*Are you all right?*::

He thought in tones of affirmative, considering it so.

The wound would heal. And the fugue had no grip on him for the moment. That his presence here had stirred it, that he found himself tangling with Katie Rae in ways physical, emotional, and metaphysical…

Well, that was something he'd figure out. Given time.

::Maks.:: Her thought-voice came chiding.

Maks released annoyance—a flip of his tail tip, his ears canting back slightly. Not at Annorah. Just…circumstances. *::I'm all right.::*

::Ooh, he speaks!:: Her laughter was a brief glitter in his mind, along with the surprise that he'd bothered to form words for her—words no one else had ever been able to perceive. *::Things don't feel well with you.::*

::Eavesdropping?:: he asked her.

::Hey! I do not—*::* But she stopped, and allowed him to feel a trickle of her admiration. *::Nice redirection. People don't give you enough credit for being sneaky, just because you stand around being quiet and capable. But that's not going to work on me, mister. Something's up.::*

Maks thought about mentioning the effect on him of being near this Chinese water deer—how it stirred him, and how he couldn't separate the natural connections forged by a healer-seer at work from what rose between tiger and deer, man and woman.

He thought about Katie's concern that he wasn't healing at a Sentinel's rate, and about the blood trickling down through his fur even now. He thought about the way the fugue had caught him at the bus station, and how it had slowly insinuated itself back into his life.

And with all those words on the tip of his tongue, mental or otherwise, he said nothing.

::Maks?::

The concern in her voice pricked at him; the hurt in it stung. She knew he was holding back on her.

His tail lashed. To tell Annorah would put her in conflict—by duty, bound to report him. By friendship, bound
to keep his confidence.

Either way, she'd suffer the consequences. Maks forced
his concerns into the background, and replaced them with
his tiger's immersion in the moment—the faint increase
in humidity as darkness fell, the rising scents of pine and
acrid soil.

And he lied to his friend.

Not in words. But in effect. Giving her only that moment, through a tiger's eyes.

::Yeah,:: she said, not particularly convinced. *::I get the
idea. But if you need anything...::*

A tiger's rumble of a purr cut briefly through the silence,
and she heard that, too, and sent him back affection, closing their connection and leaving him in privacy.

She couldn't know that he'd already asked for help, in
the best way he knew how. Not telling Nick all the details...that had been a choice. If Nick had no one to send,
no one who could help...then Maks wasn't about to target
himself for a recall.

When Katie had what she needed, then Maks would be
able to walk away.

At least, he'd thought so.

Now, with the aftermath of her touch still singing
through his body, he wasn't so sure.

He lifted his head to the faint breeze, dropping his jaw
to drag in the full scent of it, his whiskers lifting in a silent abbreviation of a tiger's curse. Humans approached—
rushing, no doubt, to get out of these woods before dark.

And Katie no doubt waited for him...no doubt worried.
And, just possibly, had gleaned enough information from
her own seer's journeys to offer some suggestion about

how they might proceed—at least until they truly understood what her visions meant.

Maks padded down a trail of his own making, a stately
trot that ate up ground at a surprising rate. No wandering this time…no inspecting. He reached the edge of the
woods before it hit him—a wave of disorientation so subtle that he almost didn't notice it. A second wave hit as he
hesitated there, checking for cyclists. He sat to make the
change, glimmering stark blue energies a brief but disori-
enting blur in both eye and mind…and then he knelt as
man, hands braced on his thighs, head bowed.

Warmth trickled down his arm and crawled over his
knuckles.

Maks the man made a tiger's expression of a silent curse,
and climbed to his feet. It occurred to him, belatedly, that
if he'd truly underestimated the severity of his failure to
heal, he'd be no good to Katie anyway.

He headed for the porch, the fugue licking around his
edges. The early rise of the waning moon created clear
shapes and shadows, all of which pulsed in time to a heartbeat now speeding up, shifting into a spectrum of sickly
greens and orange. His vision doubled, cleared…and left
him standing with one hand clenched around the rustic
wood pole of the handrail, the other unto itself.

On the other side of the screen, the marmalade cat regarded him with wise round eyes and the twitch of a tail
around its seated haunches. The lingering scent of broiled
meat drifted onto the porch…welcoming. Music played
from within; Katie's voice, sweet and low, picked up on
the chorus of something with a ballad feel to it.

It occurred to Maks to call out to her, but his voice was
buried somewhere deep inside him…still back with the

tiger. So he took another step, and another, and he made it all the way to the door.

But he didn't make it any farther.

Chapter 7

Katie sang along with Keith Urban, letting the music take her away from things she didn't want to think about while dinner waited on Maks. A ballad here, a feel-good rowdy tune there...

She knew her carefree mood was nothing but illusion. She knew she had to face the vision she'd seen, and learn what it meant. She had to allow herself to feel its clarity... its intensity.

But the seeing was a facet of herself she'd long down-played, after learning early to evade unwanted attention. She didn't mention the visions unless she had to; she ignored them completely when she could. She slid aside from them when they came upon her.

But there had been no sliding aside from this. And she didn't know if that had come of Maks—if the way he'd rattled her had caused her to lose that fine control—or if it was a result of the danger driving the vision in the first place. Either way, she'd have to look—really *look*—for the first time in…

Forever.

She stopped singing.

Katie wiped her hands on a towel and slid the plated steak from the table, poking it into the fridge. *He'll be back.*

Of that much, she realized, Maks had utterly convinced her. He was here to keep her safe.

She just didn't know if he *could.*

"This is stupid, Katie Rae," she told herself, and in no uncertain terms. "No brooding allowed."

And as soon as she said it, she realized that her uneasy sensation wasn't coming from within at all. That she'd been perfectly happy, singing along with Keith, puttering in the kitchen.

Something had changed. Something from which she'd slid away, as had become habit—except this time she couldn't afford that weakness. And then she realized she'd gotten so good at sliding away that she wasn't even sure how to *look* any longer.

Or maybe she did know, if she could face that, too. Because healing, too, started with *finding.* And she thought it no coincidence that she'd been working a modest healing on Marie's big malamute mix when the recent vision had snared her.

The one that had been full of Maks and violence and the taste of Core corruption.

"Yeah, yeah, yeah." She muttered away that particular guilt and, still standing by the fridge, did what she'd successfully avoided for so many years.

She went looking.

In an instant, she found herself surrounded by sensation, a fog edged with confusion lapping at her awareness, a despair of conflicting energies clashing to create a static of interference. It mingled with a hint of a clean, clear and vulnerable connection, and tangled with the sense of faltering strength.

"Maks?" The word startled out of her mouth—she stood, for the instant, deer-frozen, all her senses on alert. Keith Urban poured into her ear with his usual exuberance; she dashed over to slap the stereo off, listening into the silence.

Not quite silence.

Someone's breathing. Distressed, filled with pain, and not far away at all.

She ran for the screen door, flipping off the glare of the entry light—and then just barely saw him there, a dark form blocking the door.

"Dammit," she said, as close to a snarl as she ever came. "While I was *singing.*" But she didn't try to push her way out. Instead, she raced through the darkened house to the double doors off the guest room, and flung herself outside to run, fleet and barefoot-agile, through the tufty grama grasses along the side of the house. "Maks," she said, taking the porch steps in a heedless bound and coming to rest beside him, a single fluid motion. "What happened?"

It should have been obvious. She smelled the blood; she saw it. Her first touch on his arm landed on sticky, clammy flannel, dark and ominous against the cheerful plaid. But the flood of sensation she received from him…that wasn't about blood loss, or pain, or any injury at all. It was static turned loud, energy churning against itself. Her vision pulsed and doubled; her skin tingled with a vague fuzziness; it *dissolved,* leaving her gasping.

She wrenched herself away, closing herself off, and for a moment could do nothing but gape at him. "How did brevis even let you *go?*"

Just as well he couldn't answer. She had a feeling that the brevis medics knew nothing of this. And though she frowned in instant frustration at the understanding that Maks had concealed such a weakness from them, she stiffened when truth hit; she had done nothing less.

In truth, she'd done *more*. She'd hidden herself so brevis wouldn't put her in the field or assign her to the city. Maks had merely hidden himself so he could come here and help Katie.

"God, I suck." She drew her hands over her face, pausing to press the heels of her palms against her eyes. "Suck, suck, *suck*." What's worse, she was wallowing in it when he needed her.

Oh, she didn't want to do this. She didn't want to make herself open to him, to the tooth-and-claw strength of him. She didn't want to make herself vulnerable to the visions. She didn't want to reveal those parts of herself that he would surely perceive, given how deep this would take her.

Being deer doesn't mean being weak.

Maybe being deer meant being stronger than they ever suspected she'd been.

Which is how Katie found herself wedged up against the stout metal screening of the security screen, Maks's weight tugged onto her lap. It took awkward moments to prop his lolling head, to shift him so she could reach the injured arm, and so her crossed legs kept the rest of him stable and her hands free.

And then, just for a moment, she indulged. She bent over his neck and breathed in the scent of him—the scent of a man after a day of work, tinged with stress, overlaid with blood, but nonetheless…

Wild. More wild than she'd ever dared to be. And *alive*. The dry, layered scents of tiger and man, perfectly blended.

The deer in her wanted to jerk away. The human in her

fought envy. And the rest of her wanted to succumb to the allure of the powerful and wild.

Maks opened his eyes, his gaze latching straight onto hers. She froze—feeling the hitch of his breath, seeing his mouth just barely move...waiting for the words.

But this was Maks, and there were no words. His eyes simply rolled back and then closed.

Katie straightened. She took a breath, let it out, and slid into her healer, diving through his dissonant static to focus on the throb of life beneath her hands—fingers running across flannel but feeling the flesh and bone, the belly of the biceps muscle, the strap of the triceps, the groove between them and the hollow of his elbow below.

She barely touched the torn flesh of the entry wound; she didn't have to. She followed the bullet's dark tunnel toward bone and nerve and artery, seeing it raw and ragged, seeing the acute nature of it—feeling the hot pain he'd been ignoring and, for an instant, catching her breath on it.

Even as she shook off the distress of the connection, she understood. Whatever had diminished his natural rate of healing—his *Sentinel* rate of healing—had left him without the resources even to initiate healing on a wound so raw. She'd underestimated that factor, and so he had lost all the ground she'd gained for him earlier.

She gently moved energies; she manipulated blood and tissue and life. Just as she so often did with her massage, when the animals reveled in her touch and the owners had no clue. The bleeding stopped; the ragged feel of the injury faded, the torn fibers and vessels knitting, however tentatively, into a whole.

Enough.

Any more, and she might just kick up a reactive irritation. And then, since he lay quiescent, she went looking around. Looking deeper and wider. Into the throb of shifting color and hazy darkness she'd cut through to reach this healing place. Hunting the core of it and finding—

Maks! Run, baby, don't look back!

A woman's cry of despair, a big cat's wild snarl—

The echoing soprano snarl of a youngling, shifting to a child's cry—

And then a ripple of darkness, a shift of color...the cough of a tiger's warning, clamors for help...the weight of a responsibility she couldn't quite discern.

And finally, the sudden understanding that she'd stumbled into the past. That she glimpsed, in jagged shards, that which had formed the man in her arms.

That which somehow still haunted him, whether he knew it or not.

She eased away from it. She'd meant to explore a healing, not invade his deepest privacy. At least, she *meant* to ease away from it.

But the intensity of his past wrapped itself around her, startling her with the vivid overlay of intertwined determination, territorial protectiveness...the willingness to do battle. The remembered helplessness of being caught, the utter relief of realizing that he was no longer alone, the fear of change...

That new intimacy came with a lightning surge of physical desire—*initiation,* the impact of which lingered, as it did for them all. It struck echoes of Katie's own initiation— the first union with another Sentinel, so carefully matched, the coupling that released every Sentinel to full potential.

Not everyone experienced significant transformation. Katie had simply emerged much more synced to her deer, and had quickly chosen her reclusive way of life. Caught in Maks's whirlwind impression of the past, she felt him emerge on the other side of initiation to settle back into what he'd always been—always that determination; al-

ways that purpose, with the matter-of-fact physical prowess, physical awareness...lingering physical want.

It was the *want* that rose between them now, pushing
back at Katie until she jerked herself free, head rattling
back against the security screen.

No. Not free. Just looking at it from inside her own
awareness instead of his. But hunger still washed over
her skin, a flood of warmth and fluttering sensation. It
left her in thrall, aware of every whisper of air across her
skin, every tingle of sensation. Maks lay heavy against her.

He was so big. He was *tiger*. What had she even been
thinking, to haul him into her lap for healing?

What had she been thinking, to linger and to explore
the whispering fugue of confusion clinging around him?

What the *hell* was she thinking, to look down into those
open green eyes and lower her mouth to his?

Maks awoke from the tangle of the past and found himself in Katie's lap. He knew it for hers even before he fully
opened his eyes—he knew it from the sensation of her, the
long and graceful limbs, the infinitely gentle touch.

Not only in Katie's lap, but kissing her. Tired and sore,
but flushed with her healing touch—and with her gentle
nip, the scrape of a pointed canine, a kiss less fierce than
it was intimate. A kiss so totally *Katie*.

He did more than return it. He brought his hand up to
thread through her hair—and then, without breaking their
connection, he pushed himself up, finding his way to his
knees. Her arms crept up to the sides of his face, fingers
restless in his hair as she deepened their kiss. His hand
found her breast, cupped it, running a thumb across a peb-
bling nipple. He groaned deeply at her squirming response.

Not until her crossed legs fell open, not until he found

her waist and jerked her up to straddle his hips, did she so much as hesitate.

But Maks had woken to the taste of her, and he didn't care that she was deer and he tiger, or that this wasn't what he was here to do at all. He cared about Katie, sweet in his arms. He cared about the responsive tremors running through her body and the crush of her breasts between them. He cared about the fiery hot promise surging down his spine and clenching through the core of him, and he cared about the call of something—something—

Katie squirmed against him, her head falling back, a gasp of startled pleasure in her throat. Her hands slid down to clench over his shoulders; she moved against him as if there were no clothes between them at all.

He thrust back at her, all instinct and response, and she cried out as he laid his teeth against the long arch of her neck, scraping skin. He pushed her up against the door, rattling metal and not caring or heeding, only possessing—slapping his hands against that door with fingers digging into metal screening that should have been immutable to his touch.

Fire gathered within him, turning heightened pleasure to a startling intimation of pain, fire inexplicably curling around nerve and bone. It was nothing to be heeded in the face of his need, of her need—of the way she clenched strong legs around him, her pleasure crying free and unfettered and complete. Her eyes had gone huge and glazed, and whatever had taken hold of him had swept her up in its wake, turning a lurking attraction into a burst of sensation.

Maks cried out, too, a harsh sound, his body tightening with hot need, everything within him reaching, reaching—

And suddenly slapped back by a sudden punch of shifting energy, his raging physical need ambushed by an internal whirlwind of something bigger, something greedy, something *wanting*...

Something so much stronger than he was.

At the startling bolt of pain, he fell out of the exquisite whirlwind and twisted back into himself.

And there was Katie, sagging in his lap, panting—her expression befuddled, confusion quickly coming to the fore.

But even as he struggled with the wash of sensations, the dizzy combination of assault and heady desire, he stopped her when she would have shifted away.

"No," he said, and his voice reflected his conflict, leaving it rough, and harder than he'd meant to speak to her at all. "No," he said again, as her eyes widened—as she realized how quickly she'd responded to him, there on the dark porch. "There is no running from this thing between us."

He saw it right away, the rise of the deer, the deer's panic in the grasp of the tiger—the struggle impending. He didn't tighten his grip—but he didn't ease it, either, his hands flattened on either side of her head, her back against the door, no room to disentangle from him.

"No," he said again, more evenly this time. "Katie Rae, this is the safest you will ever be."

It startled her. She looked straight at him, the deer-panic receding, her focus returning. "Maks," she said, and touched his face, her fingers brushing his mouth, lingering there. "But I don't... But..."

"There is no *but,*" he told her. "There is what *is.*" Maks had spent too many years living with what *was* to doubt it when he saw it. "This—" he closed the insignificant gap between them to kiss her, the merest brush of his mouth over hers "—*is.*"

She shook her head. "*This—*" she looked down at her rumpled shirt, her sprawling legs, and the lap in which he

held her "—is probably only a reaction to the healing—
the connection I established. Or it's part of what's going
on here, or part of what's going on with you. It could be
not *us* at all."

He gave her a gentle tiger's smile, feeling the predatory
nature of it. *Possessive.* "It's still what *is*. Whatever pieces
make it that way. Let it be."

She relaxed against the door, her head tipped in thought,
her gaze going inward. "You," she said. "You're so close to
the tiger. There's more of your *other* in you than I've ever
seen in anyone else. In me."

He frowned, wondering how she could think of the deer
side of herself as *other* at all.

"I wasn't trying to pry," she said, reaching to touch his
face again, not quite completing the gesture—as if it might
somehow be more intimate than the way she still sat against
him. "I did look, but I was trying to help, to see this *thing*
that happens to you. The dissonance."

He growled a little—just a little, and not at her. One
hand rested on her thigh, the thumb straying into intimate
territory…casual and possessive.

"I felt it at the station, where I first saw you. And just
now, when I found you. But I can't separate it out from the
rest of you. I can only feel—" She shook her head. "So
close to the tiger. So unfettered."

He gave her his most deadpan look.

She pulled back her loose hair, realized the mess of the
whole, and gave up on it; the strands fell back around her
face with casual grace. When she looked at him, it was
with a compassion that startled him. "What happened to
you, Maks? There was…something. I saw glimpses… I
felt it. I—" She hesitated. "I'm sorry. I *really* wasn't there
to pry. But I think it matters."

Not to Maks. "Now," he said, "is now. This is what *is*."

But she was a stubborn deer. "Sometimes *then* makes us who we are *now*."

He felt a low, disgruntled rumble in his chest. "Katie Rae Maddox," he said. "You see what I am. It is only what I told you, when I first got into your car."

"Maks Altán," she said, and touched his face again. "You told me what you *do*. It's not the same thing."

She'd said something he hadn't expected to hear, Katie knew that much. She'd known enough to give him space after that, too—disentangling, still full of her own hot confusion.

He'd barely touched her. And yet, there she'd been... sated on the front porch, in the arms of a tiger.

One who'd known how to tame the deer, fear and all.

Later, wandering her loft bedroom while Maks slept in that cluttered first-floor bedroom—she had no idea how to put it all together. Unlike Maks, she couldn't just *accept* without understanding. She needed to know that he'd come to respect her seeings and her healing, in the wake of so many little subtle indications to the contrary. She needed to know why her vision had grown so intense...and her body so needy. And she needed to know how—and *why*—Maks figured into the other things she'd seen. Because it was her job to understand what the warnings meant.

Pretty full of yourself, Katie Rae. Her job was—and always had been—to report what she saw and let brevis sort it out. She might have more practice at that if she hadn't been looking aside from herself for so long. Squelching herself.

She couldn't quite blame her neglected talent for failing to fall into line, but it meant she had nothing to work with but disparate pieces. Maks. *Glinting metal and splashing blood, a blur of startled green eyes, a muted roar and a cry of pain.* The Core at the back of her house, leaving an amulet of silent menace. Images of oppressive dark space and terror, a deep stabbing awareness of *wrong*...

Nick Carter had no doubt hoped there was nothing amiss here at all—no doubt hoped this assignment would be an easy reintroduction to the field for a recovering Sentinel. But she didn't imagine he knew just how deeply compromised Maks had become.

And no matter how many times she put all the facts together in her thoughts, rolled them together and tossed them out again, they didn't fall into any neat pattern. They didn't tell her what to do next.

They didn't let her sleep.

Then again, maybe that was for the best. It let her watch while her wounded tiger slept.

Chapter 8

Morning found Maks back on the couch, and Katie at the end of her rope.

She didn't know where he'd spent the night after she'd left him, or how—whether it had been indoors or out, man or tiger. She only knew his misery was obvious.

But he wouldn't talk to her. And while in some part of her mind she understood that he'd been through too much in the past twenty-four hours, the rest of her thought she deserved better.

He lay slanted across the couch, his arm cradled and his breathing too uneven for him to be asleep. His brows drew together briefly even as she watched; his breath hitched.

Definitely not asleep.

The yellow cat stropped past Maks's shins; Maks cracked his eyes open in a kind of bleary surprise.

Katie leaned against the door frame between the living room and the kitchen, her hands wrapped around a mug of early-morning hot chocolate. "You should eat something."

How she understood that infinitesimal shift of his head to be a refusal to do any such thing, she wasn't sure. She raked her eyes over the length of him, taking up more room than the couch had to offer, and didn't even have to delve into her healer's perceptions to see what the day before had taken from him. "If you're hurting—" *If.* Right. "—I can help you."

She barely heard his response, a raspy murmur that added up to another shake of the head. She set the mug down on the little entertainment stand and took a frustrated step in his direction.

His eyes widened, the tiger looking out with alarm; he lurched to his feet and headed for the door, ragged words in his wake. "Can't risk it."

Her temper flared at the implication of those words. The previous evening's events had been unexpected, but she was ready for them now—and he'd been the one who'd said to go with the moment. Unless he simply didn't understand—didn't believe—the healing that had come with their connection the previous evening. "Maks, this is stupid. I can make things so much easier for you—"

He'd been aiming for the door. He walked right into the frame, groping for the handle a good six inches away. Katie froze, horrified—ashamed at herself for driving him to leave when he could barely navigate, startled at his condition in the first place. "Maks—!"

Maks froze, his hand falling slowly back to his side—as if he, too, had been confronted with his own weakness. He stood that way for a long moment, swaying slightly. When he shifted, it changed the entire nature of his stance— turned it from wild-in-flight to curiosity-got-the-cat. His head lifted just enough so she knew he'd caught the scent from her mug. "Is that hot chocolate?"

"Yes," she told him. "Would you like some?"

* * *

Maks needed help back to that couch—and he knew without a doubt that she wouldn't have left him there to heat more milk if she'd allowed herself to listen with her healer's skills. Then, she would have heard the buzz of dissonant energies bouncing around within him; she might have guessed that his vision throbbed with color and echoes.

She might have realized that he was totally screwed up—and if she hadn't immediately called brevis, she would have tried to fix it all.

Not again. Not until he understood more about it...not until he was sure he could control it.

But he was grateful for the hot chocolate. And he was grateful when she pressed a hand to his shoulder and said she had an equine house call, and a stop to make on the way home...but she wouldn't go unless he promised he'd rest right there until she got back.

She didn't repeat her offer to help. For that, he was most grateful of all. For as much as he wanted the intimacy of her healer's touch, he couldn't expose her to his own unpredictable nature.

It didn't bother him that he'd almost taken her on the porch. But that she'd lacked intent...that she'd had doubts...

Yeah, that bothered him.

It was up to Maks to figure out Maks.

But mostly he just slept, right there on the couch with the sweet dregs of the hot chocolate soothing his mind. He slept until the yellow cat—which had claimed a tight little spot between his hip and the back of the couch—leaped down to the floor.

The movement woke him from a dead sleep full of fears and portents and pain, mixing energies and confusion. He leaped from the couch in a fever dream of fury, landing as tiger...claws digging into the plain pine planking of the living room floor. The world whirled around him, a cacophony of sensation, and he flattened to a crouch, ears against his skull—the tiger armed and dangerous and completely out of control, driven by the need to strike back at that which struck from within.

The yellow cat, back arched and tail puffed huge, froze against the screen door like a Halloween silhouette, hissing fiercely—but only until he bounced out on his toes to smack Maks soundly across his whiskered muzzle. Then he dashed off, back still arched and tail stuck up in defiance.

Maks released a chuffing breath of surprise, slapped right out of his inward obsession—and only then heard Katie's car door close outside the house. He clawed his way back to the human...and got no further before she took the steps to the porch. Her car keys hit the porch floor with a jangle; the soft thump of a cloth shopping bag landed beside them. "Maks!"

Panic flared all over again—the awareness that he wasn't himself, that he didn't have the control he should. "Stay...*back,*" he told her, desperate words through gritted teeth that she never had the chance to hear.

"I'm such an *idiot!*" she said, throwing herself down beside him, one gentle hand landing on his shoulder, the healing already flowing—gentle, soothing...skilled.

Or meant to be. It collided with the turmoil within Maks, skidding instantly out of control; it flared hot and wild and surged into something too big for a human body to hold. Blue-white energies cut through the room, shards of light and shadow that left the tiger behind.

For that instant, Katie froze in stunned fear; for that instant, Maks faced her with all the wild and none of the tame, his whiskers bristling and fangs exposed in a snarl. An instant long enough for Katie's deer to flash terror and for her breath to stutter on a shriek of fear and reaction—

for Maks to feel that fear slam into the already roiling energies that burned inside his chest.

He threw himself away from her, finding his human even as he rolled up against the couch and to his knees, to his feet—and this time he made it as far as the porch before he ran into the post that subsequently held him up.

But not alone; not for long.

Katie's hand shook as it landed gently on his back—none of her healing touch, all her energies tucked inside. "I am so sorry," she said. "I should never have intruded that way. I was just so frightened for you—"

"Not your fault," Maks managed, scraping to find words at all. "I just can't—" *Can't do that again. Can't risk you.*

He heard understanding on her sudden intake of breath. "This is what you were afraid of earlier."

"Can't risk you," he said.

"Because that's not who you are," she said, and her hand pressed with gentle persistence between his shoulders. "That's not what you do."

He snorted without any strength behind it. "Right."

"This *is* my fault, Maks. Please let me help." She must have felt his instant resistance, the stiffening of his back and shoulders. "Please. I'll be careful. I won't intrude. But you relax...if you just let it..." She hesitated, and he saw it coming. *"Be."*

He said nothing, but he lifted his head slightly, looking out into the blur of the woods, and she took it for the assent that it was.

To his surprise, he felt nothing from her. Instead, after a deep breath, she said, "On the way home this morning, I talked to my neighbor. Larry Williams. He hunts a lot, and I know his friends run with Akins sometimes." It didn't make sense to Maks, but he listened, her calm tone pushing away his earlier fear. "Larry's a good guy, and the way he dotes on his own dog, I figured he'd talk if he knew anything about Akins. I was right, too—except, like me, he only suspects. But maybe with two of us keeping our eyes open…" She let her words trail off, and after a moment, asked, "Better?"

Maks lifted his head, surprised to find the woods in sharp focus. He looked at his hands on the porch rail as if they might be someone else's; he looked back to Katie, his mouth open on words that didn't come.

"I got smart," she told him, somewhat ruefully. Her hand still rested on his back. "What you need right now is *less,* not more."

Less. He sighed with the relief of it.

"I couldn't do that much," she said. "I'm just—"

He shook his head. "Katie," he said, stopping whatever she had to say next. "It's *everything.*"

She flushed slightly and moved away from him—looking, as he had, off into the woods. "I cleared away what I could—what was coming from you. I can't go get anything, not without—" She glanced aside at him, made her fingers into claws. *"Rawr."*

Maks choked on a laugh.

"Seriously," she said. "You need to take it easy. We're waiting for someone to come for the amulet, right? Well, I've got clients this afternoon, too—I don't need babysitting. So just rest. And buffer yourself. From that amulet, from incoming stuff, from…me." And she was already flushing, but she bit her lip with that canine peeking out and managed to give the impression of doing it again.

As if he, too, wasn't thinking about the previous night, waking in her lap and in the thrall of something far more primal than either of them had been able to resist.

But it didn't make him flush. It made him want. Regardless of how the wanting had ended last night on this porch.

* * *

Katie dropped another roll of elastic sticky bandages into her shopping tote and eyed a green tin of antibiotic ointment charmingly illustrated with a cow.

It had, in the end, been Maks's suggestion to come here for supplies. "Small town," he'd said, and she had understood. If she stocked up on first aid supplies at the drugstore, how many people would check on her before the day was out?

But shopping at the local farm store would raise few questions for someone who spent so much of her professional time with dogs, and who often came here for bird seed.

Maks looked much improved in the two days since his injury. He'd spent the time sprawled on her couch, sleeping fitfully, waking to prowl the grounds and grumbling when she backed him down every time he wanted to set rudimentary wards. Recovering as well as a restless tiger could.

He kept the arm close to his side but the weakness wasn't obvious. Maks himself looked rested but still wan, his color less robust than normal…his energy quiescent.

Katie should have felt the same. Deep healings often took a toll on her, but this morning…no. This morning she found herself smiling, as if in being needed by Maks— *challenged* by him—something within her had remembered how to reach out to the rest of the world…and liked it.

Old Mike at the counter didn't miss it as she spread her items on the counter to be rung up. "You look fine and happy this morning, Katie Rae."

Katie looked out into the bright sunshine through the open door and then back to Mike's lined face and shock of thick white hair. "I suppose I am."

Not that she didn't still have the visions to deal with—

to understand. Or that Maks didn't have mysteries dogging him, and a worrisome tangle of energies eating at him from within. But for the moment—*this* moment—she would smile and enjoy the day.

She glanced over at Maks, found an echo of her smile at the corner of his mouth…found him breathtaking. Tall and powerful even in repose, flannel shirt sleeves rolled up far enough to obscure persistent blood stains but not so far as to reveal the bandage, rugged features with an honest gentleness around those green eyes—

She caught her own thoughts and blinked, surprised at herself. Gentleness, in the predator who had so overwhelmed her just the day before?

A glance at Mike told her he wasn't seeing *gentle*. That in his own way, he recognized the tiger. So she said, "Mike, this is Maks Altán, a friend of the family. He's helping me with my firebreak."

Mike's face cleared somewhat, though his expression remained wary. "It's about time you had that taken care of. This all you need today?"

And then the day stopped smiling. Katie's first warning came through Maks—his faint smile, gone, his relaxed posture becoming focused. This was the Maks who had first frightened her, and who now ignited all her tightly keyed senses.

When Roger Akins sauntered around an endcap of fly traps, she could only meet him with disbelief. "Roger," she said. "For a man who doesn't like my company, you certainly do seem to find me."

He offered an insincere open-handed gesture of innocence. "Just shopping," he said. "Picking up some dog food, like plenty of other people on a nice summer day." He glanced at Maks, a gratuitous disdain briefly crossing his features, and then looked at Katie's purchases. "Is that all for you today, Katie Rae? Or maybe you need to pick up some drugs, maybe some woo-woo herbal stuff? Maybe some little potion of mercy? Or is it all in your touch?"

"No call for that, Roger," Mike said, scooping the purchases out of sight into Katie's reusable bag without ringing them up. A spare, sun-leathered woman with a horse halter in her hand came from the back of the store and stopped short at the sight of their tense little cluster.

Akins snorted. "People ought to know," he said, unrelenting. "They ought to find a way to put her out of business."

"They'd need to base their concerns on facts, first," Katie said, coolly enough. *Just like I'll get the facts that convict you. Sooner or later.*

Akins eyed Maks. "Aren't *you* quiet today," he said. "Isn't it about time for you to threaten me? Again?"

Katie was surprised to see Maks's mild amusement. "Katie Rae," he said, in the rough-edged voice that made something quiet bloom within her, "doesn't need my help to deal with you."

Maks, man of few words, sometimes knew just the right ones to use. Katie ducked her head and bit her lip on a smile.

So many of the Sentinels assumed that the deer meant weakness. Sometimes, Katie herself did just that. But somewhere in the last twenty-four hours, she'd started to challenge that thinking. It seemed Maks had always known.

Mike thrust the shopping bag at her. "Here you are, Katie."

She cast him a grateful look. "I'll bring you a list and settle up," she said, tucking her wallet away into her old leather shoulder bag.

"Can't take the heat, Katie Rae?" Akins crossed his arms, shooting Maks a look of growing confidence.

Katie ignored him. "Ready to clear some ground?" she asked, and Maks tipped his head at the entrance. If he had been thrown by her cover story, there was no sign of it. He looked like a man ready to clear ground.

But when Katie turned for the door, Akins grabbed for her with a snarl. "Don't you turn your back on—"

But by then, Katie, swift reflexes and long legs, was out of his reach.

And by then, Maks had clamped a hand on Akins's shoulder. No more than that, and Akins jerked around, his fisted hand rising for a sucker punch.

"Hey!" Katie shouted—but Akins didn't heed it and Maks didn't need it. He met the punch with the palm of his hand, stopping it short…holding it there. His fingers closed over Akins's, squeezing. A hint of a growl filled the air and Katie didn't know if she heard it or felt it or just *knew* it.

"Aw, hell," Mike muttered.

Akins swallowed visibly, his arm trembling with effort—until he realized that he couldn't finish the blow, couldn't wrench himself free, and couldn't begin to save face. He quit trying and Maks instantly released him—but not from his scrutiny. His eyes narrowed, his upper lip just starting to lift—it was still a human expression, and still unmistakable.

Akins cleared his throat. He took a step back, then two more. "Don't really like the company you keep, Mike. I guess I'll shop elsewhere from now on."

Mike lowered his voice just enough to pretend it came under his breath. "I guess you'd better."

As Akins cleared the entrance, the woman with the halter hooked the crown piece over her elbow and applauded politely. "That man needs to be muzzled." From behind her, a weathered man with a battered cowboy hat and bowed legs cleared his throat, a meaningful sound. "Pfft." The woman dismissed him. "After forty years, it's far too late to be hushing me now."

"Something to that," Mike told the man, with enough respect to say he knew the woman well. "Let me ring that halter up. You need any feed today?"

And while the men did their best to discuss beet pulp pellets and compressed hay, the woman turned an appreciative eye to Maks. "It's just as well you're not alone out there," she told Katie. "What with that creature on the loose."

"Creature?" Katie repeated, but she knew what was coming. Marie had spoken of it the day before—half joking, half believing, before Katie had been taken by her vision.

"Creature," the woman repeated, while her husband assumed an expression of practiced tolerance. She poked him. "Watch yourself, mister. John Baird saw it, and John is hardly a man given to flights of fancy. He even asked me to look up *chupacabra* on the internet. Kind of a giant dog...or boar...but he swore it rose right up on its hind legs like a bear."

"I've heard about that thing," Mike said, punching register buttons. "Took a goat right out of the Tsosies' back yard."

"Coyotes'll do that," the husband said, a blandly unconvinced offering.

"Coyotes," said his wife, "don't unfasten gates. Why, it's as bad as when those wild children were running around just west of here all those years back." She gave her husband a peremptory poke.

Katie realized that Maks had moved up behind her—a

big presence, warm and still and practically vibrating
with...

She didn't know what. Not curiosity; he was too intense
for mere curiosity. Not scorn at the legend. *Watchfulness.*
Wariness. The energy of it washed against her. Without
thinking, she eased back a step and put a hand on his arm.

"You don't hear much about them these days," she observed—as much for Maks's interest as her own—for she
knew the stories. More like urban legends in the rugged
mountains than anything else. The woman shrugged, hand-
ing Mike a twenty-dollar bill and snagging the halter up
off the counter. "I can tell you this—buncha people came
in, back then. Quiet, but they made an impression. After
they left..." She shrugged. "No more sightings or thefts."

"So," her husband said, in a flat tone of patent disbelief
that sounded as if it was a token cover for affection. "A secret team came in to grab up the wild children."

"Oh, *you,*" the woman said, and poked him again.
"We got enough homeless folk camping out in the woods.
What's so hard to believe about a bunch of kids ganging
together?"

Mike said, rather unexpectedly, "I heard they were runaways. Except there were—" He hesitated, finding Maks's
gaze on him—full bore intensity, with something new
added. Katie recognized it as a dare, and one that made
no sense at that.

Mike didn't seem inclined to take it. "Nah," he said.
"Buncha foolishness. This creature'll be more of the same."

Katie rested a surreptitious hand on Maks's wrist,
not surprised to find it tense. The healer in her instantly
reached out, sending a soothing tendril of energy.

Maks glanced at her with confusion, as if he could feel
the energy but couldn't quite figure it out. And then he

seemed to recognize his own stance, his intensity…his distinctly powerful demeanor.

Just like that, it was gone. Katie found herself looking twice—but there was no mistake; everything about him had dialed down a notch. Even Mike relaxed, although he seemed baffled about what had just happened.

Katie wasn't baffled. She'd seen the tiger, bright and clear. What she hadn't expected to see was Maks's ability to shed it. It seemed he protected others even from himself.

Katie lifted the shopping bag at Mike. "I'll catch up with you later on these things," she said, and followed Maks from the store. He stopped once he was out in the full sunshine of the parking lot, lifting his face to the warmth.

Katie felt more than saw the depth of the breath he took—the deliberate shedding of the moment. Sunshine struck the gleam of white at his temples; it washed over the line of his cheekbones, the strength of his brow, sparked a gleam of green from his eyes. And though he deliberately quashed the simmering tiger, his pure physical presence— shoulders that broad and legs that long and a torso that tight and lean—could not be downplayed. Not in the least.

Katie swallowed, and flushed. And then she quite unexpectedly heard the echo of the woman's words in her mind. *Buncha people. Quiet, but they made an impression.* She saw again Maks's reaction to the words.

"They were us, weren't they?" she asked abruptly. "And those runaways were real. Did you help bring them out?"

For a moment, he didn't react at all—or at least not outwardly. After that moment, when he lowered his face from the sun and turned to look at her, a tiger looked out from those eyes.

She swallowed again, determined to keep talking in spite of that gaze. "Who better to track down refugees in a rugged area like this? And it *would* be a great place for a batch of runaways to make a go of it. All the vacation cabins, all the seasonal visitors…" She shook her head. "City kids run to the streets when home isn't safe. Maybe, for a little while, the White Mountains gave our runaways a place to go, too."

Maks waited until she was done, and confirmed simply, "I was there."

She already knew him well enough to hear the rough quality of his voice over those few words. A job like that would make an impression on a young agent.

"You don't like to talk about it," she said.

His expression turned fierce, his words hard and sudden. "They deserve privacy," he said. "They deserve to go on with their lives. They can't do that if people think they're something to track down, to find and interview and put on display."

She met that green gaze with all the courage she had, feeling the prickle of the protective tiger roused. She managed to say, "Then it's a good thing brevis handled it so quietly."

A muscle in his jaw twitched. After another long moment, he rubbed a hand across the back of his neck, tipping his head in a quiet stretch. Then he said, "Let's go work your firebreak."

"I didn't mean—" To put him on the spot. To ask any more of him than he was already giving.

His quiet grin was back. "No help for it. Small town."

Right. And someone was bound to talk if her firebreak guy didn't actually work on the firebreak. "But your arm—"

"You can do all the heavy work," he assured her. When she scowled and poked him, he grinned, caught her hand, moving faster than she'd expected.

And then there in the sunshine, the grin suddenly faded

altogether as he stilled, staring at her—catching her gaze, catching her breath.

She wasn't lost in a vision; she wasn't plunging into a healing. It was just Katie and Maks, in a quiet sun-dappled parking lot, the trees rising up behind them. That she wanted so badly for him to close the distance between them...it couldn't be blamed on anything or anyone else but her.

Oh, little deer. Watch your step with this one.

Because being with Maks—being *near* Maks—would awaken things she'd never wanted to know about herself.

Chapter 9

"Maks Altán," Akins said, as if it was some sort of triumph.

Eduard didn't respond right away, his fingers curled lightly around the tiny espresso cup and a sticky, heavily iced bear claw teasing his nose with its sweet scent. *Maks Altán.* Of course. He'd survived. That *had* been him, taking point at the raid of Gausto's desert mansion not so long ago.

Not that there were so many Siberian shifters around to choose from. Plenty of wolves, variations on medium to large cats, a smattering of less usual predators, even fewer omnivores and grazers...

Fewer yet of the world's biggest cat. And who else would the Sentinels send into this area if they suspected trouble?

"I said—"

"Yes," Eduard interrupted. "It doesn't change anything, does it? Knowing his name?"

"You wanted to know." Akins's mouth grew sullen. As before, he straddled the back of his chair, but today his bravado looked a little thin. "They said he's there to clear a firebreak for her, but that's crap, right? I think they're doing some vertical jogging, you know?"

Now, *that* was interesting, just from a scientific point of view. His little water deer and the great tiger?

"Besides," Akins added with a smug and cocky look, "I did what you wanted. I messed with her head. By the time I'm done with her, she won't know if she's coming or going."

"And Altán?"

There. The smug, cocky look disappeared. "What, did you expect me to start a brawl right there in the farm store? I have to live in this place, you know."

Eduard hid his amusement. "I gather you had a confrontation." That was worth a precise, fork-cut piece of the bear claw. "And that you walked away."

Akins scowled. "I prodded him a little. I figured you'd want to know his mettle."

"His mettle," Eduard said, "is a given."

Akins shrugged it off, reverting to arrogance. "Doesn't matter. The Maddox bitch was upset, that was plain enough. And I got another dig at her reputation. You swear by the time this is over, she'll be screwed?"

"You'll get what you need," Eduard told him. *You just won't live to enjoy it.*

Just as Maks Altán would have to be handled before Katie could be taken, Akins would die shortly after Katie disappeared. Very shortly after. A car accident, perhaps. After which—with help from a few well-placed words— people would blame Akins for Katie's disappearance.

After all, Akins himself was so conveniently laying the groundwork for their enmity.

"Hey," Akins said, slapping the table, a sharp sound that

made several other café patrons startle and glare. "You hear about that creature?"

Ah. The creature.

"In fact," Eduard told him, folding his paper napkin in half and creasing it firmly, "I've seen it."

"No shit? I'd like to have me a piece of that. Maybe go hunting sometime."

Maybe *not* a car accident for Akins.

"If you finish this work for me," Eduard said, and nodded, "I think that can be arranged."

And then everyone would feel a guilty relief that this obvious danger to the community was gone, and the event would make the news. No one would wonder what had happened; no one would come looking for Eduard.

They'd probably look for Katie Maddox. But they wouldn't find her.

Maks flexed his arm and didn't bother pretending it didn't stretch and burn the healing flesh.

"Be careful." The sun shone on Katie's work-flushed face, and her hair threatened to tumble free from its ponytail.

"Katie Rae Maddox," he said, his words unguarded at the sight of her, "I surely will."

She narrowed her eyes as if she suspected they might be talking about two different things. Her hand rested on the sharp-toothed fire rake she used to clear a thick section of juniper seedlings; she wore a light long-sleeved shirt of baby-blue striping open over a stretchy coral tank top, and heavy jeans over clunky work boots. With her hands protected by pink-and-white pigskin work gloves, she looked just perfect.

If anything, her scowl grew. "You're grinning."

He didn't respond, because what could he say? He *was*

grinning. Just at the sight of her, and at the feel of the sun on the top of his head and the stretch of active muscle. If his arm burned and throbbed, at least it healed.

"I should work on that arm again," she told him, and she didn't have to say she was thinking about more than the injury, but also about the thing that neither of them would put into words just now. *The fugue.* And that which had happened two nights before, the astonishing connection they'd shared…not to mention the pain that had struck so unexpectedly.

Not that he'd talked about that. Not that he intended to.

He had to figure it out first.

Maks struck at the base of a small tree with a sharpened mattock, slicing it through at ground level. "Does it usually happen like that? Is that why you didn't stay to work healing in brevis?"

"You're chatty all of a sudden," she grumbled. She looked away, up into the rising slope of the national forest beyond her property; her hand tightened around the rake handle. "I think it was…" She took a deep breath. He stopped to watch her and she muttered, "Dammit," and aimed a few quick, savage strokes of the rake. The little juniper colony didn't stand a chance.

She stopped just as abruptly, and then marched straight up to him. He didn't try to contain his surprise—or his wariness. *"You,"* she said, and poked him in the shoulder. "I think it's *you.*"

"Me?" he echoed with raised brows—but just that fast, his surprise turned to thoughtful satisfaction.

She didn't flinch from him. She'd *poked* him. She even seemed bent on pushing back at him, making him prove he was safe.

If she kept it up, she'd learn he wasn't safe at all.

"I don't see things this deeply," she said, stuck in her

own frustration. "I don't get carried away by them. I don't lose my sense of self and I sure as hell don't—don't…"

She sputtered to a stop, the dismay on her face combined with a flush that had nothing to do with the sun or the work.

He reached out to her, his hand cupping the side of her jaw and ear, his fingers curling behind her neck. "It *is*," he told her. "Is there reason to fight it?"

She pushed his hand away. "Yes," she said flatly. "If it's being done *to* me. If it's not coming *from* me." She looked at him in frustration—a frank look, traveling the length of his body. "You're beautiful, Maks. Dammit, you're—" She surprised him by poking him again, harder, as if this was all his fault. "You're damned near irresistible! But this isn't the way I am—and I can't just accept it. I have to understand."

He hardly dared to move. The tiger stirred within him, provoked by her prodding just as he was provoked all over again by her proximity. "Maybe," he said, "this is you with *me*."

She snorted, a soft sound. "Trust a man to say something like that."

He spread his arms in confession.

But in his heart, he knew she was right—that there was something else.

He dropped his arms to his sides. The injured arm suddenly ached, deeper than the mere pain of use. The failure to heal. He turned his head away from her—like Katie, losing himself in the sight and scent of the pine woods marching up the ridge.

"Maks," she said, regret in that single word. She took a deep breath. "Whatever's going on, I'm afraid it's just not that simple."

He shot a quick glance at her, then bent to retrieve the

mattock, far too aware of the quick, shallow beat of his heart, the blood loss…the weakness he'd again pushed to its limit. "No," he said. "It's not." Another glance, sharper this time; he saw her take a quick breath at the impact of all the things left unspoken.

It's not. But it could be.

By tacit accord, they gathered the tools. Katie murmured something about sandwiches and a light healing session, but her reticence—and her stubborn adherence to her own truths—had brought Maks back on task. He'd allowed their work in the yard to seduce him—for those moments, he'd forgotten they were merely building his improvised cover, and he'd allowed himself to absorb this place as home again. To relax here, with Katie.

She'd been right to refocus him.

But when the utilitarian little truck pulled up in Katie's driveway, she took one look at the driver and fled.

Maks knew the man on sight, if not by acquaintance. And, like Katie, he knew what he saw—the graceful movement as the man stretched his arms out, rotating his shoulders, the sense of prowl and power.

Maks had asked Nick for help; he'd gotten it.

Even knowing that didn't stop the brief flare of territorial annoyance at the Sentinel's intrusion. *Another big cat.*

Maks was, he knew, not quite tame at heart. They'd told him long ago that he probably never would be…that wild moments like this would strike him unaware, and that he'd have to accept them and move through them.

So he did, and he went to meet the man, tools in hand and body language casual.

"Ian," the man introduced himself. Not as solid as Maks, not as tall, his hair a mussed style of premature gray with lingering streaks of black. "Ian Scott. We met at brevis—

not sure if you remember." He didn't let his gaze settle on Maks for too long. Instead he took in the layout of the place—the land, the access, the house in the middle of it. "Nick says you've got some trouble here."

"Some," Maks told him, remembering the man just fine—the amulet specialist who had worked so hard to understand the nature of the Flagstaff ambush—the man who blamed himself for being unable to provide brevis medical with answers. *AmSpec.*

All the same, he wasn't willing to cede the man any ground—putting Katie's interests before the Sentinels. Maks would make that decision—even if he wasn't supposed to. Even if he'd never so much as blinked at following brevis's lead before. A foot soldier—without nuance, without doubts. Dedicated, effective—lethally effective when necessary. A follower of orders.

But now, Maks had doubts. Because now, whether he should or not, Maks had a stake in what happened here.

In the wake of Maks's silence, Ian merely shifted in a way that evoked a twitching tail. "You want to cough up the amulet?"

Maks indicated the back of the house with a jerk of his head, then led Ian to the overturned flowerpot and its contents. The yellow cat appeared from some secret basking place, its sides warm against Maks's legs as it briefly blessed him with its presence and then ambled off.

Ian gave the flowerpot a look, offering Maks a sideways glance. "The cat," Maks said, understanding the question. "She cares about it."

Katie strode around the side of the porch—her face washed of work grime, her hair brushed into order and secured in a flipped ponytail to waterfall against her neck, her determination renewed. "Yes," Katie said, "she cares about the cat. We didn't know if the flowerpot would be any real protection, but at least it kept him from playing with the amulet."

"Not if you don't care about the pot," Ian agreed. "Katie Maddox? I'm Ian Scott. Brevis sent me to see about this thing."

"And take back some sort of report, I'm sure."

Ian's eyes gleamed with subtle humor. "You weren't supposed to suss that out. He said you weren't a field Sentinel."

"I'm not," Katie said shortly. "But I've had my share of exposure."

"He said that, too." Ian snagged a pair of ordinary barbecue tongs from the tactical bag and offered them a moment of concentration. A subtle surge of energy told Maks he'd shielded them—barriers as fine as silk and just as strong. Maks shouldn't have been able to assess them at all. He stepped back, uneasy at the dissonance murmuring down his spine. Ian raised his brows with a side glance. "I was told you weren't a sensitive."

"I'm not." His own shields were serviceable and without finesse or any particular flexibility, and he tended to use them as an afterthought. He was tiger at heart—a physical being, doing a physical job.

"Huh," Ian said, in clear if casual disbelief. But he kept his attention on his work, neatly flipping the flowerpot over and crouching to examine the amulet from beneath. "These silent amulets are a bitch. No point in taking chances."

"Silent," Katie said, moving closer to Maks. "That means it isn't just any amulet. Not something the average Core operative would have on hand."

"Not something the average Core *anyone* would have on hand," Ian agreed, using the tongs to flatten a tuft of grass and reveal the thing. Oily and black, just as before. Lurking, with an ugly kind of promise. "It's probably harmless at the moment. It doesn't feel activated, although it's hard to tell with these things."

"What's it supposed to do?" Katie didn't sound certain she wanted to know.

Ian shrugged. "That's even harder to tell. I'll need to get it to a safe area where I've got assistants working shield layers." He glanced at Maks from where he crouched. "You know why, better than anyone."

Maks made a sound in his chest. He knew why, all right.

"Well, we'll set up some wards here before I go—with three of us in the working, they'll be good and solid." Wards, once set, would self-maintain—unlike shields, which were a constant draw but were also more flexible. "Anything like this tries to get through again, it'll backfire on whoever's holding it. Sound good? It might mess with your seeings, though." He rested one knee on the gritty soil, his forearm propped across the other, the tongs dangling. Casual, with the amulet only inches away.

Maks grunted assent; Katie overrode it with her emphatic response. "Yes, *please,*" she said. "I can go somewhere else to hunt visions if I have to."

Maks turned to look at her, and she shook her head. "Seriously," she said. "I'd rather feel safe in my own home."

"I'm here," he reminded her.

"But *he,*" she pointed to Ian, "won't be. Oh, Maks, don't look like that. You would fight an army to keep me safe—I can see that. But you aren't supposed to have to face *this.* It—or something like it—almost killed you once already."

"Tell you what," Ian said, the perpetual dry note in his voice replaced by something carefully neutral. "If I ever need protection for one of my own, you're the guy I'll call. But this silent amulet situation…" He shook his head. "There are very few of us who can get a ping from one of these, even knowing they're *right there.*"

"You can," Katie said—an obvious guess, but one with confidence behind it.

"I can," Ian said, and gestured at the oily gleam in the bunchgrass. "Either someone's gone to a great deal of trouble to acquire this on your account, or you've caught the attention of someone powerful who can come up with it on his own."

His gaze drew inward, and Maks knew what he was doing the moment before he felt it—strengthening and refining his personal shields. Maks took a single step back, taking Katie with him—throwing up his own utilitarian shields for good measure.

Instantly, the fugue bit at him. Not phasing in, a sly invasion, but smacking him hard—if not so deep that he did more than stagger. It still sent him an extra step back into Katie. She made a sound of dismay—but she must have understood, for a trickle of her healing energy immediately washed up against him, tight and private and cautious.

He should have been prepared for the heat that also rose between them; his toes tried to grip the ground right through his sturdy shoes. *Katie Katie Katie* and sweet deer eyes and her body against his and—

Unexpected sparks of pain took him by surprise; one knee wobbled. He stiffened the leg, clinging to stability through pulsing, fractured colors and rising static. The pain turned into a throb, always that sensation of reaching...reaching...

Katie pinched him.

Dammit, she *pinched* him. Right in the tender skin on his side. His inner snarl pushed him through the worst of it, leaving him with the pulsing pound of fading pain. She withdrew her healing touch but kept her trembling hands at his back, as if she expected he might go down on her at any moment.

And yet she said nothing to Ian—leaving that up to Maks.

Ian seemed oblivious—or more likely, lost in the concentration that his task demanded. He dropped the amulet into his bucket, letting the thin braided leather lanyard drape over the side. "This'll tell me as much as anything, once I have it stretched out," he said, running the tongs along the length of the lanyard. "The knots they use—the type and placement—identify the amulets as clearly as any printed label. Give me a moment, and I'll have a rough draft of what they meant for this thing to do."

And then he looked directly at Maks, rising to his feet and with a big cat's sinuous grace. "I think we need to get someone else to take over up here so you can see the brevis medics."

Maks glared through the pain and dissonance. Behind him, Katie stiffened—but she was a healer, so she said bluntly, "He's probably right."

Maks thought nothing of *right* or of brevis at all. He thought of Katie. "Would you feel safe then?"

"That's not the point, Maks. You need to be well."

The glare turned to a snarl—silent, but just as potent. "They had their chance with me. And they sent me here for a reason."

"But they had no idea what was really going on," Katie protested—even as Ian carefully kept his distance.

"You told them."

"I told them," she agreed, a kind of anguish briefly twisting her mouth. "But I've been holding back for years, Maks. For most of my life." She glanced at Ian, including him in her confession. "I didn't want them calling me into the field. So no one at brevis has any reason to take my warning at face value."

A little piece of him, deep inside—beneath the waning

throb of pain, beneath that clawing sense of *reaching*—turned cold and hard. "You knew of *Core D'oiche?*"

She nodded; her hands crept up until she hugged her arms. "But not like you're probably thinking. I knew there was danger, and that it was widespread, and about when it would hit. And I *told* them, Maks, I did! But what could they do on the strength of such vague words?"

"What *would* they do?" Ian said, pretending he wasn't in the middle of a very private conversation. "If they mistakenly believed your visions to be limited and localized?"

"Well, they *are!*" The words burst out of her. "Usually, they *are!* And as far as I can tell, whatever's going on here is localized, too. It's just…" She frowned. "It's also *not.*"

Ian scraped a hand through silvered hair, turning its spiky style into something more random. "Local," he said, "but rippling outward." He gave Maks a pointed look. "I still have to talk to Nick."

Report to Nick, he meant. But Maks found himself full of certainty. "Brevis can't help me," he said. "I am what I am. I might as well be what I am here in Pine Bluff." Where Katie needed him.

"Helluva situation," Ian said. "We're all right, and we're all wrong." He dropped the tongs in his bag, picking up the bucket. "I can tell you more about this in a few moments. But there's no way around calling Nick."

Something about the way he said it caught Maks's attention. "He sent you to check on me."

"He told me to keep my eyes open," Ian said, easily enough. "And you don't get to stay alive in the amulet-handling business unless you've got an eye for detail." He hefted the bucket at them in a sardonic kind of salute. "This thing's a subtle son-of-a-bitch. I need a moment. Just a field estimate, but we'll know the category and strength of it." He glanced at Maks. "I'll let you know what Nick says."

Chapter 10

"He sees too much," Katie said, staring at Ian as he headed for the car with the tactical bag slung over his shoulder and the bucket dangling from the other hand. Though she thought—she *hoped*—the man hadn't been able to perceive what passed between her and Maks.

Or at least not all of it.

His expression turned aggrieved. "You *pinched* me."

Katie bit her lip on a smile. "I did," she said. Bold, bold deer. "And it worked, too—without setting up that feedback loop."

Maks growled. For once, that trill of fear didn't run down between Katie's shoulder blades. Instead, she laughed.

But she sobered quickly enough. "I wish I knew why that happens," she said, thinking of what she had felt in him. "You know. When I touch—"

"I *know*," he said, cutting her short—twisting to face her without quite taking his attention from Ian and his work on the tailgate of his vehicle—or the phone he had sitting on the tailgate, a phone earpiece tucked into place at the side of his head.

She opened her mouth on doubts and confusion, then shook her head, settling on simpler words. "Oh, Maks, what if Nick calls you back in?"

So many things unsaid there. *What if he sends someone else who makes me feel threatened? What if I can't figure out what's going on behind my visions?*

What if I don't want you to leave?

Maks made a quiet chuffing sound...a tiger's noise. "I'm not going."

After she'd had a moment to absorb those words, feeling them sink in past her skittery fears, he tipped his head toward Ian.

Katie understood it as loudly as words. *Let's see what he's found.*

Ian didn't look up as they approached. He'd secured the amulet inside a Mylar envelope—one that, like the tongs, was presumably micro-shielded. The braided leather stretched across the tailgate, lying on a protective quilted pad that looked a whole lot like Kevlar. His cell phone sat off to the side, its deep red case sparkling in the sun, the earpiece beside it.

"This part's easy," he told them, wielding a pair of chopsticks—running them down that braided thong and the complex series of knots near the amulet. "It's a passive working—nothing that would have literally blown up in your faces—but it's also meant to have an effect on a specific target. It's got a lot of layers...multipurpose. And it targets by proximity, but most of them do that." He frowned at it a moment, gone thoughtful. "It reminds me a little of what we found up in Flagstaff at Joe Ryan's place—the one that latched its hooks into his energy signature. That was a more active working, though."

"That's it?" Maks said, as disappointment washed over Katie. "Nothing more specific?"

Ian snorted. "You have any idea what it takes to decipher these things?"

Maks didn't look repentant. He leaned over the tailgate, ignoring Ian's raised brow of warning—but not, Katie noticed, going any closer. "I told Nick to send his best."

"That," Ian said, with neither humility nor hubris, "would be me."

"You read all that from just the knots?" Katie wasn't inclined to get closer, herself. It had been a long time since her basic amulet courses—and the Core, it seemed, had introduced a number of refinements since then.

"It's a little like palm-reading." Ian cast her a rueful glance, with something of an apology behind it. "The Core masters each have their own style…and the knots mean something just a little bit different for each of them. Their assistants tend to reflect that style, but…not exactly."

Katie couldn't help the disappointment in her voice. "Then you won't really know for sure until you neutralize it."

"Not for sure," Ian agreed. He ran the chopsticks down over the cord one more time, as if simply feeling the pattern of the knots would tell him something. "I'll get back to the Tucson lab tomorrow. As soon as I know, I'll give you a call."

"A couple of days?" she guessed.

"Depends what else comes up," he said, glancing at her as he stood, wrangling the cord and the chopsticks with absent-minded skill. "I can tell you this much. We found a lot of amulets in this style at Gausto's stronghold. No big surprise—anyone in this area would have fallen under his influence. And whoever planted this one has both skill and power to play with."

He sealed the bucket and turned around, arms crossed. Under his scrutiny, Katie eased back a step, struck by pale gray eyes edged with black lashes. *Snow leopard.* He told her, "You should come in."

She mutely shook her head. She wasn't ready to return to brevis, where once again she'd be trapped and surrounded. Not that anyone would *mean* to intimidate her, but...

As Maks might say, it was what it was.

"Nick said you wouldn't come." Ian spoke with resigned acceptance. "I brought a couple of detectors for you—it's the best we can do, if they're using silent amulets. And we'll set wards before I go. Just the house, but it'll give you a safe zone."

Katie breathed a sigh of relief. "Thank you," she said. "Maybe it'll give me the chance to figure out what's going on here."

"Or what's about to," Ian said, that single sardonic brow lifted. Dark, like his lashes, in spite of his silvered hair.

Maks lifted his head, as if something in the mountains had called to him. "I should go look," he told her. "I should find this creature your friends spoke of."

"Do tell," Ian said, most politely.

The look Maks cast him wasn't as polite as all that. "Local talk. If I find anything, I'll report it."

"You may not have the chance." Ian indicated his phone. "It doesn't take long for Nick to decide what he wants. We talked; he's calling you back in."

Maks just looked at him.

"Right," Ian said, not slow to get that message. "Well, then—my job here is done, wouldn't you say?"

"Tell Nick," Maks said suddenly, "to send us backup. That amulet wouldn't be here if Katie wasn't a threat to someone. The creature wouldn't be here if there wasn't something going on. What she's seen is important, even if we don't know why yet."

"I agree," Ian said easily. "Someone with Core skills clearly doesn't want an active seer in this area. And the rest of the precinct isn't likely to be happy about another independent—Gausto's bad behavior embarrassed the hell out of the Core's Septs Prince. They're not going to be careful about collateral damage, if it comes to taking out their rogue."

"They would have been glad enough if Gausto had succeeded," Maks said, little more than a growl.

"If you hadn't taken down his Fortress of Solitude, you mean," Ian said. "You do realize that you earned your life-time keep right then and there, don't you? There's no reason to jeopardize yourself here if you're not ready."

Maks said, "There's every reason," as if that ended the conversation. And maybe it did, for with a glance at Katie, he added, "I won't be gone long." He turned toward the woods, and didn't go far before taking the tiger.

Ian sighed, catching Katie's gaze with his own. "Nick said he wouldn't come back in." He shook his head. "You know he's messed up, right? I mean, if *I* could feel it…"

"I know." Katie's voice felt like a scratch in her throat. "He should never have come here."

And then what would I have done?

Ian shook his head again. "Here, then," he said. "Let's get the house warded, and these detectors set up." And then he looked straight at her and added, "Think about going back in to brevis. Because until you come in…he won't."

Maks pushed the pace for several miles, heading west-ward without conscious decision.

Home.

For those first few miles, he let himself *be.* Tiger, ghosting through the high pines, absorbing the sights and sounds and scents. Tiger, letting himself be absorbed by it all in return.

Eventually he let more human thoughts drift to the surface. *There's no reason to jeopardize yourself,* Ian had told him—not wasting words in doing it, and not pretending he couldn't see that which Maks had managed to keep hidden until he'd come here. Until he'd come *home.*

But staying here was about much more than *home,* and about more than Katie. It was about sensing a *wrongness,* as well as knowing he had to resolve his own inner plight before he ever made it back to brevis.

Because that wasn't going to happen while he was trapped in brick and steel. He'd been there, done too much of that. Only in those stolen moments when he'd thrown himself into the raid at Gausto's stronghold had he felt anything but restless…anything but driven.

He was a protector. Denied that, he was…

A tiger with nowhere to go.

The woods rolled out before him, welcoming him…letting him think, even as he hunted. When he recognized the first dip of land, the first trickle of a rare high-country creek, he stopped—lowering to his belly, letting his tail twitch.

Here he was.

Enough years had passed that familiar trails had wandered and the foliage had shifted. Some trees were bigger; some trees were gone—it changed that first visual imprint.

But his bones knew this land.

And he'd known, when he'd heard of the creature, that this was the first place to look.

He spent a few moments panting by the water—taking intermittent laps and letting old memories come closer to the surface.

Then. This was the place in which he'd learned to live. The place in which he had found others like himself— fully human, far too young, but also on the run. And under Maks's protection, no one was ever beaten in an alcoholic haze, battered in rage, or touched in places that should have remained private.

Now. This was no longer a benign place. Whispers of Core corruption eddied across the land, pooling west and north.

His woods had been invaded. And, these years later, the invaders had grown smarter, more subtle. The territorial workings imbued into this area would affect any man, Sentinel or not. *Keep away go home something's wrong*...a running thread of impulses, all designed to keep this area free from interference.

Not nearly as effective, once recognized.

Maks released the growl into a short, coughing tiger's roar and snarl.

Across the creek and up the hill, something *whuffed* back at him; it held the cavernous sound of something profoundly large. The faint breeze shifted, bringing with it a musky, skunk-like scent.

Javelina.

Except...not. Not with the size of whatever had made that sound.

Head lowered, Maks padded across the creek and into the land that had once been his, but was now tainted by Core presence.

The musk grew stronger; the breeze carried a low grunting noise that made way for the rapid-fire chatter of tusk against tusk.

Warning.

He got a first glimpse of it through the trees. Grizzled gray coat, hackles spiking over its neck, tusks long and gleaming...

And three times larger than any javelina ought to be.

It rattled another threat, rearing briefly and inexplicably to its hind legs before dropping back down and looking straight toward Maks.

Not deep-set little poor-sighted piggy eyes. Eerie, horrible *human* eyes.

Maks abandoned all pretense of stealth, breaking into a heavy, padding trot—tail stiff, head low, ears back and whiskers disapproving—weaving quickly through the intervening trees to take the measure of this thing more directly.

It stunk of Core. More than just javelina musk, but an overlay of the dead, dark energy routinely stolen and twisted by the Core for its workings, a sharp and stinging scent. Maks lifted his lips in a silent tiger snarl of disdain, circling to the side of the creature with a sideways cant of his head. Watching, always watching.

The javelina turned in place, keeping Maks before it—tossing its head in a mime of slashing tusk, once again offering its deep bark—but not without a gleam of intelligence, and just maybe, a hint of amusement.

There was, however, no fear.

Maks stopped his circling, lowering to a crouch; he coughed out another roar in challenge, his tail flicking behind him.

The javelina stuttered forward, bouncing off its front legs, jaws gaping and tusks fully exposed—and then it charged, those eerie human eyes laughing.

Maks crouched even lower, held ground—and sprang to the side as it passed, swiping out with one massive paw, claws sliding through the coarse hair and just barely snagging flesh. His claws dug into earth, scattering thick pine needles and musty dirt as he sprang after the creature, both front paws spread and reaching—

It whirled, meeting him with a maw of sharp and slashing tusks; he tumbled aside, rolling and coming back onto his feet to spring away—and quite suddenly *alive,* as immersed in the tiger as he could ever be and glorying in it, understanding how much he'd missed it over these past years—

He dove back into the fight, paws batting lightning fast, catching the giant peccary a solid blow to one haunch with the satisfaction that came of claws sinking into meat.

It wheeled with a squeal of fury, slashing past his face and diving at his flank. He twisted aside, avoiding that disemboweling blow with a wild leap, coiling back around—

The air split with a startlingly unnatural sound—part airhorn, part vuvuzela—and for that instant, Maks froze.

For that instant, so did the massive javelina. It took a step back, its head lifting and its mouth gaping…and its eyes again laughing. And then it quite calmly trotted away, grunting with each step—blood gleaming on its haunches and scenting air already redolent with musk.

Maks swung around in an instant bound forward—

Keep away go home something's wrong…

And this time he listened.

He stood, poised, not a little bit stunned at the implications of the encounter—how deeply the Core had insinuated itself here, how far beyond the bounds of decency they'd gone.

A creature not nearly human…but no longer anything close to javelina. Trained, responsive…deadly. And though it had so far restricted itself to livestock, Maks had no doubt it could kill humans—that it would, if it wasn't stopped.

But running headlong toward the Core handlers who had blown that horn wasn't the way to stop it.

With a final silent snarl in the direction of the fleeing creature, Maks turned and picked his way across the sullen summer creek flow, his ears flat and the very white tip of his tail twitching.

Because these past few moments weren't truly about finding a creature, or even about killing it once found. They were about the depth of what the Core was up to here—the lines being crossed, where no Core presence should be here at all.

And no one knew better than Maks just what that might entail.

Eduard spread the amulets on the table before him, lining them up before his primary power source amulet. The one fueled by the death of so many lives along his long journey, not to mention the trail of pines turned brown, the soil gone sterile...

Eduard well knew his work surpassed that of any previous Core technician.

It certainly surpassed that of any Sentinel. Sentinels, so limited, each with their own set of skills. Eduard could be any of them; he could be all of them.

But exacting science drew its price. The elements of will had to be combined...

Just so.

And if not, there were consequences. Such as the one now collapsed into a heap of muddled flesh before him.

"Take it away," he said, in some disgust. A drone in a tight black T-shirt and black slacks moved forward to scrape what was left of the stray mutt into a disposal container.

Eduard needed Katie Maddox.

Sentinel though she might be, it was her touch that had left the injured shepherd mix so attuned to itself and its own nature that it had quite nearly made a successful transition to human. And that transition, complete, would be the first step to erasing any hint of Sentinel advantage.

Eduard's lips pressed thin. Back at Gausto's stronghold, Eduard had come much closer than this. He had created the woman Jet, pulling her out from her native wolf shape. She had been stable, had learned to change from one form to another; she had been trained and active in the Core's employ, before Nick Carter had stolen her away.

But now Eduard was starting anew—knowing that the intricate foundation pieces must be redesigned to find a better balance. His subjects needed enough tenacity to survive the process, but enough bidability to be of use once successfully transformed. He now snatched dogs from the reservations, grabbing up the copious strays.

And now, he began to see that he would be unable to perfect the process without Katie Maddox to heal and prepare these often battered animals.

Once he had the process perfected, he could begin to reverse it. He could give the Core what it had always lacked—a means to meet the Sentinels at their own level.

If he succeeded, the Core would laud him for it. And he would quite abruptly no longer be working in a dark underground Quonset structure with far too many smelly animals crowded into far too little space.

A strong odor invaded his concentration—that of the little side project he'd put together to help himself define certain of the project's foundational elements. If the smell hadn't warned him, the dogs would have—half of them cowering, half of them bristling.

"The creature is not to be brought into this work space," he said, not bothering to turn around.

"Jacques is hurt."

Afonasii, with his faintly sentimental streak, had insisted on naming the thing. Eduard turned from his work to survey both the transformed javelina and the man. The giant peccary stared back with its all-too-knowing human eyes.

I made you too smart, he thought at it.

Just as well he'd implanted it with the same kind of controlling partner amulet that had once held Jet in thrall, making it so easy to invoke pain and compliance. He slipped a hand into one of the many extra pockets of his lab coat, closing fingers around exactly what he wanted— the controller. Afonasii winced in sympathy, but wisely said nothing—and the peccary stood stock still as Eduard approached.

He realized with some surprise that the creature's injury was in fact significant—for there was nothing in these woods to challenge a peccary of this size, never mind one imbued with the intelligence this one now possessed. "What—" he started, and then stopped himself, lifting his gaze to pin Afonasii with accusation. "Maks Altán," he said. "The tiger. You allowed him into our territory?"

"No, I—" Afonasii shut his mouth—shut it hard, as he looked for some answer he dared to say. "I thought you might be able to heal Jacques."

It was no answer at all, but it was enough to guess at the truth. "No? Then you must have again allowed this creature to push the boundaries of our territory."

"He works best for us when allowed to fulfill his curious nature," Afonasii said, his voice as toneless as possible. Defeated. He knew what was coming.

"Nonsense," Eduard said, his voice crisp. His fingers caressed the controlling amulet. The creature's handlers had controls of their own; they knew how to apply varying intensities of correction. "Correct him now, at an appropriate level, or I will."

Afonasii's mask broke. "But Mr. Forrakes, he won't understand—"

"Don't be absurd." Eduard looked straight into the peccary's too-human eyes. "He understands every word. Do it yourself, now, or leave it up to me—and you can most certainly be assured I won't hesitate to use optimal levels."

Afonasii reached into his pocket—his movement without commitment, his eyes on the preternaturally placid javelina.

"Afonasii," Eduard said, his voice a silk that made the man jerk to attention. "You allowed this creature to encounter our most significant enemy." No one else would pursue the Core like Maks Altán…and no one else was as suited to find them here. "As a result, I'll have to step up my plans to acquire Miss Maddox—and at the same time, to eliminate this Sentinel who has in the past eluded us with annoying ease. Do you understand the significance of these facts? Of the depth of your failure here today?"

He thought the man did. Classic swarthy Core skin tones didn't pale easily, but when they did…

Most satisfying.

Chapter 11

Katie sat in the rocker on her front porch, the yellow cat in her lap, the afternoon of this very, very long day waning into early evening. A salad waited in the fridge, along with a slab of steak and a nice batch of raw spinach that she *would* convince Maks to eat.

When her phone trilled, she jerked out of her reverie, fumbling to grab it off the porch railing without knocking it over the edge.

"Catch you at a bad time?" Marie asked her knowingly, hearing that fumble come through in Katie's somewhat breathless voice.

"Just lost in thought," Katie said. "And clumsy."

Marie snorted, not bothering to be genteel about it. "As if there ever was a day *you* were clumsy," she said, as a spate of barking sounded in the background.

"That doesn't sound like Rowdy."

"It's not," Marie said. "I'm at the vet clinic. Mr. Rowdy is getting a precautionary X-ray."

"He—what? Is he all right? He seemed fine yesterday."

"You know Rowdy," Marie said darkly. "I've been watching him like a hawk and never saw him get into anything, but he's off today and he's got a little temperature, so we're just being cautious. Especially with those surgical stitches barely out. But that's not why I called."

Katie paused to absorb this. "Then…?"

She heard the phone against Marie's cheek, the jangle of the bells on the clinic door, and then the day's stiff breeze scraping across the phone pick-up. "Sorry," Marie said. "I should have come out here before I made the call, but the waiting room was empty when I pulled the phone out." She didn't wait for Katie to respond before barging ahead. "Katie, I'm hearing things that have me worried. I don't believe them, trust me, but the way people gossip…"

Katie blinked, her quiet, tired calm washed away by stirring anger. She forgot to stroke the yellow cat, and he bumped her hand with his head. "Akins, I'll bet. Does that man have *nothing* else to do?"

"Problem is, he's convincing," Marie muttered, as if she didn't want to say it at all. "If you don't know that he's got a grudge against you—and most of these people don't—then he's *damned* convincing. And…"

Katie heard the reluctant tone in her friend's voice, gave her the push she needed. "And what?"

"Too many people saw that cat die in your hands the other day, that's what. They don't think any further—except to repeat the rest of Akins's crap. It makes for a whole bunch of people who don't know a thing and who suddenly think they know everything."

Katie tucked her lower lip under a slightly pointed canine, biting back exasperation. "I don't know what I can—"

"Get a lawyer," Marie said, as blunt as ever. "Get a lawyer *now*. I am not kidding, Katie Rae." Her stern voice made it clear she wasn't anywhere near *kidding*—but then her tone changed. "Oh, hey, I think the vet tech is looking for me in there. Call you later, okay?"

"Let me know about Rowdy," Katie said numbly, and heard only dead air. She looked at the phone a long moment, thinking black thoughts about Akins's timing, and slowly set it aside—no longer peaceful here in her quiet early evening.

And no longer alone.

Her deer spotted the tiger before the rest of her truly saw him, there at the edge of the trees—move and pause, move and pause, assessing the area for hikers and bikers. And while the deer in her stiffened in instinctive response, the rest of her felt a welcoming warmth...a relief.

The shadowed trees shimmered with his change, blue light tumbling over itself and shot through with strobing bolts. Maks strode out from the trees as he'd left her, flannel shirt over jeans, tough feet bare. He walked with an easy strength that made her think of the tiger—grounded to earth, the power for speed when needed and the patience to rein it in when not.

Only when he got closer did she see the fatigue in his expression—and then, as he shifted angle, the slashing cut across his cheek.

But the smile he gave her wasn't that of a man on his last legs. Katie felt the satisfaction of that, seeing how well her healing had taken. Thinking, too, that he could use another session.

By the time he reached the foot of the porch steps, she'd slipped the cat off her lap and gone to the top step, surprised by the swell of that little warm spot. "I'm glad you're back," she told him, giving way to it.

His eyes were dark in the shadow of the ridge; sunset

came early to this land and dusk lasted approximately forever. "Has there been trouble?" he asked, swiping at his
cheek. "Ian—?"

"Everything's fine." She leaned against the porch post.
"Ian left a little while after you did. I've been shifting ap-
pointments and working on next week's kennel club pre-
sentation."

His face twitched at a new trickle of blood. She reached
out to wipe gentle fingers across his cheek, and instantly
plunged into an intensity of seeing—*pungent scent...flash
of green and spinning, grizzled gray...slash of wicked white
tusk...*

*Power. Surging strength, self-aware prowess...the coil
and stretch of muscles honed to perfection, reflexes sharp.*

Katie found herself looking into eyes of tiger-green, her
breath coming fast, her cheeks and body flushed. *This,* she
realized suddenly, was what it was to be predator. What
it was to be *Maks.*

"Katie Rae?" he said, and his voice was calm amid all
that wild. Controlled.

Because, she realized, he was comfortable with it. With
it and with himself.

"Fine," she said, if somewhat breathlessly, still bemused
by the vision and still bemused by the fact that it had hit
her at all—still captured by its effect on her. "Maks, I—"

He wasn't so oblivious as all that. He lifted her right off
the porch to him, the one arm giving way ever so slightly,
and when he said, "Katie Rae," again, his voice was entirely differently. A little lower. A little catch that she could
hear from the inside out, the feel of it a delicious scrape
against her senses.

"I wish I understood—" she said desperately, clinging
to his shoulders and swamped in that rise of warmth, rev-

eling in it…confused by it. Knowing Maks would likely pay if she acted on it. "I don't know you," she said. "Not really. So what I felt when I saw you in the woods…was that real? Or is it driven by what I see? What I've *seen?*"

"Is that how the sight does things?" His hands lingered at her waist, settling lower so his thumbs caressed her hip bones while his fingers curved around behind, gently and unmistakably possessive. "Because why, then, would I feel it too?"

She sucked in a breath at the sharp pull of him. "For a man of few words," she said, "you sometimes choose them damned well."

His smile curved a little. "I try not to need them at all."

She groped for balance. "You're hurt again."

"Yes," he agreed, and didn't move. He merely stood there, with her, his hands quietly possessive of her—until she realized, with some surprise, that it meant something to him. Just this.

"You're *being*," she said, voicing the surprise.

He made an agreeable sound from deep in his chest. With some hesitation, she closed her eyes, feeling the warmth of his body, breathing lightly of his mixed scent, the pines still hot from the sun. She allowed the underlying tingle of trepidation from the deer; she found the delighted little quiver of response in his presence and didn't judge it or try to do anything about it.

There was no vision, no healing in process, no trickle of connecting power. There was just them. Her heart beat faster, kicking up a notch.

Maks made another little sound in his chest…satisfaction. Katie's eyes fluttered open so she could see his face and absorb that, too. She had the impulse to run her fingers across his mouth—to feel its warmth and definition.

Maks smiled faintly. It struck tender little sparks across

her body, and he must have discerned that, too, for his smile widened—

And then he stiffened, the breath turned to a sharp, swallowed inhalation, his eyes flying open to green and wild and—

Frightened.

Confused.

She felt it, too—the tight pull of fear, the tangle of not understanding, being jarred out of the sweetness of the moment into—

She felt that, too—just a hint of it. His pain. *Again.*

::Maks?:: she sent him, instinctively reaching out in a way she'd so far avoided. So personal, the mind-voice, so hard to hide the truth of what one was.

In response, she felt a quick buffet of denial, a strong impression of dismay; she gasped at it. Maks gave her a startled look, closed his eyes on the wild green, and stepped back. One step, so deliberate and purposeful.

The pain faded; the sense of him muted.

"What—" she said, barely more than a whisper.

He shook his head. Blood trickled down his slashed cheek, and though his brow drew from the faintest of frowns, she knew it wasn't directed at her. She took a deep breath…and let it go, if only for the moment. She made her voice matter-of-fact. "What happened out in the woods?"

"The Core." Short words, hard-spoken. His glance went out to the woods. "They're back."

Darkness and the stench of corruption and suffering—

She pulled herself away from memories—still haunting him, still trickling through to her—steeling her voice and her restlessness. "You found them?"

His expression darkened. "I found what they have made."

"It's real? The creature?"

The look on his face was answer enough.

"I'd convinced myself it wasn't," she admitted. "It's not like people haven't been hunting it—that they haven't taken out dogs and tromped the woods."

He said simply, "I knew where to look." He barely gave her time to absorb the implications of that statement before he added, "The Core has workings."

Understanding bloomed. "Keep-aways," she said, thinking of what Ian had said about a Core rogue. *Not playing by the rules.* "No dog would cross that line. No human, either—they wouldn't even recognize it."

Frustration crossed his features; he shook his head. "Exactly where they hide…" He let his voice trail away, and simply shook his head. "I never did know."

Sorrow assailed her again, coming to her from him no matter that he'd stepped away, glimpses of a woman gaunt and fierce, not so very much older than Katie was now. Running as the woman, running as a tiger—not so massive as Maks, wounded…determined. Someone else's blood streaking her pale throat.

Strong, throat-clamping grief—there and gone again.

Maks turned away.

She cleared her throat—still not asking. *Not yet.* "I know that you've got to report this…you've got to eat—"

He interrupted with a shake of his head, barely perceptible.

She said faintly, "You grabbed something to go, I take it?"

"And I already talked to brevis."

"How—?"

"Annorah," he told her. "On the way back. She listens for those of us in the field." He waited for her to take it in, then added, "She wants you to know that they understand—there, at brevis—that this is bigger than they expected. They're gathering a team. Until they come…we stay quiet. I'll keep you safe."

"Nick still wants you back in Tucson, I bet."

Maks didn't answer, which was answer enough.

Katie buffed her hands over her arms, feeling the tingle of her own distressed energies—gathering them up, flicking them off her hands like water. "Maks," she said, "I need to understand what happens between us when I touch you—"

Except then she instantly blushed with annoying intensity as he raised his eyebrows in a very clear *Don't you?*

"I *mean*," she told him, "the *other* thing that happens. The energy I feel, the distress it seems to cause you. I want to try a healing—a controlled one. I have no intention of letting that cheek scar for lack of treatment, for one thing—and I want to see…" She trailed off, bit her lip, and hunted for the words that would say what she meant. *I want to see if I get caught up in you. I want to see if I end up kissing you. I want to see if I can manage myself.*

Maks made a noise that didn't quite sound like laughter—closer to the chuffing sound the tiger might make. "If you touch me," he said, "I'm going to want you. You know that."

She lifted her chin, and her smile was less a smile than the faintest baring of her deer's tusks.

Not that those, in the best of times, were anything to fear.

He nodded at the woods. "Be with me, then. Work on the tiger."

Her whole body froze at the prospect. *In the woods. With the tiger.* With the night falling softly around them and the air scenting up with a hint of dew.

"Run with me," he said, and he was utterly serious… genuinely hopeful. As if for a moment, he didn't get it.

Didn't understand that her reaction came from the thought of being deer beside tiger.

But he'd defied brevis for her. He'd fought for her. He'd touched her and let himself be touched by her.

She took a deep breath, acquiescing. "The edge of the forest?"

He held out his hand. This time, he waited for hers.

This time, she gave it to him. She came with him when he moved away from the porch, barefooted in the scruffy grass and inevitable prickly weeds.

There, in the darkness just inside the tree line, he released her. Blue lightning flickered around him, enveloped him, licking out to brush her with its energies. The tingle of it rushed across her skin. Displaced air poofed out to stir her hair and clothes.

And there he was.

Just so casually as that, tiger.

And the tiger yawned, and stretched again, offering a short, raspy refrain that this time served as a harsh purr. He lowered himself to the ground, rolling over to one side.

She remembered to breathe again. She remembered who she was, what she was: Katie Rae Maddox, who could put her hands on bone and flesh and give it ease.

She knelt behind his shoulders, resting her hands behind his ruff—surprised to find the hair slicker than expected, coarse and stiff and lying smooth.

He rolled that massive head back to look at her, one front leg reaching for nothing in particular, the great paw spread to briefly knead air. And he made his little chuffing sound again, rasp-rasp-rasp, and Katie had the distinct impression he was laughing.

"You," she said, and poked him.

He subsided, but his whiskers still twitched.

"You," she said, more of a murmur this time—as, kneel-

ing there, she sank her fingers into his pelt and sank her being into her healing place.

Into Maks.

Chapter 12

Tigers didn't purr. Not like house cats; the tiger throat was made for a roar. But a tiger had a rasping faux-purr exhalation, a conversational chuff…an expressive groan.

Maks used them all.

She kneaded his shoulders, his spine, his legs…she even kneaded his toes, spreading his paws to check each joint, stretching and flexing. Utter luxury. When she was done he offered the first one all over again, stretching the toes wide without extruding his claws…a tiger's flirt.

She laughed, and when he rolled halfway to his back with his front legs splayed, utterly without dignity, she took him up on the invitation and scratched his chest and the base of his throat. "Not done yet," she told him. "It's going to take a little more to deal with your face." She crossed her legs and patted her lap. Maks rolled to his chest to stare at her. "Yes, I mean it," she told him. "I need to concentrate, so get comfortable."

He eased closer, draping his neck over her leg and letting the weight of his head settle in her lap. She stroked along his jaw; she felt along his ears, petted his whiskers… dared to lift his lip and touch a tooth. He flicked an ear and let her have her way.

Truth be told, he nearly fell asleep.

He woke fully from that doze when the energies grew strong, tugging at his face—burning. He flattened his ears back, lifting his head—or starting to.

"Don't be a baby," she said, absent words in the throes of deep concentration. He smacked his tail against the ground, offended, and settled back down. After a time, the tug and burn eased. She took a deep breath and stroked from his broad nose along his cheeks and up by his ears, a gesture of finality.

His tension ebbed away; he breathed out a deep rumble of satisfaction and pushed his head gently into her hand.

She leaned over his ear. "Men," she murmured, the teasing already evident even in that one word. "You're so easy."

His ears flattened; he rolled to his feet, and her gasp of surprise changed to understanding as the bright, shifting energies of the change bloomed around them. By the time he came to his knees he had fully become the man, barefooted, pine needles clinging to flannel.

Easy?

But he didn't have to say it; she saw his aggrieved expression and laughed out loud.

As the laughter faded, she reached out to stroke his cheek. Still tender, but no more than that. "Maks," she said. "It *worked*. I didn't know if I could do that without…" She trailed off, smiled, and shrugged. "Without getting lost in you."

Maks gave way before her, reaching out with his wordless, wild inner voice. He sent her his confusion, his desire…he sent her the very essence of who he was. Neither predator nor prey, but just Maks…and more vulnerable than she might ever guess.

Katie jerked as unexpected emotion washed through her—a wistfulness, a gentle touch of invitation…blatant honesty, but full of confusion and admiration and even pride.

None of which were hers.

"Maks?" she whispered.

He cocked his head slightly, and the emotion shifted to relief—to something of gratitude.

"That's *you?* Those…feelings? It's been you all along?" Those moments when he'd seemed silent, and yet during which she'd gotten some strong sense of him regardless.

Not silent at all, apparently. Just not full of formed words. Maybe not such a surprise as all that, given how few of them he used in general.

She touched his cheek again, where the wound was closed but still pink, readily discernible in her clear Sentinel's night vision. He pushed against her hand, just a hint of pressure—the tiger's gesture. His wordless voice touched her with a warmth—not so much a promise as an offering.

"Maks," she said again, barely audible.

She'd insisted on this healing not just for him, but for her—to know, for certain, that she could indeed still work without losing herself in her patients…or in *him.* And now she knew. Whatever kept happening between them—the spark of desire, flaring hot and sudden, the clear flood of emotion and images, it wasn't about her healing process.

And in knowing, she found herself unexpectedly receptive to the warmth of his mental touch. She curved her hand back to his nape, stroking the sensitive skin under his ear with her thumb; she thrilled to it when he closed his eyes just to *feel*—and when he shared that with her. The tingle of tightening skin down the back of his neck suddenly found its way down hers, the responses it drew from within his body suddenly bloomed within hers.

"Oh," she breathed, startled by the understanding—by the sharing. For a long moment, he let her touch him; he let her experience what it did for him—and he let her absorb that it was about more than *touch,* it was about who was doing the touching.

Katie in the sunshine, Katie with determination in her eye, Katie laughing...singing...bounding across the yard... Katie's hands clutching at him, a sob of pleasure in her throat...

She saw all that, and she saw through the matter-of-fact layers of civilized Maks to what had long lay beneath.

The vulnerability. The feral honesty.

His eyes fluttered open, fastening on her gaze—a tiger's round pupils in a tiger's eyes. She almost didn't hear him—the merest hint of spoken words in her mind. ::*Katie Rae.*::

"I'm here," she said out loud, her low voice cutting into a night otherwise silent, with only the pines rustling above them and an occasional cicada burring through darkness.

::*Be,*:: he said.

She let the touch of his emotions reach her; she fed hers back. She watched those feelings spiral, felt the tangle tighten between them until she wasn't sure if her skin tingled, or his...if the growing heat pooling along her spine came from one of them or both of them.

In the end it didn't matter. They moved in the same instant, and by the time her hands wrapped around his neck, his had cupped her face. By the time little sparks of intensity fluttered low in her belly, he'd pushed up against her. By the time their lips met, it wasn't Maks kissing Katie or Katie kissing Maks, but a fierce and mutual clash.

But just that fast, his hands tensed around her face; his breath was lost in her mouth. An instant later she felt it, too—a sharp stab of hot iron in the deepest part of herself. *No! Not again!*

He slammed personal shields up between them, wrenching himself away so abruptly that she cried out with the loss of him—and still she felt it, spreading like an inner flood from her solar plexus through her chest, down her belly, trickling into her limbs.

By the time she opened her eyes, he'd twisted aside, a harsh gasp in his throat—and she realized then that whatever she felt, it was only what little had leaked through, and that he still bore the brunt of it on his own.

"Maks!" Oh, she wanted to touch him, to soothe him, to gather him up and hold him—and she had no idea if that would only make things worse.

Because now she knew. This pain had not come on him because of her healing, or her visions, or any other thing she'd been worried about. This wretched reaction had come on him, as it always had, because of his response to *her*.

Maybe he knew it, too. He looked up at her with eyes strained and bright, and the look on his face broke her heart nearly as much as his words.

"Maybe I was wrong," he said. "Maybe we can't simply *be,* after all."

When they headed back to her house, they did it in silence—somber, but with a lingering togetherness.

The cat came to greet them with a little *mrrp,* tail high and cheerful, stropping himself against their legs.

"Feeding time?" Maks asked. The memory, brought close to the surface these past days, came from nowhere— *deplorable conditions, humans fed like beasts to force the change, jailers laughing. His mother, refusing to wean him*

*because of it. Confusion and pain and wobbly cub legs,
his mother's fierce protection while he leaned against her
warm flank...*

"What was that?" Katie said, startled.

Maks no longer found himself surprised by her perceptiveness. "This place brings out memories."

"But...that was..." She frowned. "That felt so young.
No one takes the change for the first time at that age."

And Maks said nothing, because what could he say?
She was right. But she was also wrong. Maks had taken
the change, driven by constant threat. And before long, he
had preferred it.

Katie shook her head. "I have so many questions," she
said. "But..."

"But there are other things to deal with." He took a step
closer, reaching out to stroke his hand over the shine of
her hair in the moonlight. He nodded at the house. "Wards
aren't enough. Shields aren't enough. In the woods, I can
hide you. I can keep you safe. Be human, be deer—it
doesn't matter. *Let me protect you.*"

She crossed her arms, looking away from him. "You
are protecting me. And I'll *see* anything that comes our
way, now that I'm looking."

"Would you? Truly?"

The set of her mouth gave her away—vulnerable and
dismayed, tight enough so one of those slightly pointed
canines peeked out. "Maybe I've spent too many years de-
nying the visions to count on them now. But I'll figure out
how to pull the meaning from them. I *will*." Uncertainty
crept into her voice. "Not deep into the woods, Maks. Not
when I'd have to take the deer beside your tiger."

"Ssh, Katie Rae." He stepped back, and that surprised
her clearly enough—but he could see when the deer needed
space. "Your decision."

She squeezed her upper arms in a self-hug. "I'll go hunting for a seeing, that's what. Though it's been so long…I don't even know if I remember how."

Maks didn't think about it; he pulled her in close and held her, wrapping her in his own strength. Safe enough for him, without the passion behind it. "Ian needs time for the amulet. I need time to set up my own perimeter on this land. Nick needs time to send backup. That means you have time to work on visions."

His shirt muffled her faint laugh. "Just like that."

His affirmative went out without voice, simply driven by intent. To judge by the way she briefly tightened her arms around him, she got the message well enough.

Only then did the haze wrap around him—his own personal random fog, with the edges thrumming in color separations and static building through his body. Dissonance rising, without apparent rhyme or reason.

No. Not now, when she needed to feel safe.

As if he could pretend to have a choice.

Choice…

Maybe he did, in a fashion. Because there was one thing that might cut through it, as it cut through everything else so far.

"Maks, are you—" But her hand closed around his arm. "Someone's coming." He heard it, then—tires on the scattered gravel of the dirt road, someone driving too fast over the washboard section not far from her house, headlights flashing through the darkness. Surprise colored Katie's voice, coming to his ears as if scraped through steel wool. "It's Marie. At this time of night—?" She squeezed his arm again. "Stay put. I'll go see."

The car crunched to a stop—a little too fast, sliding an instant before its halt. Just that quickly, the door opened, then slammed…too hard. Maks peered through the darkness, his night vision temporarily smeared into a surrealistic blur, the earth pulling at him through the tough soles of his oft-bare feet. He pushed his palms against his eyes. *Go. Away.*

Marie's voice rang out before Katie reached her, strident through the night. "Did you know? *Did* you?"

Katie's response was a soothing murmur, not something Maks could hear, not with the reverberation in his ears. *Go. Away.*

Because he was all that Katie had right now. The only thing between her and the Core and the dark future of her visions, and she needed to be able to *believe*—

"What about Lara Wilson's dog? What about that *cat?*" Marie's voice only rose higher, louder.

Maks focused on Katie, on her sweetness and strength... on her warmth and compassion...on the determination for which she didn't half give herself credit. He imagined the graceful press of her body against his, the long strong of his hand down her back, the perfect fit of his hand around her bottom.

The pain shot through him, expected now—and cut through the fugue, giving him a window of clarity.

"—*gangrene!*" Marie said. "How could you have known and not told me? How could you *not* have known?"

Maks breathed in hard through his nose, nostrils flaring...letting it out slow. Thinking of *Katie,* moving against him. Katie, touching him—

The two women stood by the car, Marie full of wild gestures and her voice full of tears, Katie full of quiet and calm and sadness. "I'm so sorry. I'd be glad to help—to look at him—"

"Help!" Marie's voice held bitter certainty. "Don't you think it's too late for that? Don't you think maybe Roger Akins has been right *all along?*"

Katie, with her eyes opened wide at their mutual surge of desire, his want for her throbbing harder than any fugue—

And then it struck. As Marie slammed the car door closed and flung bitter parting words at Katie, accelerating away into the night, the pain came on strong, rising from within Maks in an eager tide. He sucked in air, stiffened... bent over himself. Free of the fugue, if not of the cure.

Katie's footsteps ran over fine dirt and coarse grass. "Maks—"

He had no words, but he had all the intent in the world. He sent it her way, merciless. *I'm okay. It's okay.* He forced himself upright and put his arms around her; and this time said it out loud. "It's okay, Katie Rae."

She looked at him straight on through the night, tears streaking a face of grief and worry and fear. "Maks," she said. "You'll have to believe that hard enough for both of us."

Chapter 13

As pain faded, the fugue driven away and all the questions still lingering, Maks stayed outside to check the wards and to lay his own thin, fine security wards. Katie stalked gracelessly into the house with every intent of starting the dinner they hadn't yet had.

Instead she detoured upstairs to wash her face, tuck her hair back up and try to flush the sound of Marie's accusing voice from her ears.

She's upset. People said things when they were upset—striking out, no matter how unfair. No matter how they knew better.

Oh, please, let Marie know better.

The problem was Marie had a point.

How could you have known, and not told me? How could you not *have known?*

And Katie didn't have an answer. It had been only a day earlier...and she'd seen the dog two weeks earlier, at that. For Rowdy to be dying of gangrene today...

How could she not have known?

She found herself on the bed, curled around a pillow… trying to make sense of it all.

She found herself…

Asleep.

Splashing blood, a blur of startled green eyes, a muted roar and a cry of pain.

She grabbed at the moment, even in her sleep—sinking her will into it, looking for details—*grizzled fur, a bright, laughing eye, a dark scent of corruption*—refusing to let it go. *The glint of an amulet, the glint of a thousand amulets, piled one atop another and spilling out in an inescapable mountain turned to quivering unformed flesh and the dank smell of damp dirt and underground stone.* Present and future, tangling together, pooling into disaster…

And then something different, something more distant and yet more intense, a bigger place underground, a woman's low voice singing in her ear…a child's lullaby. Her exhortations. *Live. Stay tiger. Stay strong. Be my son, always.*

"Katie."

That voice was comfort…warm breath on her ear, a nuzzle of a kiss on her neck. The press of strength around her body.

She started awake.

"Ssh," he said. "Wake slowly. And then come and eat."

She realized that he'd cooked—the scent of broiled steak filled her house, along with the tang of sauce. It clung to him, homey and comfortable. She raised a sleepy brow at him. "I should be glad you cooked it first, huh?"

He made a noise in his throat; it sounded like amusement and reproval both. "Salad for you," he said, as though it were a punishment.

What it was, she discovered, was a good salad. Tofu, snow peas, carrots and nuts, sesame dressing. "Since when have you cooked vegetarian?" she asked, balancing the generous bowl in her hand while she took a stab with her fork, having discovered that he'd already eaten.

She found herself wishing he hadn't—thinking that it would have been nice to sit down at the table together. Companionable. And that while she hadn't hosted a non-vegetarian meal in her household for a very long time, she couldn't imagine asking Maks to put aside his nature for hers.

She found that she didn't want to.

"You have cookbooks," he said quite reasonably, opening her refrigerator as if he'd become completely at home in her kitchen in such a short time—stowing the steak sauce bottle and the salad fixings…chewing a carrot while he was at it, a crisp crunch at each bite.

Right. He'd cooked for her. Cared for her. She caught a hint of her vision, then—or maybe it had been dream, or borrowed memory. Lanky adolescent tiger, all flashing limbs and efficiency. Thrashing mule deer, kicking out hard to his ribs, but dying anyway. And the satisfaction—hunched over broken ribs, yet pleased. *Providing.*

"Maks," she started, meaning to ask—and stopped when she realized she'd been lost in thought long enough for him to pull a can of whipped cream from the fridge door, and that he now regarded it with narrow-eyed suspicion. "Seriously," she told him. "What, have you been living in a cave?"

His gaze jerked to hers. "Brevis keeps me busy."

As responses went, Katie recognized evasion when she heard it—but she set her salad down, took the whipped cream, and squirted a bit out on her finger, holding it up for brief display before she licked the finger clean and returned the can to him.

Not that he was a slow learner. He upended the can, tipped his head back, and gave himself a generous serving.

"Seriously," she said again, but found herself grinning—and doubly so when he closed his eyes to savor the taste. She laughed, reclaiming her salad bowl, and picked out a chunk of dressing-drenched tofu as Maks had a second helping of whipped cream. Inevitably, her mind returned to the lingering taste of the dreamed memories.

"Maks," she said again; he swallowed and put the can aside, leaving a tiny smear of white at the corner of his mouth. She licked at the corner of her own mouth without thinking; he only stared at her. "Here," she said, and rubbed her thumb over the spot. She saw the moment that understanding dawned. He ran his thumb over his lip, licked off the captured blot of cream and tucked the can away in the fridge.

"Maks," she said again, and maybe it was the interruptions that had loosened her tongue, but she didn't even think about the potential impact of her words. "Back those years ago. That was you, wasn't it? With the children?"

He instantly stilled—and she knew she was right. "You let me think you were here to help rescue them, but that wasn't it at all, was it? You were one of them. And you've been with brevis ever since—working there, *living* there..."

He left the kitchen. Quietly, without fanfare; he simply turned and left. But the look in his eyes wasn't anger, and the quality of his movement held no resentment—no stiffness, no anger.

They were the expressions of a man looking at something too big to face.

She ditched the salad and went after him. "Surely it's not a secret? Surely people know?"

He'd stopped on the porch, barefoot and jeans-clad and his flannel shirt tail loose, the sleeves rolled up...looking both utterly comfortable in his skin and as though he desperately wanted to shed it. His gaze locked on the woods; his hands locked over the old two-by-four railing.

"You and your mother," she said. "You were on the run...here, somewhere. But she was hurt, and she died, and you were left alone. You—" she hesitated, heard her own words for the first time. "You were just a very young boy. But you'd already taken the change."

He didn't look at her. "Before we escaped. I had to. She had to sleep sometime. And they didn't care about what a boy could do."

"But even a young tiger can leave a mark, and they knew it," Katie said, wonder in her voice. "Oh, *Maks.*"

He turned on her with a fierceness he'd never let her see before. *"Don't,"* he said. "Just *don't.*" And there behind the ferocity flashed hurt and confusion and conflict, until he spun away again.

So she kept her voice as matter-of-fact as she could. "Then tell me."

For a long silent moment, it was only Maks in the darkness, palpably aching to be wild—holding on to the porch railing as if it was the only thing anchoring him to the human. "The Core took her. She was young...she took chances. She was perfect for them." He managed to glance back at her. "They took her to impregnate, to study...to watch me grow."

"Your father?" she asked, still careful.

Maks responded with a one-shouldered shrug. "No one knows. Is it hard to get a man's seed, if you really want it?"

No point in answering the obvious. The Sentinels were, on the whole, hardly repressed when it came to their sexuality.

"You got away," she said, and the raw terror of that escape flashed through her mind—half memory, half coming in fresh from Maks, no matter that it shouldn't have gotten through to her so readily. "But she was hurt."

"She lived for a time," he said. "And then I buried her."

She stopped herself from going to him, from wrapping her arms around him. He didn't want that. Not right now. "How old?" she asked, keeping her voice level. "How old were you?"

Another shrug. "The medics decided to say four years. It doesn't matter to me."

"Four years old," she said. "And alone. And running from the Core."

"Four years old," he said, "and *tiger.*"

Of course. Too young to survive as child; too young to survive as tiger. But as both...

"They never found you?"

"They thought us dead." He glanced back at her again. "They knew we didn't make it to brevis. There was no other reason we wouldn't."

No. Of course not. Had she been able, Maks's mother would have gotten her child to safety—and if she had, the Core would have known it.

He added, "Later, they realized. But it was too late, then."

"You couldn't be caught."

He shook his head. In the wash of light from the doorway, his nostrils flared; his voice sounded strained—the memories crowding him close. "And I had others to take care of."

"The children," she breathed.

"Runaways," he said. "Like me." His memories slipped free, giving her impressions of children in mismatched stolen clothes—children raiding gardens, children huddling in a natural lava tube cave on a chill night, children hiding in an empty vacation cabin as snow fell outside.

"For how long?" she asked.

He shrugged again; it didn't seem nearly as casual as it once had. "I don't know." He glanced only briefly away from the woods. "Brevis called me fifteen, when they found us."

That made him around thirty now, given the local memory of when the children had quietly been gathered up.

Maybe.

"Maks—" she started.

He didn't let her finish. "Those things then," he said, "made me what I am now. But now…I just *am,* Katie Rae."

"What any wild thing knows," Katie said softly. "Just *be.*"

He didn't lift his arm to invite her closer. But she heard the invitation anyway, and she responded to it. He made a space to tuck her close to his side, and she wrapped her arms around him as his chin settled on the top of her head.

With both of them weary and both of them needing to be held…

It was no surprise that they ended up in the guest room, wrapped up in one another and sleeping hard, counting on Ian's wards and Maks's boundary lines to protect and alert them.

When Maks jerked awake, it was with full awareness of his entanglement, both physical and emotional. And it came with full awareness of the need to resolve the threat to Katie—to figure out the new threat to the Sentinels.

What the Core was doing here in the first place, he still didn't know. They'd abandoned the area completely fifteen years ago when the Sentinels found Maks, revealing the full nature of the Core's presence and their history of activity in this region.

But by then, Maks had been too long gone from the

strange, giant cave of his captivity—and at age fifteen and on the run for most of his life, he hadn't exactly been co-operative with those Sentinels who had gathered him up. Wherever that Core facility had been, it likely remained.

This time, Maks would find it.

For now, Maks breathed into the darkness, waiting for some hint of what had woken him.

::Maks.:: Annorah's mental voice sounded breathless, no matter the physical impossibility of it. *::You're awake.::*

He sent back a wordless affirmative.

::Ian just sent out an adveho,:: she told him, tense with concern.

Adveho. No wonder Maks had woken. No Sentinel could ignore that cry for help.

Maks pulled his arm out from beneath Katie and sat, pulling his thoughts into focus. Ian had the silent amulet the Core had set out for Katie; Ian was overnighting in Pine Bluff.

The Core wanted to keep its secrets.

He sent back a query, no more than a mental question mark—*when?*—glancing at the bedside table to the alarm clock. Three o'clock in the morning.

::Just now,:: Annorah told him. *::At the La Quinta. We're sending the chopper, but—::*

Right. No chopper would reach this tiny mountain town in time—not if Ian had reason to send out an urgent Mayday.

::Be careful,:: Annorah said. *::This is about more than muscle. And you—::*

::Also more than muscle,:: Maks said, putting the effort into those few distinct words.

::I was going to say, you're not well, and we all know it. So, yes, be damned careful!:: Annorah put bite into long-distance words better than anyone Maks knew—but

YOUR PARTICIPATION IS REQUESTED!

Dear Reader,

Since you are a lover of paranormal romance fiction – we would like to get to know you!

Inside you will find a short Reader's Survey. Sharing your answers with us will help our editorial staff understand who you are and what activities you enjoy.

To thank you for your participation, we would like to send you 2 books and 2 gifts – **ABSOLUTELY FREE!**

Enjoy your gifts with our appreciation,

Pam Powers

SEE INSIDE FOR READER'S SURVEY

For Your Paranormal Romance Reading Pleasure...

Get 2 FREE BOOKS that will thrill you with dramatic, sensual tales featuring dark, sexy and powerful characters.

We'll send you 2 books and 2 gifts
ABSOLUTELY FREE
just for completing our Reader's Survey!

YOUR READER'S SURVEY
"THANK YOU" FREE GIFTS INCLUDE:
- ▶ 2 Paranormal Romance books
- ▶ 2 lovely surprise gifts

▶ DETACH AND MAIL CARD TODAY! ▶

PLEASE FILL IN THE CIRCLES COMPLETELY TO RESPOND

1) What type of fiction books do you enjoy reading? (Check all that apply)
- ○ Suspense/Thrillers   ○ Action/Adventure   ○ Modern-day Romances
- ○ Historical Romance   ○ Humour   ○ Paranormal Romance

2) What attracted you most to the last fiction book you purchased on impulse?
- ○ The Title   ○ The Cover   ○ The Author   ○ The Story

3) What is usually the greatest influencer when you <u>plan</u> to buy a book?
- ○ Advertising   ○ Referral   ○ Book Review

4) How often do you access the internet?
- ○ Daily   ○ Weekly   ○ Monthly   ○ Rarely or never.

5) How many NEW paperback fiction novels have you purchased in the past 3 months?
- ○ 0 - 2   ○ 3 - 6   ○ 7 or more

YES! I have completed the Reader's Survey. Please send me the 2 FREE books and 2 FREE gifts (gifts are worth about $10) for which I qualify. I understand that I am under no obligation to purchase any books, as explained on the back of this card.

237/337 HDL FS7H

FIRST NAME   LAST NAME

ADDRESS

APT.#   CITY

STATE/PROV.   ZIP/POSTAL CODE

The Reader Service — Here's How It Works:

Accepting your 2 free books and 2 free gifts (gifts valued at approximately $10.00) places you under no obligation to buy anything. You may k
the books and gifts and return the shipping statement marked "cancel." If you do not cancel, about a month later we'll send you 4 additional bo
and bill you just $21.42 in the U.S. or $23.46 in Canada. That is a savings of at least 21% off the cover price of all 4 books! It's quite a barg
Shipping and handling is just 50¢ per book in the U.S. and 75¢ per book in Canada.* You may cancel at any time, but if you choose to contin
every month we'll send you 4 more books, which you may either purchase at the discount price or return to us and cancel your subscription

*Terms and prices subject to change without notice. Prices do not include applicable taxes. Sales tax applicable in N.Y. Canadian residents wi
charged applicable taxes. Offer not valid in Quebec. Books received may not be as shown. All orders subject to credit approval. Credit or c
balances in a customer's account(s) may be offset by any other outstanding balance owed by or to the customer. Please allow 4 to 6 weeks
delivery. Offer available while quantities last.

If offer card is missing write to: The Reader Service, P.O. Box 1867, Buffalo, NY 14240-1867 or visit: www.ReaderService.com

BUSINESS REPLY MAIL
FIRST-CLASS MAIL   PERMIT NO. 717   BUFFALO, NY

POSTAGE WILL BE PAID BY ADDRESSEE

THE READER SERVICE
PO BOX 1341
BUFFALO NY 14240-8571

NO POSTAGE
NECESSARY
IF MAILED
IN THE
UNITED STATES

then her presence abruptly diminished. *::There's Nick. I'll check back.::*

He didn't bother to acknowledge her; she was gone. And Maks was already reaching over to touch Katie's shoulder. She blinked her eyes open without comprehension, but her gaze quickly sharpened. He told her, "Ian. The Core. The La Quinta."

She swore, and rolled out of bed—already awake, already graceful. "My shoes," she said. "What did you do—never mind." She snagged them from the floor near the closet. "Keys," she said, a mutter to herself. "My field kit. You?"

"Ready," Maks told her.

She glanced at his bare feet, opened her mouth…shook her head. "The keys are in the kitchen. The kit's in the workroom. I need to hit the bathroom."

He found the field kit for her and left it on the kitchen counter so she wouldn't waste time looking for it. And then, because any attack on Ian might well be no more than a diversion, he went outside and checked the wards, walking the perimeter of the house wards and then running the perimeter of his boundary alarm—strengthening it, and strengthening his ties with it.

When he returned to the car, she was waiting, zipping a hooded sweatshirt against the chill night air.

"Sorry," she said as he squeezed down into the car. "I really did mean to rent you something bigger."

He pulled the door shut and tugged the seatbelt past his shoulder. "Is it far, this La Quinta?"

"Not much. Is the house safe?"

"Very much."

"Then hang on." She hit the gas and bounced the car down the dirt road, accelerating into the night as no non-Sentinel would dare, her deer's reflexes and night vision making the darkness irrelevant. They met no one else as she peeled around the corner of the dirt road to the asphalt feeder road and then onto Pine Bluff's single broad main road—blowing red lights, ignoring the speed limit, and deftly avoiding the small-town potholes while she was at it.

Maks muttered under his breath and snagged the grab handle over the door.

"Almost there," Katie said, not looking at him.

But when she pulled into the hotel parking lot, spotting Ian's little work-capped truck and slanting into the two spaces beside it, Maks put a hand on her arm to keep her in the car. "Wait," he said, and released his own seat belt.

"But—"

"Wait."

She subsided with visible impatience. "Maks—"

"Do *not*," he told her, opening the door, "remind me that I am not well."

She closed her mouth.

Maks stood beside the car, senses wide open, thinking the intent of it at her. *Listen.*

She must have heard him; he felt the quality of her attention change. His skin tingled at the faint sensation of her energies sliding over his, and outward—the taste of a healer, reaching out in her own way—discerning the night. She whispered, "Desperation…"

Maks sifted through the sensations of the place, his head lifting slightly to take in the scents, his gaze sifting through the interference of artificial lights to hunt any sign of physical Core incursion.

Nothing.

"Wait here," he told her, bending to look into the car. "Shield. Ward the car—can you?"

"Not well," she answered.

He scowled. "Stay quiet inside yourself, then. If there's a working, it has to be a seeker."

Understanding made her grim. "They couldn't use an on-site amulet—Ian would have found it, even a silent one. You're right, it must be a seeker. But those take a lot of skill."

Not news. Maks double-checked the immediate area, judging Katie's safety, knowing that Ian had already waited far too long for backup. He reached out to prod Anno-rah—once, twice.

::Busy,:: she told him briefly, even as Katie leaned across the seat to look at him.

"What about you?"

"It's a seeker," he reminder her, and the acrid stench of the working now wafted through the air to make his nose wrinkle. "Doesn't want me. I won't give it reason to. *Wait.*"

"I'm not stupid," Katie said tightly. "Go help Ian—and then call me, because he's going to need healing."

Maks took the tiger, right out there in the deep night parking lot. What he had scented faintly as the man, he found instantly as the tiger—Ian, already a familiar spoor, three doors down from the man's truck.

::Yes,:: Annorah said, popping back into his thoughts to confirm the location. *::Protect yourself, Maks—don't assume—::*

He sent a mental growl at her, chasing away the distraction and—once outside the hotel door—knew better than to take the silence as an indication of faltering urgency.

He didn't take the door as any impediment, either. He reared up, claws digging into wood—the door crashing down before him.

He found Ian backed into a corner in his snow leopard form, small ears flattened against his skull, whiskers pulled up in a hissing snarl...pale eyes just a little bit crazed. The

Core working buzzed around him in a dark cloud of malevolence—slick nits of evil, pressing down, slipping through the shields to sink right through fur and skin. Even as Maks crouched, tail lashing, wishing fiercely for something into which he could sink his claws and teeth, Ian's snarl faded away. He sank down, pressing his belly to the floor, his gaze taking on the unfocused look.

Maks pushed his way through the vibrating nits right into the leopard's space, ignoring Ian's feeble snarl for what it was—a big cat objecting to the tiger's presence with no cognizance behind the reaction.

Ian was beyond such things.

Maks moved furniture with his passage, walking right up to Ian's faltering leopard, right *over*—twice Ian's size, four times his weight…putting himself between Ian and the cloud, as if physical intervention would make any difference at all.

It wouldn't. But Maks, too, had shields. He expanded them, pushing right through into Ian's own shields…layering over them—adding to them, strengthening them.

The working's intensity stuttered as it lost its grasp on Ian—stuttered again as Ian took advantage of the moment and rebuilt his shields, leopard crouching beneath tiger claws digging into cheap carpet.

Maks ducked against the tiny vibrations of ugliness, an instinctive reaction not diminished in the least by the fact the working wasn't aimed at him.

Wasn't aimed at him.

It was aimed at Ian—but how, then, did the Core target him?

Either they know him, or…

Or they weren't targeting *Ian* at all. They were going after whoever possessed the amulet.

::Maks—:: There came Annorah's voice, as if she'd been eavesdropping all along. *::Do it another way!::*

Maks snarled back at her, knowing she'd receive the message, and swept his gaze over the room.

There—there was the amulet bucket, on the floor beside the desk. There was the tool kit, and the warded Kevlar blanket, and a worn grimoire-like book with crisp old vellum pages, sitting with precision on the corner of the protected desk.

No sign of the amulet.

Only one sick leopard, crouching in the corner...

Maks moved to the side, breaking the connection of their shields; the leopard spat weakly in protest. Maks paid him no heed. He squinted against the nits—weightless energies that bounced away without impact—and using one broad paw, rolled Ian over to his side. Ian snarled with renewed vigor and tried to claw himself upright and back over newly exposed treasure: the amulet, tucked away in a warded Kevlar bag.

::Maks, no—!::

But Maks was no fool. Not even an amulet specialist would throw himself on top of a live piece without protection, which meant the warded Kevlar bag was solid. And when not spread thin over two people, when not caught unprepared, Maks had personal shields to equal those of any Sentinel.

Even as Ian stretched a paw toward the amulet, claws unsheathed to snag the bundle, Maks flicked it out of Ian's reach, pouncing on it with ponderous grace. He pulled his shields in fur-close, bracing himself—hoping he was right—hoping he hadn't just abandoned Ian to die.

For a very long moment it seemed as though he had done just that. The nits buzzed around Ian in renewed fury, darkening the air as they sensed the leopard's vulnerability. Ian flailed, absorbing that dark power as his shields evaporated. His long, heavy tail beat against the wall; his claws scraped carpet away from the cement slab beneath.

But the onslaught quickly faltered, withdrawing to spin aimlessly around the snow leopard, sheened with the oily reflection of the overhead light.

Then it coiled, striking at Maks like a snake. It flowed around Maks's shields, seeking weakness—battering against him. Barely visible through the dark swarm, Ian rolled weakly to his knees and then slumped back against the wall, a splay of graceful limbs that still spoke of the cat within. His voice was a hoarse rasp. "Damned fool!"

Maks couldn't disagree. But he couldn't hold shields for both of them—not and keep both of them safe. *These* shields, he could hold—until help arrived, until the working faded.

Or he could have, had the faint, familiar haze of fugue not crept in around the edges, softening the steel of the shields... giving the nits a weak area on which to concentrate.

"Fool!" Ian said again, spitting it a little more strongly this time, but still unable to do much as push away from the wall.

Maks curled his whiskers back in defiance. *This is what I do.* It was who he was.

It was who he had to be.

He dug in deep, past the fugue to the discipline of what he'd always known—keeping himself invisible to the Core; keeping himself silent in all ways. Living at the edges of an organization that had to continue believing he had perished with his injured mother...living the only place he knew, the only way he knew. He dug into the memories of those days, the simplicity and focus of that single need.

Shields above all else.

Silence. Above. All. Else.

Slowly, the shielding firmed. Through the fugue, through the haze, through the distant roar in his ears.

And then Katie was there, an indistinct figure clutching the doorway and gasping at what she saw.

"Don't," Ian rasped at her. "Don't interfere. I don't know what the hell he's doing—"

Silence. Above. All. Else.

Shields...

The dissonance crashed in on him like a wave, and Maks curled around the core of what he was, what he'd always been...what he had to be. And then only the roar of the fugue remained—and the shields, snapping tight between Maks and the world.

Katie ran to the open doorway, her promise to stay in the car broken without second thought once she felt the struggle within the hotel room. But here she hovered on the threshold—unable to help Ian without disturbing Maks, caught in an endless conflict between the need to *do* and the potential to make it all worse as the working buzzed around Maks in a swarm of lethal corruption, battering against him, chewing at him.... He crouched with utter stillness, a giant form gone silent.

Her inability to sense him was the most frightening thing of all.

She could have wept with relief as the working lost its ferocity. The oily swarm dissipated...barely noticeable at first and then quite suddenly...half of the energy nits fell, enervated; half of them simply faded away.

Ian swore at the sight. "What the—" He glanced at her from a face tight and strained and let the phrase go unfinished.

"What *happened?*" Katie eased into the room, moving sideways to stay as far from Maks as possible and yet still reach Ian. Her deer, so sensible, flung her a constant litany of advice. *Run! Run! Run!*

"What *didn't*," Ian said, dry even without any strength behind his words, his head still lolling back against the wall. "They wanted that amulet nullified, I can tell you that much."

Katie could only stare at him. "Why didn't you just *give* it to them?"

He smiled at her, weak as it was, with a definite hint of self-mockery. "Because if they wanted it that badly, then it must be worth keeping." But when her eyebrows shot up, he rolled his eyes and admitted, "Because I just *did* it. And then I was stuck." His leg twitched, the muscles jerking; he hissed through his teeth, and then his arm did it, too. "This is the same working that almost got Dolan Treviño at the beginning of the year. This amulet scientist was working with Gausto. It fits, considering the silent nature of the amulet at your place."

Katie threw a glance at Maks, found him motionless and his shields hard; when she reached out to him, gently prodding him with a healing thought, she had the sense of sliding over ice. She grabbed the arching back of an upholstered chair to steady herself.

"Whoa," Ian said, though his voice caught on his own misery, and his face reflected the strain.

"I'm fine." She stood on her own two solid feet, eyeing him with conflicting needs. "May I approach?"

Ian snorted dark laughter through clenched teeth. "You surely may, little deer."

Katie took a breath and went to him—but only a step or two, because then it hit her—a hot tug, right down deep to her soul and enclosing her heart, snagging her with a ferocity that could only be—

Tiger.

* * *

Silence. Above. All. Else.

It felt familiar to Maks, this place—and not only from those early days when such silence had saved his life from the Core, shields beyond shields—so young he hardly even knew what he was doing.

No, more recent than that. It had the encompassing feel of the space he'd occupied for so long after the Flagstaff ambush. Comforting, safe…no one could reach him. No one could even see him, not even with a seeking eye.

Shields so deep, so strong, they could just as easily become a trap.

Had become a trap.

Not this time.

This time, he had an anchor. He had the warm, sweet energy of Katie Rae Maddox—and he drew it in, letting it trigger something hot and fierce and angry. He rode that surge, punching through his own shields and clawing outward, reaching—

He half expected the resulting slash of pain, and he grabbed that, too—riding it back out where he belonged and so suddenly aware that this, too—in its most raw, its most elemental—held a taste of puzzling familiarity.

But he had no time to think about it—he had only holding on, clawing out—

And bursting right back into his skin.

Maks exploded into silent light—a shimmering conflagration of energies, expanding and contracting from tiger to man—a man who flung himself up, the wild still in his eyes, the ferocity of attack still imminent.

Tucked away on the floor between his knees, the amulet's crumpled bag hardly looked worth all the trouble.

"Quickly," Ian said, as if he wasn't bent nearly in half.

"Back in the bucket—the quarantine wards will kick in when the lid connects—"

Maks just looked at him, as if the words meant nothing at all.

"Maks!" Katie said it sharply, full of fear for him—and then flooding with relief when his gaze instantly snapped to hers. She understood it then—he simply hadn't made it all the way back to words. Not with his ears, not with his mouth.

She took her chances, reaching out to him with the same intent he'd sometimes offered her. The amulet, the bucket... and *then* the words, short and simple. "Put the amulet in the bucket. *Now.*"

Maks scooped up the bag, plunking it in the hardware bucket and slapping on the lid. Only then did she glance at Ian, to say under her breath, "Not that I understand why."

Ian let slip another sardonic sound. "The bag," he said, his words jerky, "protects us from it. But it doesn't silence—*ah!* Damn!"

Katie breathed a harsher word and rushed to him, sparing only an instant to see Maks climb to his feet—to brush himself off, look at his hands as if they might belong to someone else, and then shake off the moment to join them.

"I'll watch," he told Katie, as if none of that had even happened.

It was all she needed. She knelt on the shredded carpet, opened and closed her hands a few times, and prepared to heal her second Sentinel in so many days.

Chapter 14

Maks stood watch over the deep-night parking lot, pushing out his boundaries, extending his senses...and fighting the distraction of sudden new understanding.

The Flagstaff amulet hadn't injured him. It was Maks himself who'd locked down a shield so profound there'd been no reaching him—and no reaching out.

Deep, silent shields—learned young, so ingrained as to become forgotten. That the brevis medics and healers hadn't figured it out...that made it a little easier to accept. That he'd so quickly found his way free this time...that made it a little easier, too. He wouldn't be taken unaware by it again.

That his connection to Katie Rae had been his salvation...

That didn't surprise him one little bit.

With his thoughts so absorbed, the moments passed swiftly. He heard the brevis helicopter on approach, the distant *thump-thump-thump* of the blades as it descended, grabbing a distant open space for its clandestine landing pad. He was ready when the chopper's team quietly approached; he acknowledged them with a silent nod, standing to the side of the broken hotel door as Ian batted away assistance to make it to his unsteady feet.

By then Katie had once again quietly put Maks between herself and the brevis contingent: a co-pilot acting as medic, and Dolan Treviño—a Sentinel whose daunting, dark presence had intimidated more than one field operative along the way.

Until not so very long ago, he'd been called rogue.

Maks thought Treviño was never that. Maks thought Treviño had seen very clearly that Southwest Brevis, before Nick Carter's recent ascent to consul, had been a region in trouble.

No wonder Katie had little trust.

"You've taken care of the worst of it," the medic said, looking over his shoulder to where he thought Katie would be hovering over her patient, and doing a surprised double-take until he found her on the other side of Maks. "More than I could have done—you've got a delicate touch."

"Not much scope," Katie said, her voice an apologetic murmur.

"Doesn't matter," the man said. "The right touch in the right spot beats brute force any time. Ian was lucky. You circumvented a lot of damage here."

"Yee-ah," Ian said, dark humor threaded through his voice. "Where the hell is the chopper?"

"Landed at the elementary school," the co-pilot said. "About a mile from here. You sure you don't want—"

Ian interrupted him with a silent snarl. "Let's just *go*." And he made his own way, one uncertain step after the other, through the door to the parking lot. The co-pilot shrugged at Treviño, who lifted a shoulder in return. After a moment, Ian's voice filtered back to them. "Where the hell is the bloody damned school?"

"Cranky," Treviño decided, rare amusement in his eyes. He raised his voice. "Turn left. Unless you want some help?"

Ian's crude mutter left no doubt as to his disposition on that account; he turned left and wobbled toward the road.

The co-pilot lifted his hands in a gesture of *what're you gonna do* and hastened afterward, leaving Treviño to hook a grip though the bucket handle as if it didn't hold the amulet equivalent of dynamite. "You're not coming in," he said to Maks, as if he knew the answer and had to say it anyway.

Katie's hand crept into Maks's; Treviño's eyes were far too sharp to miss it. His gaze went to Maks, all sharp sapphire and full of knowing. Maks offered the faintest shake of his head; it was enough.

"You shouldn't be up here alone," Treviño said bluntly.

Katie's grip tightened. Maks squeezed her hand in return. "He means he doesn't want to go back and leave us."

Her relief trickled through him.

"It means I'm a bastard for going," Treviño said, studying them both. "But, hell, there's dumping going on in the Chiricahuas and the earth is fu—" He glanced at Katie and moderated his tone, a courtesy he afforded few. "The earth is bleeding out."

Katie spoke quietly from behind Maks's shoulder. "I'm glad you could come at all."

Treviño met Maks's gaze head-on. "Maks will keep you safe," he said, but he didn't look away until Maks lifted his head slightly, telling Treviño all the things he was looking to know.

Yes, she's mine now.

Yes, I can do this.

Yes, I will *do this.*

Katie stood quietly, watching. Seeing the exchange but, Maks thought, not quite understanding it. Wary and thoughtful and so damned brave.

Treviño spoke as if that exchange hadn't occurred at all. "Things should quiet down a little now. I wouldn't be surprised to find the Septs Prince has put a price on this rogue's head. The Core can't pretend they're playing nice as long as the fool is stirring up so much trouble."

"We're on guard, now," Katie said, her light touch landing at the center of Maks's back, easing down to rest at his waistband. "They've lost their advantage."

Treviño glanced at Maks again. "They never had an advantage, Katie Rae Maddox. Haven't you figured that out yet?"

Katie said, "There's a lot I'm figuring out. Tell Nick..."

"You'd be surprised what Nick already knows," Treviño said, a wry half smile on striking, hard features—the black jaguar in his harsh beauty, not a bit of his edge diminished since he'd taken Meghan Lawrence to his own. "Look for a couple of solid secondaries tomorrow, Maks."

Maks, already wary at the thought of more Sentinels intruding on Katie's space, made his ruffled tiger settle.

Treviño saw it...let it go without remark. "You did good," he said to Katie. "Don't sell yourself short."

Katie didn't move from the shelter of Maks's shoulder. "I know what I am, Mr. Treviño."

Treviño grinned—feral, that expression. "You're in the field, now, Katie. It's more a question of what you'll become."

Katie didn't miss the significance of Treviño's words. She didn't miss the significance of the glance he sent Maks as he left, either. A warning, that look. *Don't be stupid* and *watch your back* rolled into one.

Understanding, in that final flick of a gaze at Katie.

And then he was gone and Katie let out a breath she hadn't known she was keeping to herself. "Dolan Treviño," she said.

"Yes," Maks agreed.

"Southwest's bad boy," she said.

"Yes," Maks agreed.

"You've worked with *him,* too."

"Yes," Maks told her.

She shook her head. Maks, she was beginning to see, had been there in the shadows all along—all the big operations reported in brevis e-bulletins. Sanitized of detail, they listed only the results and the lead field operatives.

But not the quiet, dependable tiger on whom they'd always counted.

He gave her a questioning look, and she smiled, rueful and small. "Brevis is coming," she said. "I'd best have something to tell them. It's past time I went vision-seeking, don't you think?"

"We," Maks told her, and held out his hand again. They headed for Katie's car in the surreal peacefulness of deep night. For all the power and fury so recently expended here, the incident had been oddly unremarkable from the outside. Two powerful Sentinels, locked in a furious but silent battle, Katie's quiet healing...the rescue team, coming in fast and quiet, and gone the same way.

Deceptive as it might be, the night felt safe.

Until Maks hesitated at the car, and his troubled nature brushed against her awareness—Maks, speaking without words.

"What is it?"

He didn't respond right away—not out loud. Katie

watched him, trying to reconcile his uncertainty with the strength standing before her.

He said, "I always thought that…the thing that happens with me…"

He stopped, looking away, and she understood then that it was about more than hunting for the right words. It was about getting through them.

"Maks—" she said, thinking he didn't owe her this—not explanations, not excuses.

He cut her off with a sharp shake of his head. "This is important, Katie Rae. We thought everything started with the ambush. But now…after what just happened in there… I think it started before."

She lifted her head with a little jerk, understanding those implications immediately. If brevis had been treating the wrong cause, they could easily have failed to find the right cure.

He said, "There was a power surge. On the Peaks."

She knew something of that from the bulletins. Described only as a deep surge precipitated by the Core's interference with the natural wellspring of energies within the San Francisco Peaks, it had nearly killed Joe Ryan—and it was then that Annorah had been pulled as a field operative, although no one seemed to know why. "I know of it."

"That's when," he said, his certainty growing even as he told her of it. "That's when it started. I thought—" There it came, the tension in his shoulders and jaw, the deep breath he took before he continued. "I thought I had shielded carelessly at the hotel. But now…"

She finished it for him. "Now you think you were already broken."

He nodded, short and tight.

"That's good," she told him, and smiled at his surprise. "Seriously, Maks. Brevis couldn't help because they were starting in the wrong place. But if we know the *right* place…" She smiled at him, a spontaneous thing of hope—of expectation. *We can do this. I can help* you, *too.*

He didn't smile back; he was too troubled for that. But he lifted one hand to trace the line of her cheek, and then— a move so spontaneous she didn't see it coming—he leaned down and kissed her. Gentle, thorough…warming the space between them, warming Katie right down to her toes—a sweetness filling her from the center out.

Sweet enough, gentle enough, so only as they broke apart and Maks touched her lip with his thumb, lingering there, did she realize what else had happened with that kiss.

Katie Rae Maddox, possessed by a tiger.

Probably they should have gone straight home.

But *probably* didn't take into account Katie's need to decompress, the sun rising in the early-morning sky to announce the day, or the lure of the town's one and only gourmet coffee shop. It could be, Katie had to admit to herself, that the pastries were the real reason for her detour here on the way home.

Maks, while patient, still seemed somewhat bemused at the whole coffee obsession scene.

At least, until he walked through the door. And then suddenly he was the tiger again, gone on the hunt with his gaze piercing and the strength bristling from his body.

He'd gained something from their moments in the hotel, Katie could see that clearly enough. A certain confidence—a certain awareness of himself. As if identifying the correct nature of his injury had somehow lessened his conflict over the event.

Or maybe it was more than that. In all of their short, intense time together, she'd not yet seen him project the silent, unmistakable menace that infused his posture as he took another step into the shop. His head went up, his shoulders stiffened. *On the hunt.*

"Well, well." That voice was as familiar as it was unwelcome. "Look who's come out to play with the common folk."

Katie stopped short as the door jingled shut behind her. *Akins.* He straddled a chair at one of the tables, a plain small cup of coffee before him and an abandoned coffee sitting across from him, along with a small plate where sticky frosting lingered. "Maks," Katie said. "Let's not be here. It's too early in the day for this."

"By all means, run away," Akins said. "Wouldn't want to face a conversation about what you've been up to." Half of the little shop's patrons gave Katie a curious glance, and the other half burrowed more deeply into their reading, texting and private conversations, unwilling to take part in the unpleasantry.

She reached out to touch Maks's arm—and realized instantly that Maks wasn't hearing her at all. He'd focused entirely into the finely honed creature of his other: hunter, protector...untamed.

Akins eyed her from over his coffee, and his expression was entirely too smug. "'Course, if you run off without even a token denial, some folks might start to think there's truth to the whispers around here."

Katie gave him a startled look, her attention too divided to produce the disdain his remarks deserved.

"Oh, you know," he said, and waved the coffee cup in a vague gesture that made her think it was empty. "Animals that die after you've handled them. Animals that get sick. You didn't think that word would spread so fast?"

Marie's dog. And how could she deny the cat, or the dog from months earlier, wracked in pain and ready to go? She hadn't actively released him, at that...only showed him the option existed, when his owner was clinging so hard as to keep him past his time.

The instant of doubt must have flickered on her face; Akins pounced with a mean triumph. "And then there's last night. The things you touch don't do well, do they?"

She cast a glance at Maks, a panic rising in her throat. *No one knows about last night. They can't possibly.*

But Maks didn't so much as look at her. Maks had turned into someone she hadn't seen before—someone to whom she would never leave herself vulnerable in healing, would never share a bed in exhausted sleep. He circled the table, his eyes both feral and distant, as if he tasted something she couldn't quite perceive—as if he quartered in on that scent.

Akins's grin turned nasty. "Haven't you heard about last night, Katie Rae?"

"I told you, you're not welcome to call me that." She kept her voice low in the hopes of hiding its faint tremble; by now half the coffee shop listened in undisguised interest.

"Not much left of your neighbor," Akins observed, words that reached Katie without yet making sense. "It's really kinda surprising you didn't know that. Or, you know, maybe you knew all along, and that's why you laid low." He glanced at Maks's bare feet, brows raised. "Or laid *something.*"

Unexpected temper fired through Katie's nerves. She slapped the cup from Akins's hand with a speed she rarely revealed. "You," she said, and this time her voice was low for entirely different reasons, "need to learn manners. And you need to figure out that nothing you say about me will *ever* change the things you've done."

Akins's superiority, his amusement, vanished into the rising color of his face, his flushed neck. He stood so quickly that the chair went skidding; several customers shifted away in alarm, and one older lady abandoned her coffee to exit the shop.

"Hey!" the barista said, her tone full of no-nonsense. "Roger Akins, it's time for you to leave."

Akins didn't seem to hear; he lurched for Katie.

"Hey," said the barista, and this time she stepped out from behind the counter with a fire extinguisher in her hand.

But Maks wasn't as preoccupied as he'd seemed. He moved—faster than Katie, faster than anyone had any right to expect. His hand clamped down on the back of Akins's neck, squeezing tightly. Akins stiffened in surprise, his eyes wide with pain—Katie could all but hear the crunch of compressed tissue.

A tiger's killing grip.

Maks leaned close to Akins's ear, and said, *"No."*

Akins gurgled a protest. Maks shook him slightly, instantly silencing him. *"No."*

Slowly, carefully, Akins raised his hands in a gesture of surrender. Maks cut a glance at Katie, who understood well enough—a request to move to the side, no longer between Akins and the door. No longer within Akins's easy reach.

Katie eased away. Maks gave Akins an abrupt shove; the man stumbled forward a few steps and stopped, turning a resentful gaze on Katie.

"And, might I add," the barista said, with more scorn than fear. "Stay out."

Akins snarled a last, nasty word at her and left, shoving chairs aside with crude violence. One teetered and fell in his wake, and then he was gone.

The remaining customers applauded with quiet decorum, and bent their heads together to exchange murmurs, not realizing how clearly their secretive body language gave them away—that it was Katie they talked about, as much as Akins.

Katie told the barista, "I'm sorry. I didn't help."

"He was being an asshole," the woman said. "From what I've seen, he's addicted to it. Now. You want some coffee? You and your friend? He could have his free if he can teach me that Vulcan neck pinch."

Katie glanced at Maks—already distracted again...on his hunt. "I think," she said, smiling slightly, "that you just have to be Maks." She ordered her coffee, and for Maks, on an impulse, frozen hot chocolate.

She tipped heavily.

She found Maks prowling by the back exit at the end of the short restroom hallway, and presented him with the imprinted paper cup; he took it without looking. "What's going on?" she asked, keeping her voice low enough that he could pretend not to hear if he didn't want to.

She wasn't expecting the answer, or his direct stare, coming back so quickly from whatever preoccupied him here. "You tell me."

"I—" she said, and flushed. *Be the seer,* he meant. "Not *here.*"

He only watched her.

"I mean," she said, "I *will.* But not here."

After a moment, he seemed to accept those words; he took a sip of the slushy drink she'd brought him, and his eyebrows went up.

Then he shook his head, his bafflement clear enough. "There's a scent here," he said. "A taste. Bitter hot metal..."

She frowned; she might have asked. Instead, that taste flooded her mouth, obscuring the lingering flavor of rich coffee, filling her nose as much as tingling off her tongue. She flailed in it—found herself suddenly afloat in invasive darkness, in damp memories of dim, foul places—

the briefest glimpse of a woman's face, faintly familiar, the sound of emotional agony. The grunt of a man taking a hard blow resolving into torn curtains of wild green.

She blinked, and found herself looking into that same green—the watercolor clarity of Maks's eyes. He'd plucked the drink from her hand as she sagged against the wall.

She cleared her throat, glancing somewhat furtively in the direction of the shop floor.

"No one came," he told her. "No one heard." And he didn't ask, but he wanted to know—she saw that in his eyes, too.

"I don't know," she told him, her voice low. "I could taste what you described…I know people were being hurt, people were in despair. I don't know why…"

The look on his face struck her with unexpected dread, plucking at something in her chest. "You *know,*" she said, bringing it down to a whisper. "You know what I'm seeing. You were part of it, once."

He shook his head. She didn't know if it meant *no, I don't* or simply *not here.* She knew she wouldn't get any immediate answers, either way. "Let's go home," she said—and pretended not to notice his reluctant glance at the exit and the hunt that drew him.

They might even have made it, if they hadn't met a cluster of people in the steep little parking lot, gathered at the tailgate of one of the newly parked SUVs and inadvertently blocking Katie's car.

Maks didn't think twice—reading the high emotions of the group, reading their expressions and body language— as Katie stopped, he stepped forward and sideways, putting himself in front of her so cleanly that she didn't at first realize it—and then she did, and her hand touched his arm in an unconscious gesture. Not only seeking reassurance, but connecting them.

The parking lot slanted hard toward the main road, leaving little room for graceful evasion. Especially not when someone in the gathering—eight or nine people, all looking shaken and sounding strident—did a double-take and said, "Hey, aren't you the neighbor?"

Akins had made a reference to *neighbor,* too. And while Maks knew better than to respond, already eyeing his best option to make an opening to the car, Katie had all the wrong instincts for a moment like this.

Hers were herd instincts, healer's instincts—to reach out, to become part of…to help. And so she asked, "Whose neighbor? What's happened?"

"As if you don't know," muttered another man. "I don't care if your house *is* a quarter-mile down the road—there's no way you didn't hear him screaming."

"What?" Katie's tone rose a notch. "Larry? You mean Larry Williams? What happened?"

"Akins said she would play innocent." A third man—a big man—pushing away from the back of the SUV and eyeing Maks as if he was pretty sure he could take him.

"I'm not *playing* anything," Katie said, and took a step closer. Maks still stood angled before her, not quite facing the group, but she was by no means hidden—all tall and slender strong grace, the courage finding its way back out no matter what she thought of herself.

Courage, but not stupidity. When Maks shifted ever so slightly to draw a line on her progress, she ceded it to him.

The only woman of the bunch stepped forward and tipped her head at Katie. "Williams is dead," she said. "He didn't show up at early shooting practice, so we went looking—"

"We found him, all right," the third man said, crossing his beefy arms over an impressive chest. "Shredded to pieces."

Katie looked at the woman; she nodded. "Blood everywhere. Looks like it took him a while to die, too."

Katie closed her eyes, the natural flush of her cheeks fading. "The crea—" *Creature*, she'd started to say. But Maks shifted into her before she could finish.

Maybe not quite soon enough.

"There, you see?" the second man gathered up the other two with his gaze, while those further away, still having their own conversations, hesitated at the changing pitch of the conversation. "She knows something."

Maks could feel Katie's fatigue, could see it in her face. And they had things to do before she could rest—property lines to be secured, house wards to strengthen…a discussion to have. *In the shop…a scent…a taste…bitter hot metal…*

Katie shot him a glance—not just checking in, but reading him—seeing his impatience. She told the men, "I'd like to get to my car, please."

The closest responded with an expression that wasn't quite a sneer—but it came close, and his meaning was clear enough. He opened his mouth, but before he could speak the woman slapped out with the back of her hand, a solid thump against his ribs that he didn't even seem to notice. "Oh, my God," she said in disbelief. "Are you really about to say 'make me'? Just because you're bigger than everyone else?"

The man crooked an eyebrow at Maks.

Yes, bigger. Yes, broader. Yes, meaner.

But not tiger.

Maks growled.

Or maybe he didn't, not literally. Maybe there'd been no actual sound. But somehow it hung in the air between them, startling the group, yanking surprise from the woman, wary expressions from the men…and from the biggest of them, all the mean turned to surprise.

"Really," Katie said gently, "I'd think you would want us *on* your side."

The rest of the group had already made that decision, easing back to the tight space between the vehicles. The big man didn't have to move, but he shifted toward the tailgate all the same, giving then room to pass.

Katie walked through the space like a queen claiming her own, and Maks paced her—his attention on the big guy, on the abashed crew between the cars—not taking them for granted. Katie barely hesitated as she again told the woman, "Please. Be careful."

The woman gave her the driest of looks. "Somehow, I think I'd better say the same to you."

Chapter 15

The day's sharp, early sunshine broke through the sheltering trees along Katie's dirt road. She eased off the accelerator as they approached a wide, sparsely graveled crossroad, and with a glance at Maks, made her decision, taking them off the single lane road that led to her house and around the corner.

"Your neighbor lives this way," he guessed.

"It was coming after me," she said tightly, not looking at him this time, full of certainty. "You know it was. But I wasn't there, so…" She braked to a gentle stop as the house came into view—an old wood-siding house in need of paint, the roofline distinctly uneven. Crime scene tape wrapped around the porch; the door was sealed. A homemade doghouse sat inside a fenced kennel area, but there was no sign of the German shepherd to whom Katie had occasionally spoken. *Please be safe. Please be with a friend.*

"Katie," Maks said, his voice a rumble that filled the

little car until she gave him a startled glance. "Even if it had wanted you, what happened isn't your fault."

His words didn't stop the guilt enveloping her. "Even *if*?"

He didn't look entirely comfortable. "Katie," he said, using her name again as if it gave him some place to start. "It came for me."

She arched an eyebrow at him, knowing her response was entirely unfair. "Oh, so now it's all about you?"

"This," he said, affirming it. *"This* was about me."

Something about the regret in his voice—the anger underlying it—made her look twice. He was, after all, the one who had seen the creature. Fought it.

"Because of yesterday?"

He nodded, his gaze on hers. "They know who I am."

"That it was a Sentinel, you mean." She said it without question, certain enough of the answer.

He shook his head. "That it was me." *The one who got away.*

The sense of his unspoken meaning came through so clearly, she had to hesitate, assuring herself that she hadn't actually heard the words.

Maybe it shouldn't have mattered so much to her that she could perceive such things of him…but it did. Because she didn't know if it spoke of Maks or of her own skills—or of *them.*

She felt so very much like a deer at the moment. Circumstances piling up on her, turning frightening…bringing to the forefront the fact that she was simply not a brave creature, after all.

She made herself take a deep breath and stay in the moment. "We shouldn't have come," she said. "We already knew what we had to know."

"We can go," Maks said. "I'll come back later."

As tiger, he meant. Hunting traces that human eyes—and noses—would miss.

Not that he'd missed much back at that coffee shop, human or not. As she started the car again, she looked over to the take-out cup in his hand—empty of its frozen hot chocolate, white fracture lines running through the brown logo where his grip had grown tight during the encounter outside the shop.

"What was it you saw at the coffee shop?" she asked, wheeling a tight circle away from the house and then quickly cutting right toward her own driveway. A lone cyclist approached them from behind, faster on two wheels on this road than they could be on four. Katie quickly rolled down her window and when the cyclist wished her a good morning, said, "Be careful out there today. You're alone, and a man was killed here this morning. Horribly."

She wanted to say, *You're alone, and there's a massive rampaging mutant javelina out there*.

No doubt words that would have had the cyclist running, all right. But not from the right thing.

As it was, he stopped, threw a look over his shoulder, and frowned. "Are you saying the guy is out in the woods?"

Close enough. That wordless impression came from Maks, who leaned forward just enough so the man could see him. "Yes."

"Maybe you could spread the word," Katie said—although she had the feeling that when the man got back to town, he'd find "the word" already there waiting for him.

The cyclist grumbled—but he turned his bike without dismounting and pedaled back toward the paved road, lifting a hand of thanks on the way.

Katie let out a breath of relief as she drove the short remaining distance to her driveway. "He won't be the first. No matter how the word spreads. And we can't stop them all."

"Call brevis," Maks said.

She cut the engine, casting him a surprised look as she pulled the keys from the ignition.

He hesitated, looking out into the woods and then returning his gaze to her. "The one behind this knows he has little time. Now he'll push. Maybe make mistakes. Even more so, after I——" But he frowned, and stopped there.

"After?" she said, hearing the familiar light thump as the yellow cat jumped up to scale the back hatch, a bit of a scramble as he made it to the roof, pattering unevenly overhead. "Come on, Maks, don't——"

But Maks cursed, an unexpected snarl, and she followed his gaze to the windshield—gasping, fumbling her keys, as she saw the bloody trail of prints smearing down to where the cat sat on the windshield, claiming the car with all his usual nonchalance, the ragged stump of his tail attempting to curve around a floppy hind leg that looked to be held on by skin alone.

Maks drove.

Crammed into her small car, grimly cursing the mechanics of it, he followed her distracted directions to the vet clinic. Katie held the cat wrapped in a towel on her lap, crying and healing him at the same time.

Maks didn't need to be told that she couldn't begin to save what the cat had lost, but he felt what she did for the little animal, sending him strength, easing his pain, supporting his body against shock and blood loss.

Just as Katie didn't need to be told what had done this to her independent companion. But when she came out of the clinic afterward, biting her lip, her eyes red and her nose and cheeks pink, she marched up to where Maks sat against the hood of the car and demanded, *"Why?"*

It wasn't something Maks wanted to say. "The creature was playing," he said. "And it was giving warning."

"Killing my neighbor wasn't enough?"

"That," said Maks, "was frustration. The warning was probably meant for me."

For a long moment she simply stood before him, one leg lifted slightly…the deer wanting to run. But she didn't, even as a tear spilled over and down her cheek. Maks said, "Katie," and opened his hands to her, and she came into his arms and let him wrap himself around her, holding her close right there in the parking lot where anyone who saw the blood and the tears would know everything they needed to know.

When she drew a huge breath and let it out slowly, and then another, he took the luxury of letting his fingers sift through her hair, pulling it from the elastic band to scrape it away from her face with gentle fingers.

His words weren't as gentle. They couldn't be. "In the coffee shop," he said, and when she drew another breath, sharper this time, he knew she understood—in the shop, when he'd gone on the hunt. "Before we entered, there was a man with Akins. I know this man."

Her voice didn't quite make it above a whisper. "And he knows you."

Maks nodded, his head against the side of hers; she pulled back to look at him. "He saw you, didn't he? He saw us coming through the front window, and headed out the back."

"Yes." Maks thought back to that cruel, bitter scent—

the memories that flooded back to him, the feelings that engulfed him.

Just that fast, her eyes widened; she absorbed the sense of it, the fury and the pain and the loss, and she *knew.* "From back then," she said, voice still ragged but full of certainty. "He was part of what happened to you."

"Yes." One of those who had engineered his mother's kidnapping, the breeding program that only she had survived long-term, the endless hunt for Maks after his escape—right up until the Sentinels had found him and his little ragged band of runaways and swept through the area, taking down what Core they could find. "More than that. At Gausto's workshop on *Core D'oiche,* just as we broke in…I thought I scented…" He shook his head. So much chaos, so many smells in that horrifying cellar workshop— the death and gore and creatures distorted, infected and dying…the acrid corruption of Core workings, burning his nose.

Yet for that one moment, he thought he'd scented his past.

Katie understood.

She understood that Maks's expression, grim and predatorial, frightened her—not for her own sake, but for his.

She understood that the game had changed. The Core wanted something from her; the Core was coming after Maks…and the Core was incubating something new and horrible. And somehow, Roger Akins was involved—sitting there in the coffee shop with the man who had come from Maks's past to invade his present. To invade *her* present.

And she understood that she'd done little to help figure

it all out—that her visions so far consisted of murky warnings and dire but detail-free mutterings.

Such thoughts followed her home from the clinic, which she left with the reassuring murmurs of the staff in her ears and the promise of a call as soon as the yellow cat was out of surgery—and there, she discovered something else.

The good people of Pine Bluff understood things, too.

Oh, not that they had the details, or knew she harbored a tiger in her house, or knew that the creature in their forest was a Core construct, wicked of eye and distorted of nature. But they knew *something*.

Akins's efforts to taint her reputation...the cat's death in her hands...and now, Rowdy's sudden illness. Not to mention the gruesome death of the reclusive and somewhat paranoid man who'd lived beside her.

"No, don't worry about it," she told the kennel club events coordinator who'd called as she'd stepped in the door. "I understand. Maybe another time." And then she ran through a quick sequence of voice mail messages, all saying essentially the same thing—"just can't make it to my appointment."

"Well," she said, putting the phone aside to find Maks watching her, silent and aware. "I'm busy today anyway."

"Resting," he suggested, with a glance at the stairs that led to her bedroom.

She immediately shook her head. "I'm done with sitting around, waiting for inspiration to strike or for brevis to run up and take care of things. Unless I can offer some direction, there's not much for a team to do, anyway. So I need to go hunting."

She might have imagined the hint of a smile around his eyes. She didn't imagine it at all when he leaned over to press a kiss on her mouth, sweet and gentle and far too brief. She found herself unconsciously following as he moved back, and missing his touch when they separated.

When had that happened?

He said, "I have perimeters to do. Then I'll do my own hunting."

She bit her lip. She didn't mean to; now, if ever, she wanted to be full of strength. "Should you?" she asked. "After yesterday…after the day before…" She touched his cheek, where the faint scar still lingered…but wouldn't, for much longer.

"Whatever is, *is*," he said. "But the injuries…you took care of that."

"I only jump-started you." But she'd done it in spades, free to use her healing openly for the first time in so many years—surprised, in retrospect, at how effective she'd been. Just as she'd helped Ian. "You should take it easy."

"I'm done sitting around," he said.

She bristled in indignation for him. "Hardly that," she told him, straightening, her hands finding their way to her hips. "You've been—" But she saw the humor in his eyes, and stopped, and gave a rueful shake of her head. "Okay, okay. I get it. Yes, I've been doing more than sitting around, too. But seriously…I'm just too wired to rest right now."

"Then come out with me," he said, simply enough, and tipped his head at the security screen. He barely waited for her hesitation before he added, "Not the woods. The yard perimeter."

Sunshine and fresh air and silence, after a night of chaos and the early-morning hours of frantic worry. Balm to a deer's soul. A warmth blossomed in her chest that had nothing to do with the sensual heat he so easily sparked to life.

She gestured at the door. "I don't understand this perimeter thing of yours," she said as she followed him out.

"It's not a warding; it's not really a shield. It's not something I realized any of us could do."

For once, it felt good to say it that way...*us*. As if including herself as a Sentinel suddenly made a lot more sense when Maks was there with her.

"No one really understands it," he said, a little wry self-awareness there. "I don't think about it much. It just—"

"Is," she finished for him.

"It won't stop a Core working," he told her. "But I'll know if anything or anyone crosses the line." That it wouldn't physically stop someone—or some *thing*—from approaching was something Katie already knew. No one's shields did that.

She walked with him as he moved along his perimeter, and while Maks stepped in careful concentration, Katie relaxed enough to enjoy the newly blooming wildflowers—gumweed and asters and penstemon gone to riot. As they circled around the side of the house nearest the road, she thought to say, embarrassed, "Watch your step here. This is where clients let their dogs stretch their legs. They're supposed to pick up, but not everyone is good about it. Although Marie was the last one out this way and she's pretty—"

Good, she'd been about to say, until it struck her again that Marie had last been here to strike out in her anguish over her dog's sudden illness.

Maks didn't respond—not to the warning or to Katie's sudden pensiveness—but he did stop short, eyeing the grass with interest, and focused on something shiny.

Like her deer, Katie had a much easier time seeing motion than she did unmoving detail; she held back, letting Maks take a step, then another—and then his curiosity turned to something more grim, and he knelt to pick up a stick and poke at something until suddenly Katie could see it in the grasses, black and knotted and leather.

An amulet cord.

Confusion warred with the cold clenching sensation in her stomach. "I don't understand. There's no amulet?"

In answer, he nudged the stick into the grass until he could lift it with the cord hanging limp from the end—two ragged ends, and no amulet. Katie felt nothing from it— no acrid corruption, no malaise—and still no inclination whatsoever to touch it. The deer was smarter than that, and so was Katie.

"Why would the Core leave a cord here with no amulet?"

Maks took his gaze from the thing long enough to give her a meaningful glance. "They wouldn't."

Katie frowned. "Then where—"

Except *where* was suddenly obvious.

One great big goofy dog with a penchant for swallowing rocks and the occasional child's toy.

"Marie's dog," she said, filled with horror at the thought, and unable to deny the obvious reality of it. "That poor animal! No wonder he got so sick so fast, even though he was healing beautifully from his surgery." And no wonder she hadn't felt it when she'd treated him. When he'd been on her table, he hadn't been sick at all. "Surely they can find it—surely they can remove it!"

But she knew better even as she said it. No doubt they'd already taken X-rays; either the amulet had done its damage on the way through, or it had, in the way of these evil things, integrated itself into the dog's body, leaving nothing to remove.

"Maybe," she said, trying again, "I can still help him."

If she dared. Because what if the dog died, and Marie blamed her anew? If everyone knew? Katie gave the side yard a startled and distrustful look. "We don't know that it was the only one."

"We'll look," he said. "I should have done it sooner."

Her own vehemence startled her. "As if you've even had the chance. It wouldn't have helped Marie's Rowdy, anyway—you were flat out when he got here. You didn't have a chance!"

The look he shot her held flat disagreement, but he said only, "We'll ward a bucket for this. Someone at brevis will know what the knotting means."

"Brevis," she said, breathing the word out. "We have to call them. They have to know about my neighbor—"

"They know." Maks straightened, breaking his perimeter to place the knotted cord on a rock where it would be easy to find again. He glanced her way to discover her patent uncertainty, and said it again. "They know, Katie."

Well, she supposed they would. A police scanner or two, an ear already perked to this corner of the region. "They don't know about my cat!" she blurted out, not really meaning to—feeling absurd as soon as she'd said it.

The look on Maks's face didn't make her feel absurd at all. "They will."

"They will," she agreed. "Because this time, I'm going to call *them*. Enough is enough." She crossed her arms, scowling down at the cord. "And I'll have something to tell them when I do it. Finish up here, Maks—I don't want to go *seeing* without someone on watch."

He did a double-take and gave her the sliest hint of a smile. She marched up to him and launched a quick poke in the chest, her finger giving way before hard muscle. "You like it when the deer gets pushy?" she said. "You haven't seen anything yet."

She didn't expect him to spread his arms slightly in a

nonverbal mea culpa, or for his smile to spread something unmistakable. She didn't expect to find herself smiling back, flushed with the pleasure of having this man enjoy her—deer and human, healer and seer. Struck by impulse, giving way entirely before it, she threw herself across the scant distance between them, giving him a fierce hug.

He staggered back an exaggerated step, just a hint of laughter rumbling in his chest; his hands rested against her back, warm and strong. "What?" he asked, and the laughter was still there in his throat.

"Just because," she told him—didn't have any other answer than that, and didn't care. "Just because."

He held her that way a long moment, his breath tickling the top of her ear, his heart thudding comfortably against her chest. She became aware of the strength rippling beneath her hands—the way it lay waiting, completely and comfortably silent so the deer might feel welcome. One hand stroked down her spine, brushing all the way to the very base of it—holding them together so she could clearly feel the tension in his body change—and clearly feel his response to her.

And just as quickly, she could feel the pain that speared through him. In response to her, always in response to her. As if she'd broken something when she'd done that first deep healing, there on the front porch.

She eased back from him. "Oh, Maks," she said, the conflict strong in her voice. "What have we done?"

"What was right for that moment," he said, and his voice held no conflict at all. Nor was his touch hesitant, as he released her to cup her face, briefly search her eyes, and then bring them together in a kiss of the sweetest intensity, mouth gentle, tongue a mere tease, a soft bite on her lower lip as he pulled away. "We'll figure it out."

Katie found herself holding her breath on that comment—and letting it go with a sigh, relief and satisfaction and worry all bundled up into one. "Okay," she said. "Do what needs to be done here. I'm going to call the vet, and then let's go hunting. The seer's way."

He bit her lip again, a little more smartly this time, and stepped back from her, silent. Not that she needed words.

With Maks, she was beginning to understand that the best moments came without them.

Chapter 16

Katie stared out her bedroom window into the bright afternoon and fought the ragged edges of panic.

Not the panic of a deer on the run, not the panic of things impending.

No. The panic of a seer who couldn't see.

This, then, was the price of so many years of squelching her abilities—limiting herself to peeks and vague hints.

She'd been so sure that if she sat herself down in calm silence, amid the familiar scents and comforts of her own bedroom and knowing that Maks stood watch for her in the living room below, she'd be able to reach out to the seeing part of herself.

Boy, had she been wrong.

But if she couldn't reach out to those visions, then she'd simply sit here quietly with herself and ponder what they already knew.

They knew her visions had sent her dread and violence

and darkness, each on a level she hadn't experienced before...except once, leading up to *Core D'oiche*. She knew they involved Maks—those glimpses of his eyes, in ferocity and pain. That he faced some undefined battle, she could pretty well figure.

But she thought he'd already figured all that out. The creature had to be stopped...the Core agent had to be stopped. Who else to do it but Maks, whether or not he should be out in the field at all?

Maybe he's better.

That hopeful thought came unbidden, and she scowled it down. *Wishful thinking.*

But if not better, then different. That, she thought was true. Things were changing for him—because he was here, and because they had touched one another.

After that, what she knew started to get mixed up. Maks might think the attack at her neighbor's was all about him, but Katie knew better. The visions had started before he got here...the amulets had been planted even as he arrived. No, Maks's presence had served as a catalyst, not an instigating factor.

Akins, too, had started in on her before Maks's arrival... and now he had half the town convinced that she'd gone angel-of-mercy on her clients...with just enough truth mixed in to be convincing. *And Marie's dog...*

And Akins was also now somehow associated with the Core rogue who had once held a young Maks prisoner. It had been less than a decade since the children—since *Maks* had been discovered; surely the children hadn't been on their own for long. Just long enough for the rumors to start flying. And before that—

She frowned, trying to make sense of what she'd seen of Maks's escape. He'd been so young...three? And already turning tiger. And now he was...what? Maybe thirty? Not a youth, but fully mature, his features with the hard, beautiful edge of a man in his prime.

And yet, he'd said he'd been a teen when they picked him up.

She just couldn't make it come together.

Katie closed her eyes and reached out not just to her visions, but also to Maks.

Nick Carter hesitated in the doorway of the private room, unnoticed, phone tucked in his hand. Gleaming steel and linoleum, pleasant beige walls and a full choice of music, large-screen television. Southwest Brevis medical not only kept its facilities up-to-date, it also kept them comfortable.

Ian Scott had the music turned up to something angry, guitar licks shredding through the room in an audible extension of his mood. He wore a classic hospital gown over black ninja bottoms, and he'd kicked the covers of his bed into a tangle. A laptop sat on the swing-arm table over the bed and notes sprawled across his lap, pencil tapping against them. His hair—a moderate length of spiky silvergray that would do David Bowie proud—was in greater disarray than usual.

Nick drew a breath and knocked on the door frame. He couldn't hear over the music, but Ian's lips formed a short, sharp response as he grabbed the remote by his thigh and cut the music. "You'd better be here to release me."

"Ha," Nick said, "and ha. Sorry, Ian. We're not taking these amulet workings for granted these days."

Ian snorted with impatience. "Who's to know better than I? This was the same thing that took Treviño down—only Maks stopped it before it really got started, and Katie pretty nearly put me back together on the spot. She's a quiet powerhouse, that one is." Ian cocked his head. "But you knew that, didn't you?"

"So much for my poker face." Nick crossed his arms, leaning his shoulders against the door frame. "Let's say I knew there was more there than she's shown us. But it's her choice."

"She's not going to have a choice now," Ian said, tossing the well-chewed pencil onto the desk. "Whatever's going on, it's come to *her*. And you've bloody well hung her out there to dry."

"Not so much," Nick said, offering an expression that would have spoken volumes to anyone who was paying attention. But Ian was too caught up in his own restlessness and frustration, not completely aware that some of that itch came from what his body still struggled to shed. "I just talked to the local Core *drozhar.*"

That got Ian's attention. "Our friendly new local Core precinct prince? Did he spin some lie about being a good little enemy?"

Nick laughed, short as it was. "Close. But you know the man sounded just frustrated enough. Wanted me to clear out my people so he can go in and clean up."

Ian's response was as succinct as his reaction to Nick's knock at the door.

"I said something similar." Nick's grim smile reflected the satisfaction of the moment. "After *Core D'oiche,* their cred is nonexistent. Thanks to them, we've very nearly been revealed to those who would hunt us all, if they knew of us."

"Or cage us, or kill us, or use us," Ian muttered.

All of that.

Ian shifted the pages on his lap, a restless movement. "Okay, then. The Core sucks but they're not going to mess with us, Katie and Maks are still out there on their own. Why am I still here?"

"They won't be on their own for long," Nick said. "Lyn Maines will have a crew up there by midday tomorrow—Treviño will join them as soon as possible. Meanwhile, I need to know if you can identify this. No one else in the lab could do it." He held out the phone, thumbed the display and moved closer to the bed with it.

Ian, being Ian, took the phone from Nick's hand, cocking his head at it. "No effing wonder. Who took this picture, and with what?"

"Maks took it," Nick said dryly.

"Well, that explains it." Ian angled the screen this way and that, hunting the best light. "Pestilence," he muttered, flipping over a piece of paper to grab his pencil and sketch a few strong, confident lines that suddenly turned into a pattern of knots.

"Pestilence," Nick repeated, angling himself for a better look at the sketch.

"More or less. Think of it as bad mojo. A drawing of illness."

"A friend's dog apparently swallowed it."

"Ah," Ian said in instant understanding. "The dog, I presume, is now dying of whatever would have killed it somewhat later in its lifetime anyway."

"An internal gangrene," Nick said. "The animal apparently has a habit of eating…*anything.*"

"That sounds about right." Ian paused, a time during which he might well have been grinding his teeth. "Let me out of here, Nick. They can use me."

"As I said, there'll be a team there before end of day tomorrow," Nick repeated, more patiently than he might have under other circumstances. Cultivating driven brilliance meant dealing with driven brilliance. "And your assignment, until medical clears you, is to keep your leopard ass in this bed."

Ian stiffened, one hand reaching unconsciously for the laptop in a protective gesture—as if Nick might take it in an attempt to force him to rest. A gesture that did, of course, completely reveal his intent to do anything *but* rest.

"Pointless," Nick muttered. "It is absolutely pointless to be brevis consul when no one listens to you anyway." And then, more loudly, "Yes, you can keep the toys. And you can work remotely—as long as I don't hear from medical that it's a problem."

From the way Ian narrowed his eyes, Nick doubted very much that anyone would be so bold as to suggest the work was a problem.

Already Ian had looked back to Nick's phone. "Maks took this, hmm?" This time his reaction wasn't to the photo itself, but the implications of Maks Altán voluntarily using such technology. One more glance at the image, and Ian handed it back to Nick. "Told you he had fallen for this one. First crush, isn't it?"

"Something like that." Not that Nick had been at Southwest when Maks had been brought in, but he knew his people. And he knew that when he'd arrived only a handful of years earlier, Maks had been presented as their most reliable personal bodyguard—a man who didn't know how to play and who rarely offered anything of himself other than loyalty.

"He shouldn't be out there alone, then." Ian's expression went distant, as if seeing those things he'd left behind in Pine Bluffs. When he looked back to Nick, his gaze had turned sharp. "He's in over his head, Nick. Best you tell him to lay damned low."

"Maks is more than people make him out to be," Nick said mildly, aware that Ian spoke from concern and not censure. Who in brevis *didn't* like Maks? He'd even won over prickly, confused Marlee—the inadvertent traitor who still lived under a house arrest. "But he's been told to lay damned low all the same. See to it that you do the same."

"Already here," Ian told him, his sardonic bite back in full.

Nick gave him a raised eyebrow that could only be considered unconvinced, and tucked his phone away into his inside suit coat pocket as he left the room.

He'd barely cleared the room when the thick distortions of a shredded guitar solo blasted to life. Nick ducked his head on a smile, and went to see if he could make the impossible happen. *Lay damned low, Maks. Help is on the way.*

Katie's visions had stymied her, but she found herself slipping easily into her connection to Maks. He could have been in the living room, he could have been beside her—he could have been back in Tucson. It didn't matter. To her, he was *right there.*

Warmth and solid strength and implacable power couched in a gentle touch...

Her body reacted as though she could feel it all—that touch, the press of him against her, the burst of response in them both. She released a deep breath, long and slow... savoring it all before she reached out to what she knew of him, the trickles of past...the pieces of his story. Absorbing it, reveling in it...seeking truth through it.

The bedroom door slammed open.

Katie startled up off the bed, rolling to land, limbs akimbo, between the bed and the wall, then scrambling to press herself up against the window, her mind in a panic— *Did the Core get past Maks? Is he okay—*

But it wasn't the Core, at that.

It was Maks.

And he definitely, definitely wasn't okay.

Not when he stood in her damaged doorway, one hand clutching either side of the frame as if it was the only thing keeping him on that side of it. Not when he breathed as though he'd just bolted miles through the forest to reach her, his eyes wild and dark, just a flash of green around the pupils. Energy pulsed around him, palpable to Katie's healing senses—full of dissonance, battering at her even from there, full of fever-pitch arousal.

If he tried for words, he failed—but his entire expression was a plea, and she understood it instantly. *What have you done? What are you doing?*

"Maks," she whispered—having no more words than he did, appalled by what she'd done—what she'd woken in him.

Except...

Look at it, Katie Rae. The response to you. What it's done. What it always does. Maks, touched by her quiet strokes of emotion and sensation, and then battered by how his body reacted to them. The energies, tugging at him—an escalation of the very state in which she'd first seen him at the bus stop.

Not integrated. Not with his emotions, not with himself. His energies clashed with one another, fighting for dominance...fighting for clarity. Completely out of his control.

"Katie," he said, grinding the words out loud this time, his fingers biting into the door frame. *"What are you doing?"*

"Loving you," she whispered, and knew it for truth as soon as the words came out. She pushed herself away from the wall as he trembled visibly in response to her words, her presence...her healing touch, reaching out to him again from where she stood...trying to sooth. But he responded with a jerk, a swirl of that baffling dissonance, the tension of it bringing out every strong line of his face, every bit of wild that a man who shared himself with a tiger could have.

A thrum of fear ran through her. What if she'd woken something that neither of them understood? That neither of them could control? Pure determination kept her from pressing back against the wall; pure survival instinct kept her voice calm, her mind racing. For when she tried to pull back on the touch she'd shared, however inadvertently, he lifted his head with tight protest—the tiger snarling behind it, too battered to think straight.

Just like every time she touched him—roused him. Every time he responded to her. This tiger who'd spent his youth imprisoned, on the run, and devoted to the protection of others—and who'd come only late to the learning that every other Sentinel received from birth.

Dissonant energies, lack of balance, a certain lack of awareness...

"Maks," she said, taking a step forward—enough to reach the bed, where she placed one knee as if she might just keep walking right over it. "Did brevis see to your initiation? Have you—"

Have you been with other Sentinels before?

His eyes widened faintly; he seemed to grab at the words as a lifeline, and took a deep, shuddering breath, reaching inward for—

There. He jerked again, losing all that breath in a grunt of pain—holding himself straight, arms braced, and panting until he got past the moment, able to lift his head with a complexity of expression Katie simply could decipher. *Desire, barely banked; pain, barely withstood. Pleading... for understanding, maybe. For help.*

His words were ragged but honest. "Yes," he said. "They

said they thought going tiger early had unbalanced me. They said initiation might help."

She swallowed. "And did it?"

The conversation seemed to give him a focus; he gave her a faintly thoughtful look. "They…" He shook his head, trying to hang on to words. "They thought it would change me. It didn't. They said…" Another deep breath, and now he allowed himself to lean against the door frame. "They said it was like that, sometimes."

"Sometimes," she murmured. Initiation was an unpredictable thing. It didn't matter how many times a Sentinel had experienced the act of sex…it only mattered the first time it happened with another Sentinel. That moment came of planning, consulting with family and the young Sentinel…and with the candidates who might be assigned for what was a very personal rite.

Sometimes the initiated youth came out of the experience essentially as he or she had gone in. And sometimes new strengths emerged—new talents. Before initiation, Katie hadn't been identified as a seer.

Before initiation, Maks had apparently already pretty much been Maks.

He seemed to struggle with something—words or pain or feelings. After a moment, he said, "They thought that my life had already brought out my skills."

"The early changing," Katie said. "The boundaries you can set, the silence you can take. Your skills as a protector."

Maks nodded. He looked at his hands, as if surprised to find he'd let go of the door frame. He swallowed hard, and this time she knew—could see the conflict on his features—that emotion was what gripped him now. "I don't understand what's happening. I don't know what to do about it. And I don't know how to keep you safe." He looked away from her, his jaw working, his words strained. *"From me."*

Chapter 17

Another shudder ran through Maks, leaving his body torn between sensations—great desire, great confusion, great pain. His mind was torn between understandings—knowing he wanted, knowing he couldn't have, knowing that in the middle of it all he was still broken in some critical way.

He couldn't bring himself to look at her again. Not that face that was purely Katie. Not her sweet nature, or her compassion, or the very strong courage running throughout.

Because you can't have her, Maks.

Not when the very thought of it roused such a tumult—the fugue mixed with the inevitable shards of pain.

At first that pain had taken him purely by surprise—until he'd learned it could clear his head. It also served as a warning: no matter what he wanted or how he wanted or what he felt when Katie reached for him, he couldn't have it.

"Maks," she said, full of concern, and of course he was lost to her, and none of the reality of it mattered one little bit.

"I want you," he told her, though he was pretty sure she already knew what he wanted. "I want you in a way I've never wanted anyone. It does these things to me…I don't understand. I can't—" He broke off, shook his head—dared a glance at her and then looked down at his hands. Could feel the claws there, waiting in another form. Could feel himself, so close to something so big, something so out of control—

I don't know how to keep you safe.

Something that scared the hell out of him.

He thought she'd understood—but she couldn't have, not when she crawled right over the bed to reach him. Her hands came as a cool balm when she placed them along either side of his jaw. They didn't stay still long; she stroked through the hair over one ear, a light and infinitely pleasurable touch that tightened the skin down his nape and all the way down his spine. Her calm breathed into him.

The sensations swirled up in him as if he'd never conquered them at all—the fugue, closing in to make his skin pound and his heart race and his vision double; the surge of desire, a straight shot down his spine, curling and twisting and tightening. The first hint of hot pain, grabbing his breath. He reached for her wrist, stilling her hand. "I can't—"

"Neither could I," she told him. "I went looking, just now, and I didn't find any answers—all I found was you. It makes me wonder if all I ever saw was you." Her expression sobered; she made no attempt to disengage her wrist. "You with the Core, you with your mother…you in darkness. You and that creature—although I can't say for sure if that was about what happened yesterday or if it's still to come. You…and me."

His gaze shot to her face. She found herself beyond blushing. "Even in the car, the day I first brought you here. You felt it, I'm pretty sure."

Mutely, he nodded.

"The thing is, as much as it's always been you…it's something darker, as well. It's not all *about* you. And that's the part I still can't figure out. Because when I reach out, I find…" She shook her head, took a deep breath, let it out slowly, and admitted it again. *"You."*

Regret flashed through him—second guesses. If he'd been straight about his condition, Nick never would have sent him here—and then maybe Katie could have seen further—seen *past* him—to figure out her visions. If he'd never come here, she would be safe—in the care of some-one who wasn't compromised or hauled back to brevis. Even if his inner hackles rose at the first possibility and he knew she would have hated the second.

"Stop it," she said, simply enough. "Whatever you're thinking, it's wrong. You're the one who said it, Maks. Whatever is, *is*. Let it be. Whatever's happening to you… let it be. It's the only way we'll figure it out."

He stiffened in resistance. *I can't*—

Maybe she'd gotten *too* good at perceiving his mind's voice. She said, "You may have to." She looked up at him, full of thought. Maks flinched under the scrutiny of it— of the perceptiveness there.

"Listen, Maks. You were born in captivity. You took the tiger younger than anyone knew was possible. And when you escaped, you survived as the tiger until you found those first runaways in the woods and made them yours."

He remembered that day. How they'd been so terrified of him, thirteen-year-old twins escaped from an abusive home and on the run from the petty thefts they'd committed to survive. How he'd lost touch with the spoken word, but still coaxed them into trust with persistence and gestures and his own abiding intent to protect them. He'd been bigger than the twins by then—still lanky, shoulders already showing promise.

"And you gathered more children, until after several years, the Sentinels realized what was going on, and they came and got you."

A day of terror, that—of facing his first Sentinel, a man well-grown into his lynx and strong-hearted enough to face an adolescent tiger without escalating the situation, even when the tiger struck out in fear. A man who had hidden his surprise at Maks's youthful human form...a man who had told Maks, *I'm taking you home.*

"But they never figured out who your mother was."

"No." It still hurt, after all these years—a ragged, forever pain, watching his mother die—never knowing, in retrospect, her story.

Katie said gently, "Didn't that strike you as strange?"

He jerked away from his memories to look at her, guileless and gentle, and inside him something swelled, reaching...

He pushed it back. Ruthlessly.

She said, "How many Sentinels go missing, unrecorded? How many women of childbearing age?"

He shook his head, floundering, a pounding in his ears.

"Because they were looking in the wrong generation, tiger mine." She moved closer, twining her fingers in his. He growled, deep in his chest, and she only laid her free hand against his chest. "Because brevis might have *guessed* at your age, but they didn't get it right. How could they? No one else has ever changed so young. No one else has spent their childhood hiding as their other. Maks," she said, her voice going low. *"How long does it take for a tiger cub to grow up?"*

And he only looked at her. Only looked, while the truth of his life lay out before him for the first time, and the impact of it swirled into the sensations already battering at him.

"You may have *looked* fifteen at your initiation, but you weren't. Not in years."

"Then…" He couldn't quite say it out loud. Because initiation did more than bring out a Sentinel's full potential… it balanced him, clearing pathways for the mature energies. It made order of an undisciplined connection to the earth.

But only when the body was ready.

As if she'd followed his thoughts, she said gently, "I don't think your initiation took. I don't think your body had yet reconciled your chronological age with your physical age."

He frowned at her, trying to think past the ongoing battle for control, the reaching sensation that filled him beyond full and still ached for more. "But I've been with others since. Surely, if it hadn't happened that first time…"

She shook her head. "*Something* took—something partial. It had to have, or they would have known. Haven't you ever felt an initiation? It's unmistakable. More children are conceived on initiation nights than all the other nights put together." She smiled, a little bit rueful.

Initiated, but not initiated. All this time.

"Initiation does more than bring out the potential of a young Sentinel," Katie said, and yes, she was damned close now, hands on his shoulders, moving down his arms, tracing his collarbones. "Because it does that by clearing certain channels of energies. Without that, we can't be balanced. We aren't quite whole…or stable."

He struggled to absorb the implications of that statement. *Initiated, but not initiated.* "Then...Flagstaff..."

"Until then, you were managing," she said. "But I think the energy surges there—*before* the hotel—knocked you out of balance. Then, once you were released into full activity again, the imbalance got worse."

He only frowned at her. It made sense to a point. But this—*this*—between the two of them...

She must have felt it—that resistance to the idea. It didn't seem to bother her.

Not judging by how close she'd come to him now, and the whisper of her breath against his jaw as she just barely nipped skin, sending shards of sensation through his body and making it—

So very hard—

To think...

She said, "I know you've been with other Sentinels..."

"Often enough," he managed.

"But you haven't been with *me*."

His hands landed on her upper arms, tugging her in close. He went for her neck, so slender and thin-skinned, the life pulsing close to the surface and her vulnerable nape right there. She didn't stiffen; she didn't fear. She clung to him, and the sensation of *reaching* crowded him from the inside out, filling him beyond endurance. The pain followed on its heels, but not enough to deter him. Not now.

Her words were a different story, muffled as they were. "Let me help, Maks."

He froze. "I'm not your patient. I'm not your *project*."

He wasn't prepared for her self-deprecating laughter. "Like I haven't wanted you since the start. Like I haven't already pretty much imploded in your arms, right there on my porch. Have mercy, Maks!"

Right there on the porch. Hot and wild and rocketing her

straight to completion, the feedback between them taking him so close…before the pain hit.

"Katie," he said, his mouth brushing her neck with the words. "Katie Rae."

"Yes," she told him, shuddering with the words. "*Please,* Maks."

Yes. Every part of him wanted her, inside and out. He wanted the connection, the sensations, the completion. Sweet, brave Katie Rae—he'd known her, *seen* her, since that moment her vision had pulled them together in her car. It had only taken him a while to recognize what he'd learned of her in that moment—from her compassion to her courage.

The rush of understanding surged through him, bigger than he was; the tiger sprang free, roaring through his being. He gasped with the enormity of it, losing track of the house, the room, the doorway—of everything that wasn't him and wasn't Katie.

And then the pain slashed through him, leaving him only a glimpse of Katie's startled face—flushed cheeks and kissed lips and wide eyes. He wrenched himself aside from her, agony in his chest—but not from the pain. He could handle the pain.

But not the loss of control.

Maks, the strong one. Maks the protector. Maks, so close to his tiger that he'd lived an accelerated childhood in his tiger's skin.

Maks, who didn't dare release his tiger on the woman he loved.

Katie stood in her bedroom doorway, rumpled and kissed and aroused beyond measure, flushed with the overflow of energies as much as from Maks's hands on her body and her hands on his—and suddenly alone.

Just one brief glimpse of the wild, naked desperation on Maks's face, that's all she'd had—and then he was gone.

And she knew just why. She'd felt it, a near-subliminal impression of fear and understanding—her connection with Maks obscured by sensation but wholly, vibrantly alive.

Fear.

For her, and what he might do to her. For what he might turn into. Fear for his own sanity, in the clash of fugue and pain and desire.

Tiger, fleeing from himself.

But if she was right...

Maks, without complete initiation, would only destroy himself from the inside out. Energies turning on themselves, talents blocked and unrealized, a body tearing itself apart.

It wasn't a chance she could ever take.

As ever, the deer was swift. She ran down the stairs in his wake, her shirt rumpled and half-unbuttoned, and out into the daylight of her porch.

He hadn't even hesitated. Halfway across her yard, barefoot, flannel shirt flapping open—she caught only a glimpse before the achingly bright swirl of energy formed around him and the tiger emerged on the exposed open ground beside her house.

So many times she'd demurred from running the woods with him; so many times, she'd felt that flicker of self-protective unease. This time, she flung herself into the deer—small but infinitely quick, a reddish-brown blur of movement across the scattered bunchgrass and needle-covered ground.

Powerful as he was, he wasn't built for a lengthy sprint. Eventually, she'd catch him.

Eventually, she did.

Far into the rugged woods, he'd stopped—the pines closing thickly around him, a rough thrust of granite blocking his progress and nurturing a stand of smaller trees— twisty little Gambel oaks and bushy mountain mahogany with a burst of low spreading fleabane off to the side.

He stood in the midst of it, spraddle-legged, panting with head low and eyes dazed.

And Katie, because she'd felt his fears, did what she had to do. One step after the other, slender legs and vulnerable neck, she moved closer to him. She knew when he'd spotted her by the cessation of his panting—and knew it again when he raised that massive head to look at her.

If she was wrong…

One swipe of a paw. One crunch of those jaws…

But she wasn't wrong. She'd been in his memories; she'd been in his *life*. She knew what formed him, as well or better than he could understand it himself.

I'm not wrong.

And still it took all her courage for that next step…and then the next. And then she was there at his shoulder, her petite black nose nuzzling into the fur of his ruff.

The tiger groaned, a deep and wrenching sound, and threw himself away from her—taking the change, blue-and-white strobing light obscuring the very moment he became Maks. He staggered to his feet until he met the thick trunk of the closest ponderosa and braced himself against it, head bowed.

Katie stepped after him, moving right through the change as he had done, the air gentle against her legs where she'd leaped right out of her yoga pants during the change. Just as the deer had done—just as barefoot as he—she took one deliberate step after another, all too aware of the tension in his back and shoulders, the muscles standing out in relief.

His skin was hot with the energy, damp with effort, the muscle hard beneath her tentative fingers.

"You can't go on like this," she said quietly—so matter-of-fact in voice and word when she wanted only to run—or to wrap herself around him. "*We* can't go on like this."

He gulped air, shuddering faintly beneath her touch.

"Whatever's happening with the Core, we have to fix this—we can't deal with them until we do." Her voice grew a little more fierce. "Not just for you, Maks. For *me*."

He shook his head, a barely discernible motion. Not rejection—she knew it as she knew her own self.

Fear. He threw it at her in his desperate attempt to explain—for he was beyond the words that had never come easily to him.

She understood perfectly. It shouldn't be like this—not the fugues he had endured, not this massive swell of never-channeled energy. Not the pain of blocked channels, finally challenged.

Or maybe she hadn't understood at all. For as Katie's touch brought on another surge of desire, Maks dug his fingers into the chunky orange-brown bark of the pine and managed hoarsely, "Can't…keep you…*safe*."

She moved closer, sliding her hand around his ribs from behind; she lay her cheek against his back, feeling the tremendous struggle of will and body.

"Maybe that's my job," she said. "I'm the healer, Maks. I'm the one who can make this work." Her other hand slid between them, skimming down his body, scraping nails lightly against the denim between her touch and the back of his thigh. His leg trembled; he made a sound deep in his throat. She tucked herself up closer, running her other hand over his chest, finding the smattering of pale chest hair. He sucked in a breath and the reaching power surged higher, a rushing noise in her ears. She told him, "I'm the one who *wants* to make this work, because I want you. I want you so badly it scares the hell out of me. Don't you dare think of this as a *project*."

The way he stiffened had nothing to do with desire, and everything to do with the energies battering at him, seeking release. The sound he made then came of a different kind of desperation—and the fear she felt from him was now a different kind of fear.

And oh, she didn't blame him at all. The power gathering inside him was nothing she'd ever felt before—nothing anyone should ever have to feel. There was a *reason* for initiation, a reason it was crucial…a reason they'd tried it for Maks, never guessing that his scrambled maturation would leave him not more settled, but less. So very vulnerable, with the unchanneled energies tangled and echoing and waiting for a chink in his formidable armor.

"Ssh, Maks. It'll get better." *She hoped.* "It'll get better. Think about me. Think about what you did to me out on the porch, the way you made me feel…" She brought one hand up the back of his thigh, dipping between his legs from behind; she brought the other down straining abs to trace along the inside of his waistband. His head dropped back; bark flaked away under his fingers. The sight of him, the feel of him, the echo of his internal energies, swirling against her own…it hummed through her in a promise so strong she nearly tore the jeans open, nearly went for him right then and there.

Instead, humming, she licked his skin, warm and salty, right along his spine. "*Please,* Maks…"

She could survive the consequences if he didn't complete his first, partial initiation to join with her now. She would ache, and she would feel bereft, and she would never be the same, but she'd survive.

But Maks wouldn't. Not for much longer.

"Please," she whispered. "For me." Shameless, playing on his body…playing on his lifelong need to protect. Her hand slipped inside his jeans—and she froze when she realized there was nothing between her skin and his.

Maks jerked in response, and he snarled, and he turned so fast she didn't see it coming. By the time her body protested the loss of his, he was fisting his hand in her hair, wrapping one arm around her to cup her bottom and *lift*. She didn't think twice before wrapping her legs around him. He shoved her back against the tree, and by then he was kissing her—growling and kissing her, every plunge of his tongue in her mouth echoed by a jerk of his hips, energies reaching…reaching…shot through with pain that brushed against her without affecting her, all her careful intentions shot to hell as she pushed back against him. Her fingers clenched around his arms, his shoulders, his neck; her body spiraled way past control and straight to—

She cried out with the surprise of it, all hot and sweetly abrupt, and came back to herself with her heels digging into Maks's muscled ass and her shirt pulling up under her breasts. Maks sank to the ground, taking her with him. Finally he rested on his knees—still kissing her, his face buried in the hair at her neck, his teeth nipping as often as not.

"All the way, Maks," she said, almost too breathless for words as she groped between them, hunting the second button of his jeans.

Way too much work. She shoved him, hard and demanding—he went sprawling, his legs awkward, and she rode him down, her knees making contact with the pine-needle carpet. The moment he landed, she rose up and went after his pants.

She threw back her head and cried out with the relief of it as they slid together—as Maks gasped, his eyes gone dark and distant and his hands clutching convulsively at her hips. But his second cry came of pain, and his distant gaze grew wild, and even as she bent over to reassure him, he cried out again. His hands left her body to clutch at the ground, and his hips rising under hers were arched in agony and no longer in pleasure.

"Maks—*Maks*," she said, stroking back his hair, stroking along his arms and chest. "Ssh, Maks, be with *me*, Maks—" as if she said his name often enough, he might hear it.

But Maks heard nothing, twisting under her in an awful parody of the delight this moment should bring him, his eyes wild with the tiger's primal, furious fear.

Nick Carter sliced through the brevis lap pool with a vengeance—hard, efficient strokes that pulled him through the water at speed. And though his wolf hated swimming—hated the feel of it, the buoyancy of it, the insidious invasion of nose and ears and mouth—this afternoon the water felt like silk, caressing and soft. It put him in mind of Jet's hands—the wicked mood, where he knew he'd pay for gentleness with unpredictable ferocity and demand. Jet of the truly wild nature, untamed by the Core and untamed by her time with Nick and with brevis. Jet with her unabashedly direct sexuality, beautifully athletic body—

Nick snorted out a mistimed breath, slung his head free of water, and planted his feet at the bottom of the waist-deep lap pool.

Mercy for him that the water wasn't any lower against his body.

What the hell—?

The pool room's metal door clanged shut. Nick sluiced the remaining water from his eyes and found Annorah standing at the end of the lap lane with a towel in hand.

"Saddle up," she said, and tossed the towel at him, taking for granted that he'd pluck it out of the air before it hit either the water or his face. "We got trouble. Or haven't you caught on yet—" She interrupted herself, her head tipped a bit to the side, and a bit upward, and snapped, "I know, already! Quit tying up my head!"

Nick wiped his face dry, gave a token scrub of the towel over his hair and wrapped the soft white terry around his neck. Annorah's fluster and flush had his attention like little else could. She'd come a long way since the spectacular failure in the field that had left Maks, Ruger and their team in critical condition and nearly resulted in Joe Ryan's death…but she'd also always been a rock when it came to this part of her work.

Apparently, not today. She shifted uneasily—uncomfortably?—her sable hair in the kind of disarray that meant she'd been poking at her own head, and that meant plenty of action. Nick gave his cell phone—over in one of the locker-like cubbies with his keys—a quick glance.

"Don't even bother listening to that pile-up of voice mails," Annorah told him, hands on hips. "They all say the same thing, I can guarantee it."

Suddenly he understood—her demeanor, his own thoughts…the reason he wouldn't quite haul himself out of this pool to check his cell phone after all.

"Initiation," he said dryly, his hands tightening on the towel with reason. "One hell of an initiation. There's a reason we schedule these things. Does anyone know who—?"

"It's Maks," she confirmed, seeing the understanding on his face. "But it *can't* be."

What the hell was going on up there? And how had he so misjudged the decision to bring Maks back into the field? He struggled with thoughts thick under the influence of heat and sex and heavy, thumping desire. "Can you reach Katie?"

Annorah shook her head. "She's the only Sentinel up there besides Maks, so I expect she's very, very busy."

Nick pressed the towel against his brow with the heel of his hand. *Hell.* It made no sense. And if this impossible initiation went sideways, it was going to go sideways in a big, big way.

"Nick—" Annorah said, her tone both pleading and pushy.

"I know," he said grimly. "But I can't get that team up there any faster than they're already going. Katie will have to handle this."

Annorah's expression said what she thought of *that* clearly enough—protective of Maks, not trusting the un-familiar Sentinel who had most likely triggered this situation in the first place.

Because it took a trigger. Even when planned, it took a trigger.

"Meanwhile," Nick said, somewhat darkly, "don't open any closet doors without knocking first."

"No kidding," Annorah muttered, shifting uncomfortably again. "Or enter any offices, or use the elevator…"

The pool room door slammed open again, this time with somewhat more force—and there stood Jet, short ruffled black hair and golden eyes, barefooted beneath the drawstring crop pants and jersey-cut T over magnificently straight, strong shoulders. "Nick!" she said, and her frown was partly question, part demand.

No, Nick had no intention of getting out of the water. "Close that door on your way out," he told Annorah. "And lock it."

Chapter 18

Power thundered in Maks's head, pounded through his body—a raw, scraping sensation, twisting around nerves and wrapping through his torso. Deeply, deeply, a distant pleasure lingered; just as distantly, a broken voice cried for his attention. *BE, Maks*—

Oh, Maks *was*. Maks was pain and thundering hunger, spiraling energies and a dangerous, dangerous rise of uncontrollable powers. He fought it with every bit of his strength and will, the tiger rising wild and fierce—and underneath it all emerged a wrenching fear—the awareness that he couldn't win, and he couldn't withstand, and he wasn't alone and he couldn't keep Katie safe from this.

He barely felt her lips brushing his face or her reassurances brushing his ears. The pleasure of their connection—her weight centered over his hips, her body surrounding his, her legs twining back to hook behind his thighs—touched him only through the veil of battering pain.

He cried out in protest, his body arching, panting... tiring. Her hands landed at his shoulders, holding him down—or trying to.

Be with me, *Maks*. The whisper came in through his mind, now, persistent and growing louder. *Be...with...me!*

Katie. Katie sprinting across the yard, fleet and graceful. Katie laughing beneath the pines, hair in disarray and tools in hand. Katie advancing on Roger Akins, gentle nature turned to her own special ferocity.

Katie on his lap, body trembling with pleasure, expression vulnerable and honest and just plain coming undone.

"Katie..." he said—if just barely.

She was right there, her hair brushing his face, lips brushing his mouth, broken whisper brushing his ears. "Be with me, Maks."

"Can't—" he said, so tired, shards of fire jerking through his body—his body, jerking in response.

She kissed his face, his mouth, his brow. "Can," she told him. *"Listen* to me."

He strained to listen, to hear, but found nothing—until he started listening not with his ears, but with his inner self. There, he found her—the first, distant waves of gentle peace, lapping over the pain.

Katie, the healer.

"You see?" she said. "With *me*. Not alone."

Katie touching him...*touching him*...

Maks groaned, and this time it wasn't pain at all. He released the ground to shove his fingers in her hair, angling her head to take her mouth—and all the while she was touching him, *touching him*...

He gasped, and this time it wasn't pain at all. He skimmed his hands over her, finding curves and soft skin and settling at her hips, and he drove into her with a sudden

purpose. This time they cried out together, and the twist-
ingly sweet spiral of tension and pleasure rising to share
itself between them—Katie's sensation of being filled min-
gling with the very male experience of being enclosed,
hard muscle against soft skin, Katie's breath gusting out
along Maks's neck—and the same heat, the same pull, the
same liquid rush of—

Reaching...reaching...

The energy surged within Maks, took root within Katie.
It pushed at his edges, filling him—the pain driven away
by pleasure, the rising power churning and shoving and
finding its way, spilling over to fuel the drive, the need,
the physical yearning—

Two bodies gasping in accord, straining and reaching—

Climax took Katie in a sudden slam of sensation; she
stiffened and trembled, her hands digging into his shoulders, her voice caught on a sob—the pleasure, the pain,
the triumph of it so close—

And so very big, so very much power, such a demanding, battering rush—Maks floundered, breath caught in
his throat, doubt crowding his heart, wild fear holding him
back and ecstasy clawing just out of reach—

Katie looked down at him with the fierce protective
gleam of a woman in love, and took matters into her own
hands. A final twist of her hips, a final deep thrust, driving them utterly together. *Reaching, reaching...*

THERE!

Power roared through him, driven by elusive ecstasy,
and a rough, ragged and helpless cry tore from his throat—
not once but over and over as he rolled her, drove into her
from above, and buried his face at her neck to clamp down
on a tiger's bite—not gentle, not kind—but claiming.

And Katie bit him back.

* * *

Katie stirred beneath Maks's weight. She had the impression they'd been there for more than a few moments, collapsed together…wrung out and sated. But more than a few moments was time enough to worry, given what Maks had just been through. She thought she'd brought him through it—she thought he wouldn't have found his release if he hadn't, with or without her, managed the intensity of this initiation.

But she wasn't making assumptions. Who knew what happened when a man's body had been left half-completed in that process of cleansing its channels of power? Years of stabilizing in that uninitiated state, years of failing to trigger the complete process simply because once the body had been fooled, it took more than an accidental alignment of two compatible Sentinels.

It took finding someone who connected on all levels… and who understood.

And it had taken a healer to keep him alive.

Maybe one day she would tell him how close he'd come. One day, when the thought of it no longer terrified her.

And after she'd made certain he had, in fact, survived— here in the woods with his weight pressing her into the pine needles and a bee buzzing thoughtfully at the spread of her hair against the ground. He hadn't moved a muscle, and she had the sudden, overwhelming fear that maybe he wasn't even breathing, maybe she'd failed to save him after all—

And then he licked the curve where her shoulder turned into her neck, there where he'd so thoroughly bitten her. The caress sent a happy chill down her spine. She ran her hands over his back, lingering at his backside and reaching around to touch and fondle until his muscles bunched beneath her and he twitched and hardened within her. He body gave a satisfied sigh of its own, relaxing to the full ness of the sensation, and they locked together for long, silent moments of *being* with one another—feeling the connection with exquisite detail—each flicker of movement, each slow, rolling shudder of delight.

Finally, Maks propped up on his elbows to look down at her, thrusting gently once he was there.

"Oh," she said. "I mean, seriously? After that, you're going to—*oh!*"

"Oh," he said solemnly. "Yes, I think so."

She moved with him, slow and quiet, letting her legs relax, letting her hands roam along his body to feel muscle tense and release, discovering just where her touch made him hesitate or catch his breath. "And here I was, just hoping you were okay."

"I'm okay," he told her—and then tipped his head, a gleam coming into his eye. "You were there. Didn't you notice?"

"Ha," she muttered, "ha." And then murmured a low hum of pleased contentment, as he used one strong arm to position her hips, tipping her up so he could fill her more deeply and still, the long, slow strokes. "Mmm, yes."

After a moment, as his breathing quickened and she'd thoroughly bitten her lip, she said, "We should talk, though. There could be some big changes—"

"Talk," Maks said, "later."

"But we don't know…we should be sure…we should—"

He hitched her hips up a little higher yet, raising up on his knees just enough to—

"Oh!" she said again. *"Oh!"* And her fingers dug into his backside as she wiggled to take him deeper yet, increasing the pace of their movement, watching his face as his eyes closed and his nostrils flared and his mouth tightened until she, too, closed her eyes and panted and clutched at him again.

Maks slid his hand between them, brushing his thumb against her in the perfect counterpoint to the rising sensations between them. Just like that, she lost control; she grabbed the rhythm and took him with her right over to the edge.

The next time she opened her eyes, she found him watching, the faintest of smiles on that beautiful face... and one brow ever so slightly raised.

"You're kidding," she said.

He shrugged.

"Maybe we should take a moment," she said, though she had to stifle a smile. Maks, full of energy...healed. And like all Sentinels, quick to recover, even in this. "Seriously. That was a huge energy shift...a tremendous change for your body. Maybe I could sit—?"

One hand slid beneath her shoulder, another beneath her hips, and suddenly he was on his knees and she sat astride. He brushed pine needles from her hair, but she wasn't paying any particular attention—not any longer.

She was looking at the startling beauty of the shield around them both, one that glimmered bright through her healer's eyes. Faintly blue, marbled with coruscating light, a dome of energy through which the sun beat in moderated fashion and the rustle of bird and tree came muted. "Maks!" she said. "That's—that's beautiful!"

His expression told her that he'd noticed it long before she had—but that he'd expected it no more than she.

Katie bit kiss-swollen lips on a smile. "Of course," she said. "Of course this was what was waiting for you. The world's most beautiful shield." She reached out to it, let her fingertips brush through it; a frisson of energy—clear, bright, strong—shivered over her. "What else, for the man who endlessly seeks to protect?"

"I protect," Maks said, "what I love."

And this time, when he moved within her, Katie threw her arms around him and went along for the ride—and this time, when she felt his teeth at her neck, she knew it for what it was.

"Can't," Katie groaned, "believe we did that."

Maks's shirt was a loss...torn off in his earlier struggles. Katie's pants were still on her porch, her underwear now a torn and misshapen scrap.

At least she still had her shirt.

And she wasn't the least bit worried by their failure to use protection. Sentinel nature kept them healthy, and a healer who couldn't prevent her own conception wasn't much of a healer at all.

But she had needles in her knees and hair, she had no pants, she had no underwear, she was perceptively tender throughout, and they were how far from home?

Maks, suspiciously straight-faced for a man not prone to deception, observed, "We're staying safe. And out of trouble." He glanced at the shield. "And silent. That, too, I do."

Katie just snorted softly. "Very glib," she said, "for a man of few words."

She wasn't surprised to feel his humor or his wordless affection. But as much as she wanted to stay in this little circle of safety, reveling in what they'd accomplished and who they'd become together, she found herself struck by restlessness—knowing the Sentinel team was on its way, knowing the Core still hunted her.

As if he understood, Maks rose to his feet—rebuttoned and brushed off, his hair scraped into place with his fingers. The entire effect was arresting enough to make her breath catch all over again—the gleam of the shield's subtly altered light against his skin, the dusting of course hair across his chest and trailing to casually low jeans, the powerful ease with which he held himself.

His arm still bore bruised and raw flesh, but between her early efforts and his own renewed body, it had healed beyond even a Sentinel's normal progress.

And it certainly had not faltered as he had held his weight from her.

Katie sighed and stood, swiping away pine needles and ruing her lost hairband, fighting a fleeting return of uncertainty—what to tell the team, how to interpret her seeings—but only until Maks took her hand and took her chin and kissed her, just the right balance of sweet and possessive.

Okay, then.

Katie smiled back up at him, prepared to take the deer, and *the world spun away in clashing abstract colors, a dark and turbulent storm—the splash of warm blood across her face, the raw, hot smell of it, cloying in her mouth.*

Hands at her waist, hands at her back, a hard, warm body taking her weight.

Wild green eyes, the snarl of a tiger enraged, the flash of golden orange and white and brown, claws scraping her vision. A pungent scent, a barking cough, a swirl of action—a woman's cry of grief, familiar and haunting. And then an entire chorus of grief, animal skins fluttering to the ground like sodden laundry. Wolf and bear, panther and boar, wildcat and stoat and...deer. Diminutive little deer, crumpled up and discarded, and a nation of grief splashing in to wash it all away—

"Ssh," Maks said, a rumble in her ear, the vibration of it passing through to her body as she pressed up against him. "Ssh, Katie Rae."

And then an entire chorus of grief, animal skins fluttering to the ground like sodden laundry...

Only then did she realize she sobbed against him—not subdued little public sobs, but big choking wails. She realized she bore none of her own weight, but that Maks had pulled her to him with such effective strength that he cradled her upright.

"Tell me," he said, quiet but inexorable, and she instantly loved him for not making a fuss about the sobs—for accepting them and for assuming she could pull herself from the vision and go on.

For understanding that the moment held more importance than the sensitive nature of one certain deer.

Although such emotion was not, she quickly realized, as easy to turn off as a faucet. So she spoke through the gulping breaths, needing him to know—to share the burden. "There was blood, and you—and violence, and such a strong smell, and it was so— Oh, Maks, the sadness, I don't even know how to say the sadness, and there were skins—Sentinels, empty Sentinels and darkness—"

"Ssh," he said again, as her words stuttered out to a few belated gulping sobs. As she took her own weight again, he stroked a soothing hand down her back. "It's not usually like this?"

It took her a moment, during which she scrubbed her face against her shoulder—and then she understood. "The visions, you mean?" She looked up at him, blinking, and he gently wiped his thumb under her eyes, one then the other—a gesture so absently tender that she nearly started crying all over again. "Usually? No. I should say, never. I don't know—" *Why,* she'd been about to say. Except she looked around herself, and knew. Maks's arms around her, Maks's shield rippling gently around them, Maks's touch still echoing within her body. "I'm safe," she said, the wondering tone evident even to herself. "I'm *safe.*"

Maks frowned, puzzlement in the expression.

Katie didn't bother to say what was now so obvious to her. All those years of absorbing intimidation and insinuation and subtle harassment…it wasn't only the deer who'd fled those things, never quite escaping them. It was the seer she'd buried so deeply. She took a deep breath, straightened, and wrapped her arms around Maks in a way that this time gave as much as it took. "I'm safe," she said. "You've made me safe, and for the first time, I truly *saw*." Though she frowned in the wake of that statement. "Not that I understand a bit of it."

"It was a warning," Maks said. "That's enough." He lifted his head, looking out over the woods with his eyes slitted in a particularly feline expression, tasting the air as he let the shields fall away to a bright spatter of sunshine through the trees. His attention shifted outward; for a long moment, he stood that way…still and focused.

When he took a deep breath and let it out in a long, slow exhalation, Katie knew he was back. "Where did you go?" she asked. "What did you do?"

His expression changed—pleased and open, the hint of a grin. "The boundary," he said, and removed his arm from her shoulders to gesture an enlarging circle, echoing it with his unique wordless mind-voice so she quite suddenly understood.

"You enlarged it?"

"I spread it," he agreed. "Now, I watch these woods."

She eyed the woods in appreciation—she eyed him with appreciation, while she was at it. "You gained more than just those shields, then."

"More than the shields," he agreed. "Now, be the deer, Katie Rae. Take us home."

Katie as deer hesitated on the edge of her yard, checking for hikers along the trail, visitors along the drive, and intruders around the house. Then she bounded through to the house, slender legs navigating the stairs with such grace that Maks suspected she took advantage of her solitude to run the deer on moonlit nights.

Maks followed, barefooted, torso bare to the light breeze and strong mountain sunshine. He strode easily across that same ground—his senses aware and extended, sweeping around the house and through the woods in a buffer zone he hadn't even imagined but which now came naturally—his boundary zone, spread wide—monitoring not only the edge of the enclosed territory, but also a broad band of territory inside it. It tickled constantly at his attention, draining constantly at his resources—not a defense without cost.

But with a Core rogue after Katie?

Maks would pay the price.

Chapter 19

You, Eduard thought as he spoke to Akins over the phone beneath the canopy of mighty pines, *will not be alive much longer.*

The thought allowed him to keep his voice even as he put one foot to the ground, stabilizing his dirt bike just outside the hidden primary structure—although his phone casing made a faint crackling sound from stresses he hadn't meant to apply to it.

It could be time to adjust the self-maintenance workings. He'd found it so, over the years—as he'd gotten more efficient, more effective, his personal amulets had become ever more subtle. And now that he'd developed the silent blanks, he doubted anyone could even detect the workings any longer; only those who knew his age and his medical records had any idea.

It pleased him that so few had any notion. And being pleased calmed him, so it was easier when he said, "The beast is not for you. Let Altán take it on alone—though you may feel free to cheer his death when he does."

Not that Eduard would leave anything to chance; he'd help the beast as necessary. He was on his way to Katie Maddox's home even now—heading overland through the forest with his escort. They rode electric trail bikes—silent machines, clandestine on the trails where no such vehicles were allowed.

He had no doubt that Altán would show. Even as a youngster, he'd had an uncanny awareness of any trespass in his woods. Now that he was protecting Katie Maddox, Altán would never tolerate the presence of the beast on his turf.

"Well, hell," Akins said reproachfully; he, too, navigated the woods—on foot, circling in on Katie Maddox's property from the back, where he'd meet Afonasii and the creature. *Jacques.* "After it takes out Altán, then? It'd be a hell of a way to start rebuilding my place in this town. And you gotta let a guy have a little fun, Ed."

"Perhaps then," Eduard said, satisfied that Akins would die easily enough when that time came. "But if Katie Maddox is there, you'll no doubt need to restrain her."

"Ree-strain." Akins's breath gusted into the phone as he navigated what must have been a rugged feature of the trail he strode. "I like the sound of that. You're sure you don't want her broken in for you?"

"That," Eduard said sharply, "I will do myself."

"Hey, okay, okay, whatever. Just offering. It's not like I don't have plenty of experience. I do train dogs, you know."

Fools and idiots. Katie Maddox was a resource—not to be squandered or shattered, but to be broken in subtle ways that left her useful.

Fools and idiots. But he would only have to tolerate this one for a short while longer. Once Katie was his, Akins would die—with all the evidence in Katie's disappearance pointing his way.

"Well," Akins said, raising his voice above the crack of a dead branch, "if those hunters reach this creature before us, there's nothing I can do about it."

"Don't worry about them," Eduard said. He certainly wasn't. If a few of them were found dead with Altán, then so much the better.

"So listen," Akins said, far too casually. "If Katie Maddox *isn't* there, how about if then I take care of—damn!" That last came through a sudden rustle, followed by a most unpleasant clatter. Eduard held the phone away from his ear and could still hear Akins's raised voice. "Hey, you still there? Dropped the damn phone. Ed—?"

Eduard flipped his phone closed. One quick stop at the nearby secondary workshop to ensure that the isolated amulet blanks for his ambitious new project were maturing nicely, and he'd be on the dirt bike, headed out to finally take care of the Sentinel who had defied them so young—and for so long.

It was time to watch Maks Altán die.

::*Maks!*:: Annorah's voice blasted into Maks's mind, startling and a little strident. Maks stumbled on the porch, catching himself even as he heard Katie's displeased sound of surprise from within the house. If she'd been caught in the broadcast of Annorah's call, it could only be deliberate—Annorah didn't make such mistakes.

::*There you are,*:: Annorah said, her mind-voice all kinds of irritable.

::*Have been here,*:: Maks told her, making the significant effort of words simply because the other felt too intimate just now.

Annorah's defensive disgruntlement came through before her voice did. *::Yeah, well, I've had some personal stuff to deal with.::*

Maks said nothing, not even a wordless shrug. The only safe answer. And the only one he was willing to give, even to this friend of his.

Annorah had no such conversational reticence.

::Do you have any idea how widely we felt that? Do you have any idea how many babies were conceived this afternoon? There's a reason we schedule these things, never mind one of that...that...volcanic nature! God, Maks, the Core could have done an amulet air-drop and we wouldn't have seen it coming.::

Maks said nothing—a little more loudly this time. From the kitchen, Katie cursed softly, out loud, though no sign of it came through the conversation.

Annorah's voice softened. *::But you're okay?::*

Ah. He understood now; he let her have that much, wordless though it was, and then added, *::Better.::*

::I see that,:: she said, after a pause in which she must have been sorting her impressions of him. Then she gathered herself back up. *::You've still got plenty of questions to answer, mister.::*

::Nick?:: he requested, ignoring that. Because he thought that *Nick* was the one with questions to answer. Why hadn't brevis realized that Maks's extensive early time as the tiger would affect his growth? Why hadn't brevis looked harder for Maks's mother? And now that they knew the right timeframe...

He wanted her found. He wanted her honored, and her family to know.

But Annorah cleared her mental throat. *::Nick,::* she said delicately, *::is still otherwise occupied.::*

Katie broke into the conversation. *::Well, when Nick comes out of whatever closet he's chosen, you tell him that*

*brevis put Maks in the field with an incomplete founda-
tion—and because of it, exposure to the Flagstaff variations left him vulnerable to that ambush. We fixed that—so
Nick can just back off.::*

Annorah seemed to think about it. ::*I'll let him know,::*
she said finally. ::*Meanwhile, the team will be there tomorrow. Keep your head down until then, Maks.::*

But Maks ended the conversation with some finality,
finding the words more readily than most.

::*Not,::* he said, ::*if the Core needs hunting.::*

"The Core," Katie said, with little hope of being heard—
truly *heard*—"does not need hunting." She stood on the
cool, hard stone tile of her kitchen—bare feet, bare backside, tea bag in hand just as it had been when Annorah's
call had so abruptly intruded.

Annorah was gone now, leaving only Maks in this conversation—bare chested and just as barefoot as she—as he
stood in the vague boundary between kitchen and living
room and looked at her. She had the palpable sense that he
was gathering words—that he needed just the right ones,
and that they came hard to him.

"The Core," he said finally, "is this *man*. This man has
killed your neighbor, conspired with your enemy…seeded
your yard with poison. This man has created a monstrous
creature. This man," he said, taking a step forward—and
the look on his face was all fury and intent, "has come
back to the place he once hunted me like a beast. Where
he helped imprison my mother like a *beast*."

He came up softly before her, tiger in certainty, and his
words resounded inside her mind as well as in her ears.
"This man," he said softly, "now hunts you. And so I will
hunt him in return."

She wanted to protest—to pull her selfish needs tightly

around herself. She wanted to say, *but I've only just found you* and *but you've just been through so much* and *but you're only one man* and even *but if you just wait until tomorrow...*

But she knew what Maks knew—that whatever his end game, the Core rogue, now exposed by their near-encounter at the coffee shop, had little choice but to act as quickly as possible. The rogue would know what they knew—that if the Sentinels weren't coming after him, his own people, embarrassed beyond endurance, *would*.

And she knew as well as Maks that he was strong and well and capable, his long-delayed initiation completed, his energy flows balanced and free and his true talents released.

She clenched a fist around the hapless tea bag and took that final step between them—but rather than put her arms around him, she simply came close enough to rest her head against his shoulder, her body against his.

After a moment, he sighed, and smoothed his hand down over her hair. Another moment and he stepped back, used that hand to angle her head and bent down to kiss her—a long, thorough and possessive kiss.

A kiss that said enough without any words at all.

She didn't lower her face when he moved back, leaving only a whisper of space between them. "Then I'm coming with you."

He took a sharp breath, and she didn't give him a chance to come back at her with words. "There's only one place I'm safe," she said. "And it isn't here, alone, without the tiger and his impossibly amazing shields."

The truth of that hit him hard and honestly; his jaw worked as he absorbed it. Another man might have looked away. Maks caught her gaze and kept it, and his long, slow exhalation came with the slightest of nods. This time, she

didn't need to hear the audible words to hear his understanding. More than that, acquiescence. *Then I'll wait.*

"Even if it means you lose him?"

No words at all this time, just that steady gaze, green
and full of wild—silent affirmation.

Katie, in wonder, absorbed the truth of it. The meaning of it. She let it spread through her body, let it spread
to her smile—

He stiffened, gone as still as any big cat on the hunt, his
attention instantly elsewhere, and her relief slipped away.
He closed his eyes and turned his face from hers as though
he listened to something distant, completely captivated.
Katie hesitated, awkward in her own kitchen with the tea
bag crumpled in her hand and the stone cool against her
feet, and she shifted uneasily. When he turned back to her,
she was ready for anything.

Or so she thought.

"The boundary," he told her. "They come. The creature. Those who hunt it. Those who handle it." His eyes
gleamed, a brief flash of the predator. "The one who made
it."

"All of those—you can…?" She couldn't quite finish
it—couldn't quite believe it. "You can tell *who?*"

"I can read their imprint within my boundaries." His
grim voice left no doubt. Where moments ago he would
have waited, would have foregone the hunt…now he would
not tolerate invasion, would not tolerate a threat to this
area. "Clothes, Katie. If you are to come."

She hesitated—not second-guessing herself, but needing to know that he didn't, either. "I could be in your way."

"The deer knows better."

And the deer did. The deer knew how to hide, above
all else.

What else had she been doing here in this little town, so far from brevis and anything it might ask of her?

Katie tossed the tea bag into the sink and dashed up the stairs, pawing through the big drawer that held the clothes that would remain stable through the change and pulling on underwear and a pair of worn woodland-pattern BDUs, slipping out of her worse-for-wear shirt to tug on a jersey T. She wasn't quite as comfortable as Maks without shoes; she slipped on a pair of brevis-commissioned sandals that would change with her.

She found him waiting, just as he'd been—the open flannel shirt with sleeves rolled up, sturdy jeans riding his hips, bare feet comfortable on her carpet…eyes closed and head slightly lifted. "Here," he said, without looking at her. "The creature comes here."

"And the hunters just follow along, no doubt." Blithely pursuing prey they weren't truly equipped to manage.

Maks shook his head. "Fools." He opened his eyes, looking off at that distance with a narrowed gaze. "Fools and enemies." He jerked his chin at the door, a subtle gesture, and sudden panic clutched at her throat—not at the thought of what waited for her, but at the certain knowledge it would try to come through Maks to get her.

"Wait!" She went to him, hands flat against his chest—looking inward. She followed the new flow of his personal energies—not quite surprised to find a taste of herself there, but touched by it all the same. She briefly rode the essence of him, finding only a steady strength. The things she feared—knots of weakness, thready spots of energy-driven pain—were nowhere to be seen. There was only his arm, healing at a normal rate now that it was of no great threat to him.

"Good?" he asked—both of himself, and of her.

"It's all good," she said, but *wild green eyes, the snarl of*

*a tiger enraged, the flash of golden orange and white and
brown, claws scraping her vision*—strong hands, holding
her up, tugging her close.

"Tell me," he said.

As if it mattered. As if he not only truly believed, but
depended. It warmed some small part of her, making her
smile—here, now, when there was little to smile about.
"Nothing new," she said. "Just a reminder. It's dangerous,
this thing."

"So," said Maks, "am I."

They ran the woods together...tiger and deer. The tiger,
loping along faster than suited his nature, drawing on reserves of power only recently available. The deer, her
spurts of speed more extended than suited her nature, her
petite jaw dropping to offer a delicate pant...her modestly
elongated tusks peeking out.

In his glimpses of her, Maks saw not prey, not deer.

He saw only Katie.

And in his mind, in his body—in the new combina-
tions of awareness that combined scent and touch and inner
vision—he saw anew those who had intruded upon his
boundaries. Hapless Dogo Argentino dogs, used to hunting wild boar but not this monstrous abomination so many
times larger. Overconfident hunters, eager for both the action and the accolades. Distant but closing in, two figures
moving in tandem, and too fast to be on foot. They tasted
of dark, bitter corruption.

Closest of all, the initial intruders—the creature and one
human companion, tasting of less potent Core.

Close enough so Maks slowed to a trot amongst the
pines, and then close enough so he stopped altogether, panting in the high afternoon heat of the southwestern altitude,
the tiger in him wishing for a deep river and a cool swim.

The deer rustled not far away, a deliberate sound. Too deep in the tiger for words, Maks sent her concepts instead. The imminence of the creature, the perfection of their position there along a minor outcrop, thanks to a smattering of young trees and bushy undergrowth, high ground and good cover.

Good cover, especially, for one who was never meant to join such a fight.

I'll wait, he had told her. He'd meant it, and he'd hated it, and he'd fully intended to do it—but not if it meant letting the Core rogue and his creature stage the battleground.

Now, she would have to wait. And keep herself safe.

The coruscating light flickering through leaf and needle told Maks that she'd understood—that she had chosen to be human in this place of impending conflict.

Not Maks. He crouched silently at the edge of their outcrop, picking up the creature's approach with his ears as well as his inner senses. Its path had been as direct as possible across this rugged terrain, its goal clear. He sent one more thought Katie's way—warning, and a reminder that they'd moved so quickly, so intently, that no one at brevis knew they'd moved at all.

She sent him affirmation, moving back slightly so he could see her, even while remaining hidden from below, and tempered her thought with fierce command. *::I can take care of myself. You watch your own back.::*

That, he didn't answer. He'd already reached down deep, hunting for that same, earth-centered feeling he'd discovered in the aftermath of initiation—drawing on it to shape the same profound shielding effect. A shield for each of them, impervious to any workings the Core rogue might launch, to any amulets the creature's handler might invoke. His claws extruded into the ground, rooting him there... rooting the shields.

::*Maks,*:: she said, as the shields took on strength and substance, ::*do you hea*—::

And she was gone—her thoughts, so clear to him, vanished behind the strength of what he had wrought.

His tail lashed with the surprise of it—and then he had no time to think about it at all as the huge javelina trotted out into the sparsely wooded space below, its flat human eyes taking in the scene with eerie alacrity, its fleshy snout twitching. It came to a halt, huge and grizzled, the pungent stench of it filling the air. When it lifted its head, it was to look straight up at Maks.

Maks growled with low feeling, a rumbling warning. By the time the creature's handler made his noisier way toward the little bowl of pines, the mutant javelina had aligned itself to face the outcrop—and in those eerie eyes, in that twitch of a nose, Maks thought he saw unwelcome awareness—and a realignment of position toward Katie's position.

The javelina's acute sense of smell...

No doubt this monster had it in spades.

Maks didn't think; he acted. While the tiger crouched, quivering with the need to attack, Maks dug in and held back, drawing on the roots he'd established—yanking hard against resistance, knowing only that he needed *more,* that Katie needed to be completely invisible to this thing.

Something gave way—within him, beneath him, staggering him with the suddenness of it. In body, he crouched even lower, legs spread to steady; in mind and energy, he tumbled into a geyser of hot power; it gushed free to splash and form where he'd aimed it—*Katie*—and just as abruptly faded away.

Before he even shook his thoughts clear, the javelina barked a challenge—a gleeful sound, its front feet stamping hard against the needle-padded ground, its demeanor eager.

And then he saw Katie, bathed in a watercolor effect that he didn't at first understand—not until he realized he had wrought for her shields so strong that they obscured the detail of her. Shields so strong, they cut off not only access to her mind-voice, but to her physical presence.

She looked at him through the intervening leaves, her face pale, her expression wary—the deer, startled into fright, and quite nearly into flight. Unable to bespeak him, unwilling to reveal herself to the creature, she instead showed him exactly what he'd done—reaching to push against the trunk of the closest substantial tree.

But her hand never quite touched the bark, and the energy flared between wood and flesh, building to brightness at the pressure point.

Physical shields. Shields the Sentinels had never been able to develop, no matter how they studied and tried.

The javelina barked another challenge—more eager than before, a note of triumph in a sound that should have been nothing more than dumb threat. A note of laughter.

And Maks realized he no longer had any shields at all.

It made instant sense. The shields he had created for Katie were so profound, so impossibly, *physically* present...there was nothing left for a second, separate shield.

To judge by her expression, her gestures, Katie realized it, too. Her mouth might have been clamped tight on the words that would give her position away to handler as well as to beast, but her face was eloquent enough.

Maks had no choice—he couldn't leave himself unshielded to an enemy who had shown himself to be exceptionally clever with amulets and workings. Still braced against the earth, he backed off on the energies he drew from it, damping down slowly until the distinct lurch of

balance told him he'd gone far enough—and when he
looked, he found her as before—protected, but not by the
impossible. Impervious to workings, but not physical assault.

Then no one gets that close.

The javelina made a disgusted sound, a snort and
stamp, and Maks understood that, too—his own shields
had shifted back into place.

"What the effing hell is your problem, Jacques?" The
Core handler bent to prop his hands against his knees,
breathing hard. The man had *minion* written all over him,
in spite of his classic complexion, his hair drawn back
into a tight, short club at his nape and one ear and several fingers adorned in heavy silver—all the signs of an
active posse member. "Keep your tusks to yourself until
we reach the girl. Forrakes is damned serious about that,
and I'll be fucked if I'm going to take the blame for your
games again."

The creature snorted, a scornful noise, and tossed his
head in a scooping gesture that needed no interpretation.

"Keep that to yourself, too," the man muttered, straightening to brush off his black T-shirt. "If he ever figures out
you're as smart as you are mean, he's going to kill us both."

Not words said lightly. And words said by a man with
no clue that they were no longer alone.

Maks rolled a growl up his throat, settling into a
couchant position, front paws flexing to dig claws into
the ground. The man jerked his head up—locating Maks,
spitting out a string of startled curses—and then turned a
furious glare on the creature. It snorted in such a way that
made its disdain obvious.

But when it slanted a sly glance back at Maks, its expression was nothing but threat and promise.

Chapter 20

"He's got a gun, Maks—you know he's got a gun." Katie pressed up behind her tree, frantic for Maks to hear her—and certain he wouldn't.

He'd know, though. He'd been in the thick of things with the Core in Europe. He'd been in Flagstaff, he'd been in Tucson. The Sentinel battle lines.

Surely he'd know the man had a gun, no matter that he couldn't see the lump of it at the man's back.

Just as surely he'd heard the dogs approaching…knew they were close.

Why, then, did he narrow those green tiger eyes and lift his lips in a whisker-bristling snarl, focused only on the creature below?

She thought about speaking out loud; she thought about tossing a pebble to get his attention, and pointing at the man in a ludicrous game of charades. She even gathered the pebble in her hand, feeling the faint frisson of energy in her shields as she tightened her fingers around it. Marveling at it, and at what Maks had done only moments earlier.

No one made physical shields. *No one.*

But she relaxed her hand, dropping the pebble and leaning against the rough, deeply scaled bark of the tree.

He hadn't brought her here so she could expose herself to the enemy, making his job all that much harder. She'd trusted him to take care of her…and he'd trusted her to let him do it.

"Maks Altán, I believe," the man below said, and this was not, could not be, the man whom Maks had scented in the coffee shop, the man who had been part of his early life. This man was too young, too much a foot soldier. Too blatantly eager to have made his way to the upper levels of the Core hierarchy and its pervasive *Survivor*-like society. "You've saved me a lot of trouble by showing up here." Unbelievably, he put a companionable hand on the beast's shoulder, impervious to the thing's obvious disdain. "You're going to make us look very good, indeed."

She got the impression that he had a pressing need to look very good indeed. The tension in his body, the fact that he'd been sent out here by himself, on foot, with only this beast at his side—it spoke volumes. The fact that Maks focused his attention on the beast and not the man…that spoke volumes, too.

She looked down at him, this man who had come for her, and at the monstrously huge creature that accompanied him—the jutting curve of its tusk, the gleam of malice in its eye, the quick movement of its feet as it settled itself before Maks, more nimble than any creature its size should ever be.

Lord, it stunk—the normal javelina musk mixed with bitter Core energies and a hint of the corrupt putrefaction behind any Core working.

But normal javelina had poor eyesight. This one...
This one was looking straight at her.

For an instant, chaos swirled around Maks—new awareness, new power, new sensations. The local hunters moved
in, splitting up as the dogs grew increasingly agitated. The
distant figures moved closer on their dirt bikes; the creature's companion tried to look menacing and only came
off as a man with too much to prove.

The creature looked straight at Katie, having found
her with eyes and nose no less preternaturally sharp than
Maks's. It took a step in her direction—tossing its head
until it slung slaver onto its companion, and if it couldn't
reach her, it could still endanger her—simply by revealing her presence.

Maks shoved all the rest of it out of his mind and leaped.
The man stumbled back, cursing in a human snarl; the javelina sprang forward.

Maks had barely landed when he leaped out again, all
the strength of his powerful haunches driving him into
the beast with the bone-jarring slam of two heavy bodies.

They rolled across leaf and pine needle litter while Maks
closed massive jaws around the beast's shoulder, ducking
in under those tusks. His body took the brunt of sharp
hooves as he curled his hind feet up, hunting for purchase
to deliver a disemboweling thrust.

They slammed up against a tree and Maks sprang away,
out of reach of the deadly tusks. The creature scrambled
to its ungainly feet, legs absurdly delicate for its bulk but
well protected by the length of those tusks.

He gave it no time to recover, but leaped again, angling
for its back and a grip on its stout, short neck—and then he
twisted wildly aside as it whirled to meet him with head
tilted and tusks foremost.

A canine bellow split the surreal silence of their battle, and as Maks tumbled aside and back to his feet, three huge white dogs charged into the space. They surged around the Core handler to charge at the creature, blithely harrying it as they would any peccary—expert teamwork at haunch and neck and shoulder, trying to close jaws over flesh that was simply too bulky to offer a grip. One dog latched on to a hock, only to be kicked away; another lost its footing near the beast's head and instantly flew through the air, blood spraying behind it.

Humans thundered onto the scene an instant later, and by then Maks had invoked the change to human form, too deeply conditioned to reveal himself to the hunting party.

At the sight of the dogs—one crumpled against the outcrop, another against a pine, and the third hanging from the jaws of the creature—the foremost hunter cursed shortly and brought his rifle to his shoulder, with no apparent awareness that the Core handler stood off to the side, or that Maks was only barely outside of his sights.

The man managed a single shot before the Core handler shot him in the back.

A third hunter hung back—the big guy from the parking lot, shouldering his rifle with quick efficiency to fire a quick round into the creature. The sharp report echoed around the mountainside and kicked hard against the man's shoulder, but the impact barely staggered the creature. The handler took a shot at the hunter, missed—and lost his chance, for the hunter flung himself back behind the largest of pines, his curse hanging in the air.

Maks, the protector. Maks, stuck as human, as frail as any of them against a creature of such size. Maks, watching men die…

He picked up a sizable rock, the same as any human; he flung it with the strength and accuracy of no human. It bounced off the creature's rump, bringing the thing spinning around, eyes narrowed with hatred and jaws dripping bloody slaver.

Oh, my God, what are you doing? What are you doing? Katie dug her fingers into the bark of the pine that hid her, anchoring herself—wanting nothing more than to scream out at Maks—to *stop* him.

He stood at the edge of the small, lightly forested area beneath the outcrop, a second rock in hand, the challenge clear in his expression, his stance, his intent.

Or so Katie thought. But that second rock didn't bounce off the creature's tough, grizzled coat at all—it hit the Core handler's thigh like a bullet, taking the man down in a cry of agony.

The creature roared in offense, a thunderous squealing battle cry. It flashed tusk and eye in fury, charging straight at Maks.

"Look out, man!" The hunter's cry echoed and so did the shots from his rifle, a quick one-two that did nothing to stop the creature. One shot sprayed bark from a tree behind the creature; the other must have hit it in the haunch—but its stumble was only momentary.

Deer rifles, Katie realized. Deer rifles on an animal worthy of a big-game double rifle. And a creature so thick, so muscled, so *quick*... "Maks," she breathed, unable to hold back at least that much, even as another rifle shot cracked through the air, this one kicking up dirt. The Core handler snapped off a careless shot, driving the hunter back.

But Katie should have known Maks would be just that quick, bare feet bounding effortlessly over pine needles and granite as he scooped up another of the outcrop's fist-sized rocks and whipped it at the creature's head, hitting it hard between the eyes. The thing stopped short, pawing awkwardly at its head with a sharp hoof, and by then Maks was rearmed—but running out of space against the outcrop. When the creature charged, he sprinted to the side, running lightly along the outcrop—cat-like in his progress across nearly vertical rock, tiger-like in his power. The creature instantly reoriented—Katie held her breath, seeing then that Maks had the perfect vantage from which to fire another rock right down on its head, directly at its eye.

Instead, he jerked his head up to look at her, narrow-eyed—no, not *at* her, just to the side of her, and even as she flinched away with shock that he had betrayed her position, she realized that wasn't it at all.

I'm not alone.

She froze against the tree, making herself deer-still... deer quiet. She caught a glimpse of movement from the corner of her eye—

Another shot rang out, this one from below—*the handler!*—she couldn't help but flinch, and then to gasp as Maks jerked, his expression gone startled, the wild eye of an animal wounded. Only for an instant, as blood bloomed low along his side—and an instant was all he had, for the creature was upon him.

And still Maks twisted aside, slamming the rock down between the creature's eyes, rolling...leaping up again to latch on at the side of the its neck like the tiger he was—with one very human hand snagging the stubby javelina ear, using it to cling tight while the other hammered the rock against face and eye and even tusk. The creature screamed in protest, blood streaming—

Movement, from the corner of her eye...

Core. A Core posse member, dressed in his woodlands camo T-shirt and pants, oblivious to her presence as he took stance with his semiautomatic pistol, one hand steadied over the other, the aim deliberate and confident.

Maks.

Katie shrieked, an inexperienced battle cry, and dove for the man—Sentinel in strength, deer in agile speed, woman protecting her own.

The man went down before her, and her advantage faltered, giving way to expertise as she scrambled to take possession of the gun. She ended up tussling in her own defense, rolling through prickly scrub oak, jamming up against a tree with her teeth bared and her feet kicking out at him, lightning-swift strikes while she scrabbled for the gun in the pine needles.

He snatched at a leg, lost it, snatched again—got it, fingers gripping tightly around her ankle as he braced himself and yanked her away from the tree. She bumped over the ground—and felt herself astonishingly airborne as he whiplashed them around to launch her over the outcrop, the gun clattering right out with her.

Airborne all too briefly, before the ground came up to meet her.

A tusk broke beneath the rock in Maks's hand; his breath came in panting gulps as his flank quivered in growing pain and heat. His leg gave way, muscles too shocked to function. But the creature still stood spraddle-legged beside him, a thing of massive muscle and unnatural strength stunned into brief acquiescence.

In the growing tunnel vision of his determination, he heard the shriek above him; he heard the scramble. He heard, too, that one of the hunters had gotten the drop on the Core handler, shouting a demand of surrender.

Only when Katie's slender form twisted through the air did he understand the shriek, the scuffle from above. Only as she landed, crying out with the impact, did he see the black shape of the gun clatter down after her and understand what she'd done...why she'd done it.

His own shields had kept her from warning him any other way. And now she was down in the thick of it, the bullets flying and his strength compromised and the Core handler desperate—

He clung to the side of the creature's neck, gore splattering his hand and the rock it held, sweat stinging his vision into a blur, hot blood running down his side—and he knew he couldn't protect her. Not like this.

Reaching down to the root of his newly channeled power came more easily now, and he did it now without second thought—pulling his strength from that place, spinning it into a shield...forming the shield around Katie. Already she tried to rise, hunched over the injuries from the fall, but her ankle instantly gave way beneath her.

The shields buffered her fall. At first she was too panicked, too deep in the deer to notice—or to hear the cry of one of the hunters urging her to stay down. She flailed back up to her feet and went down again—but this time, she realized the shields had changed. This time, she pushed away the panic of a crippled prey animal and flung her head up to look at him, her hair a flow of cinnamon-sparked movement in the sun. This time, she caught his eye—and he didn't need to hear her with ears or mind to read the expression on her face. *Oh, my God, Maks, what have you done?*

Because he couldn't protect her with these new physical shields and still protect himself with any shields at all.

It didn't matter. He told her as much, clinging to his stunned opponent with a slipping grip—he fought brute strength, and needed no shields. It didn't matter, because she was everything, and protecting her was what he *was*.

His leg quivered beneath him; the hunters shouted at

him. Or he thought they did, wanting him away from the thing so they could take it down—but for that instant, he had eyes and ears only for Katie Rae Maddox, waiting to see that she understood. Needing to know it.

Because six hundred pounds of raging Core monstrosity wasn't something a wounded tiger could take on.

And the monstrosity knew it. It roared to life beneath Maks, one side of its head battered to pulp and the other still full of fury. Instead of trying to toss Maks away, it reared up, suddenly wrenching itself around to slam Maks against the rock base of the outcrop. Maks saw it coming, twisted in midair to take the impact with bent legs…and the weak leg slipped out from beneath him, skidding down the rock and leaving him vulnerable to the impact.

As quick as that, the beast was upon him, tipping its ruined head to clamp down on his shoulder—tusks shattering his collarbone, slicing through flesh and out again. Maks froze in the shock of it, stunned into instant, cold, clear knowledge of a mortal wound.

Gunfire rang out, spattering the rock over his head; the hunters cursed in disbelief. The dark, bitter taste of a Core working told Maks what the hunters couldn't possibly understand.

The Core rogue was here. Here, and armed in his own insidious way, protecting his creature with workings that spoiled human aim and human intent.

As a man, Maks would die. His shields around Katie would die. The hunters would all die, and Katie…the rogue would have Katie.

As a man.

He reached for the change. Not painless, this time, as the energies surged through his body, changing torn muscle, reforming broken bone. The hunters' curses of shocked surprise came to him as though from a great distance; the creature reared back, understanding its great danger.

The tiger now raged beneath him—still shot, still wounded, but possessed of great, raking claws, possessed of massive teeth and powerful jaws.

Freed, Maks rolled to his feet and launched himself at the creature in one swift move, clamping his jaws at the base of its skull..

The creature staggered under his weight, equal to its own.

The creature renewed its efforts, clattering across the rocky base of the outcrop, aiming to swipe Maks against stone, against tree—

Gunfire rang out, a meaningless assault with the hunters under sway of the Core working—except the creature jerked with it. Its handler cried out in fury and threat; another shot abruptly silenced his voice, even as several more slammed into the creature, their combined effect finally bringing it to a stop.

Maks braced himself, digging in again, finding purchase—shifting his hold, shifting his body, *wrenching*—

A dull, resounding *snap* of bone resonated through his jaws. The creature shuddered once, made a sound of astonishment, and toppled over, pinning Maks.

For a moment, he didn't care. He cared only about catching his breath, feeling his pains, reaching for the internal flows of power that would start healing, hoping it could even be done in time.

And then he opened his eyes, and found Katie on her knees in the rocks, her attacker's gun still gripped tight in both hands and her face strained and determined—the healer turned killer, and stunned by her own actions.

A lone hunter knelt beside the beast's dead handler with grim regret—only a moment, before he called out to his friends, hastening to see to them, too, and completely unaware that the dead handler hadn't been the only human enemy here.

Up above, a Core posse member lingered on the edge of the outcrop, his hands empty of weapons but his expression meanly satisfied all the same. Not far away, Roger Akins regarded the dead creature with stunned disbelief and resentment, and then turned to Maks—the tiger—with a highly calculating eye.

And not far from Akins stood the Core rogue.

Not so imposing at that—a short man, with a complexion paler than most Core, his black hair neatly trimmed instead of caught in a queue, his ears and fingers free of the usual heavy silver. His clothing, however, was black…right down to an old-fashioned morning coat festooned with neat pockets. *An amulet specialist. A man who could make silent, subtle amulets and seed them into Katie's life, who could send targeted workings after Ian.* And his features…

They were far too familiar; they hadn't aged at all. Not the years they should have, since Maks had escaped, since he'd lived as a fugitive…since he'd been reclaimed by the sentinels. But recognition hit Maks hard. His curse came out as a snarl, whiskers bristling and ears flattened, his intent obvious.

If he hadn't been trapped. If he hadn't grown even shorter of breath, a rasping sound in his throat and the hard taste of blood on his tongue, an odd sparkling at the edge of his vision. If his body hadn't been battered into numbness, the pain only now beginning to take hold.

If he hadn't been the human when those tusks had pierced him.

"I want the tiger," Akins said. "You can have the girl."

"Can I?" the Core rogue mused, nursing some secret humor. Neither appeared to notice—or care—that Katie could hear them or that she still had the gun. She froze, there on her knees, her gaze flicking between the two men and settling on Maks, his silent name on her lips. *What have you done, Maks?* mixed with *what should I do?*—and her healer's need to rush to him.

Her lover's need to rush to him.

Maks stared steadily back, ignoring the struggle to think, to breathe, to hang on to the grit of determination. *Stay put,* he told her, using the only voice he had—the expression in his eyes. *Stay separate...stay away.* Because for the moment, even if a very short moment, she was safe. And if the hunters moved in again, maybe she wouldn't even be alone.

But the lone hunter to witness the outcome of the fight was still with his friends—having obviously absorbed the fact that the creature was dead, that the inexplicable tiger was trapped...that Roger Akins stood there with rifle ready. In the hunter's world, the tiger had come from no where; Maks the man had fled, or already lay dead out of sight.

"Roger," Katie said, her voice low and strained, the shielded air shimmering faintly around her—the shield Maks couldn't drop as long as she stood alone. "Roger, come away from him. You don't know who he is—you don't know what he'll do—"

Akins sneered at her. "It's too late to play nice," he told her. "You lose. And you can damned well bet I'm going to gloat about it."

"Later," the Core rogue murmured, gazing at the creature, brow drawn in concentration.

"Come *on,* Eddie. The creature was supposed to be mine. The least you can do is let me kill your fucking tiger." He propped a rifle in the crook of his arm. "Let me take it down while those pussy hunters are off crying over themselves because something shot back for a change. That was the deal—I get my reputation back."

Eddie. Maks's memory snagged on it. *Not quite right. Ed...*

No. It was *Eduard...*

Eduard seemed to find humor in Akins's words. "You were seen fighting the beast," he said, unconcerned and moving closer. "That should be enough for your reputation." He moved another step closer to the creature, his hand reaching into a pocket.

Maks gave him a silent whisker-tipping snarl, anchoring claws in thin soil to haul himself out from beneath the creature—to try. Scrabbling with all his strength, weakened by the shattered collarbone...he sank splayed claws into the nearest small tree and only succeeded in uprooting it.

He gained an inch, maybe two. His blood splattered the rocks; his breath rasped in his throat. The pain blazed up to rip right through him, telling him for sure what he'd until now only guessed—that only his Sentinel nature still kept him alive at all.

"Oh, hell," Akins said with some disgust, as if Maks wasn't there at all—as if he wouldn't have torn them apart before he went down for good, had he gotten loose. "Just *fighting* it isn't the same. No good, Eddie."

Eduard's eyes glinted, a sudden hard obsidian. "Then, yes. You may shoot the fucking tiger. *When* I'm done with him." And Katie's expression changed, too, the pleading one, her grip shifting on the gun...her stance shifting to something more balanced, there where her injured ankle kept her on her knees.

"It's not the same," Akins muttered, but even in his obstinacy it was clear that he, too, had seen that look—that he respected it.

"No," Eduard said, with such little interest that it was plain how very much he simply didn't care. "It's not."

Akins stood back slightly at that, not missing the disdain of the words, or—belatedly—the distinct threat threading through Eduard's manner.

Eduard pulled an amulet from his pocket, then another. He strode to his creature, barely sparing Maks's panted snarl of greeting a glance, one of the amulets tucked into the palm of his hand. That the creature dwarfed him didn't seem to bother him at all, and as Akins looked on in obvious impatience, Eduard upended his hand above the coarse, grizzled hair of the creature's side, and the amulet snapped to it like a magnet. The creature jerked in response, quivering; the movement tickled a cough up from Maks's lungs and then instant, blinding pain and suddenly he couldn't get enough air, just couldn't—

Couldn't get enough—

"Shee-it," Akins said. "It's not dead yet!"

"It's thoroughly dead," Eduard said. "Keep your rifle on Altán, you imbecile. If you think he can't still kill you, you're a fool."

"Keep my rifle on—what—?" Akins stared stupidly at Maks, at the quivering creature.

"The *tiger*," Eduard said impatiently.

"It's all but dead," Akins said, full of scorn.

"You *are* a fool," Eduard muttered, and under his hand the creature juddered, its skin suddenly crawling with movement. The weight of it eased; Maks shifted slightly, finding purchase with the single back leg that responded. He breathed past the pain, finding a shallow rhythm that sucked in just enough air to tamp down the panic of suffocation.

He could still reach Akins. He could still reach Eduard. He could still watch them die.

"Hey," Akins said, watching the javelina, suddenly understanding. "I mean, what *the hell,* Eddie—"

Gone. The javelina was gone. The amulet in Eduard's hand turned even darker, sucking in the light around it... dimming the very air—the taste of it churning the blood in Maks's throat into something foul. And yet he gathered himself. Not outwardly, where they could see, but within, steeling himself for the effort. Outwardly, he was the dying tiger, sickened all the more by the Core working.

Akins looked as though he might throw up. "Eddie..."

"Eduard," the Core rogue said tightly, his hand closing around the amulet with hard satisfaction. "It's *Eduard.*" He tucked the amulet away, pushed the other into his palm, and advanced on Maks.

"No," Katie said, her voice just as determined as her expression. "You leave him alone. You've done *enough,* both of you."

"Katie Rae," Akins said, with a patronizing approval. "Who knew you actually had backbone?"

"Leave him," she said, *"alone."* And she pulled the trigger, over and over.

Akins flinched, ducking wildly—and Eduard paid her no mind at all. The bullets flew wild, and if Katie realized that Core workings sent them astray, she couldn't absorb it—not when it had probably taken everything within her to pull that trigger in the first place. In an instant, the semiautomatic's clip had emptied, and the slide locked back into place.

Akins straightened. "Why, you little bitch. You would have done it, wouldn't you? Killed me over an animal!"

"You're the animal," she said, and her chin only quivered once before she lifted it.

Eduard stepped forward. Akins headed for Katie, steps full of purpose. And Maks rolled to his haunches.

No more warning than that, and he leaped—not for Eduard, practically within reach, but past him. For Akins. Akins, who headed for Katie—who had invaded her life for his simple, greedy, human reasons.

Akins, who knew nothing of shields and the Core and larger battles, but everything of cruelty.

One crippled, agonizing, shortened leap, as he brushed right past Eduard. Another, and Akins would go down. Akins screamed, hoarse and short, as he saw it coming.

But that final leap never came. In his mind, it did; in his intent it did. In reality he sank down instead of surging forth, his limbs no longer his to command, his wounded flank drawing at him. He tipped his head up, roaring protest; it echoed along the base of the outcrop and out into the trees.

Eduard stepped away, hardly ruffled, his eerie features full of satisfaction. Maks didn't understand it at first—not with all his focus on fighting the tug of darkness, the hot strokes of pain radiating down his body. And not with all his intent on reaching Akins—on reaching Katie, who had thrown away the gun and scrambled to her feet, standing on one leg with the other toe barely touching the ground.

And then he saw Eduard's empty hands, and understood all too well. *Core amulet.* The same working that had already sucked the creature dry and gone was now attached to his own flank.

Akins drew himself up as if he'd already convinced himself that his scream had never happened, and reached for Katie once more. She didn't seem to care, didn't even seem to notice—not as she stared in horror at Maks.

Eduard snapped, "Have a care, Mr. Akins! She is not to be damaged further!"

Akins snapped, "She would have *shot* me," and grabbed for Katie.

Didn't grab her.

Tried again, with both hands, anger rising—grabbed her hard.

Didn't grab her at all.

"What the hell?" he demanded.

Katie laughed, a sound on the verge of hysteria, and wobbling with fear—but not for herself. "Maks, take them back. Take back the shields. This man won't hurt me! God knows why, but he wants me. *Take back the shields,* Maks, please!"

As if he ever would. Not until the hunters returned, realizing finally that things were not exactly as they'd thought them to be—that not all the humans were on the same side, and not all of them meant well. That Katie needed their protection.

"Maks," she said fiercely, "I will never forgive you!"

It struck deep; he lifted his head to look at her, suddenly aware of how heavy it had gone, and that he'd let it settle to the rocks at all. Her image doubled, reverberating overtones of red…*the fugue.* He found her gaze anyway, and growled at her…a beseeching sound.

"No!" she said. "I won't!"

His growl turned into a deep groan, driven out by faltering lungs and the world turning inside out, right there on his flank, and Eduard's inexplicable words at his ear. "There, there," he said, with no comfort in his voice at all, "it'll be over soon. Inconsiderate of me, I know—we do this after the source body is already dead, but I simply couldn't resist a little plundering of your most excellent living energies."

"Hey," Akins said, no more than a distant voice in spite of his proximity—because now, for Maks, there was only Katie, only the graceful slender nature of her, swaying slightly on one leg, one hand reaching out to him. Akins's voice was only a grating in his ears. "I don't know what the hell, but you said I could—"

"Tsk, Mr. Akins. I've told you that you'll have your turn. I'll leave enough of him for you to put a bullet into, among other things."

Maks's rasping attempt at a snarl nearly obscured Katie's gasp—he could only imagine her expression. He could no longer see it, not with the whirlpool sucking at his life and returning only darkness. He reached out for the feel of her, knowing he'd find only the slick surface of his own shielding—shields that would fail soon enough.

Only until the hunters got back...

That was all the longer the shields had to last.

Maks let go of the outside world and dug inward, hunting the roots of the shields—so deep, so central...the place where everything clicked hard into place. If he poured of himself into it, *everything* of himself—

Everything.

Maks burrowed deep among his own roots of power— pieces of him trickling out to awareness of Katie: the tension of her body, the strangled cry in her throat, the piercing throb of her ankle. A tiny piece of himself wrapping around her—taking protection there, even as he protected her.

For as long as it lasted.

Chapter 21

"You bastard," Katie said, glaring at the bizarrely formal little man in his morning tails and supercilious attitude, wishing the gun still filled her hand, replete with bullets. "I don't even know you."

"Don't you?" He cocked his head as though disappointed in her. "Think back several months, Miss Maddox. The profoundly ugly reservation dog with the liver damage. No doubt it got into something it shouldn't have eaten, that's what you said at the time."

Thin, scarred, a dull yellow creature with prick ears and an upright curve of a tail. And this man...dressed in jeans and an ugly polo shirt, his hair less styled, his eyes behind outdated glasses, his manner mild. Undercover Core.

"I see you *do* remember," he said, approving. "I was quite impressed with the work you did. I need your assistance in one of my own endeavors."

It didn't make sense. She shot a glance at Akins, who

stood in pure frustration—a bully unable to bully, his fist clenched at his side, his rifle in the other hand, his face flushed with emotion.

The Core rogue interpreted that glance very well, even as he watched Maks's helpless throes with satisfaction. "A tool," he said of Akins. "About to complete its usefulness."

Akins might not know what that meant. Katie did. The Core rogue would not leave mundane witnesses to his workings.

In fact, Akins muttered, "About damned time, Eddie. Lady, you've been nothing but trouble," as he raised his rifle to Katie, interpreting those words as wrongly as he possibly could. He looked after the hunters, as if wary of their return—but those who hadn't been hurt were still caring for their own, not understanding Katie's peril or Akins's true nature. Not even beginning to understand the Core, or that the tiger who had come from nowhere was her Maks.

Maks, who now twisted in agony, a bloody froth at his mouth and a heinous Core amulet over one hip. He needed her healing, and he needed her voice, her caring…the caring touch of a love discovered.

Katie was tired of being the prey, tired of hiding…tired of taking her cues from a single side of her inescapable deer nature.

The deer was swift. The deer was persistent. The deer could fight back when cornered.

Maybe this time she wouldn't wait until she was completely cornered.

She lurched forward, the merest hint of weight on her bad ankle—the one so badly twisted by the Core minion who even now made his long, crashing way back down the outcrop.

"Where do you think you're going?" Akins snapped at

her, bullying for the sake of it. "Sit your ass down and face facts. Your manly friend ran off and left you here. Cowardly sonuvabitch."

"Shut up," Katie told him, her words full of calm, striking intensity. She took another hop toward Maks, who had subsided, no longer even twitching, but simply deflating, there in his twisted posture; urgency drove her. *It can't be too late. It can't.* Not while she still had the shields. "You, Roger Akins, are a mewling, nasty little schoolyard bully, and you're in over your head. You don't matter to me, and you don't matter to him." She jerked her head in the Core rogue's direction, her hands busy with her balance.

Akins snatched at her again, unable to stop himself; his hands slipped away from her, closing on nothing. Katie stopped long enough to give him a bitter smile. "You see? In over your head. You know *nothing,* and you're about to die. You won't have the tiger, you won't have your reputation, and you won't have *me.*"

He snarled a long string of curses, stepping back, lifting the rifle—not, with a glance at the Core rogue, to aim at Katie.

To aim at *Maks.*

She had no idea how long the shields would last; she had no idea if they would stop a rifle bullet point-blank. But she didn't throw herself at the rifle, hoping to wrench it aside; she didn't wait for Akins to heed the rogue's snapped command. She threw herself at what mattered most, a single bound across rock that wrung the last bit of effort from her ankle, that covered more ground than Akins or the rogue or even Katie herself had thought possible of a one-legged woman. And as the rogue shouted in alarm, warning Akins off, as Akins snapped the rifle to his shoulder to put Maks in his sights and pull the trigger, Katie threw herself over the tiger, covering his body with hers, her face pressed up close to his bleeding flank and to that appalling amulet.

Akins's shot rent the air, a spike of sound.

Katie barely felt the impact—high against her back, where it would have shattered her spine. She barely heard the rogue's escalating anger. She felt only Maks, the rough warmth of him through the fading shields, the thickness of his fur, the muscles gone limp. The amulet pulsed malevolent darkness inches from her nose, a thick and gathering malaise.

Katie didn't think twice. She slipped her still-shielded hand between Maks and the amulet—*shoved*—and flipped it away with violent disgust.

"Maks," she whispered, resting her face against fur. "I know you're in there. I *know*..." For the shields still slipped between them, paper thin and growing thinner.

"What the fu—" Akins's voice had gone up an octave. "Eddie, whatever the hell this thing is...get it off, get it *off*—"

Katie's fingers sank deeply into fur—too deeply, the hard outer coat making way for the soft undercoat, the sensation of it both luxurious and alarming...the shields were fading fast. And she mourned the biggest irony of all, that she couldn't reach him for healing until the shields were gone and it was too late—and then this rogue and his men would snatch her up and leave Maks to his death.

"Off!" Akins shrieked. "Ohmigod, get it off!"

She saw it, then—that he'd followed her to Maks, that he'd been close enough—no doubt reaching for her—that he'd been directly in the path of the amulet as she flung it away.

That he, human in all ways, had neither the great strength nor reserves of a Sentinel. He went to his knees even as she looked, his face contorting with pain. "Eddie!

Eddie, get it—" His words degenerated into a panting howl; he writhed as Maks had writhed, going down to the rocks.

The rogue stood over him. "Eduard," he said coldly. "You may call me Eduard. And then you may die."

And the shield between Katie and Maks, the shield whose very presence meant that Maks was still there...

The shield slipped away, and Katie buried her face in the tiger's fur and keened bitter grief.

Maks hid from the pain, hid from loss, hid from the truth. Broken tiger, unable to protect that which he loved. *Again.*

Not that he'd stopped trying—still pouring the last of himself into that shield.

And there, in that deep place, he felt a warm breath. Barely perceptible, a steady and calm wash of peace. A tug of comfort. It came with an insistence—a little bit pushy, a whole lot persistent. It came with a taste.

Katie.

Katie Rae.

The love of Katie Rae.

The *healing* of Katie Rae.

If he let her.

Let someone else take care of you, Maks, she'd told him, and the undercurrent of it ran through the this new connection. *Let it be me. Now.*

Maks breathed of her.

The darkness grew less dense. His ear flicked at a ragged sound—an intake of breath. Fingers clenched in the fur over his shoulders. He smelled the salt of her tears and of his blood, and the raw nature of her stress, but the bitter corruption of the Core workings could not reach them here.

Shields, Maks. He poured of himself into them, just

as Katie poured of herself into him, and he pushed them out—no longer skimming along their bodies, but retaking a buffer space.

Eduard's voice intruded into the healing. "You should have died," he said, oddly reproachful. "You would have saved me some trouble, and saved yourself a lot of pain. The woman will be mine; I have need of her."

"Maks," Katie breathed, and she made his name sound like a caress. "You're still there. But the shields..."

And because there was nothing between them any longer, he could show her, even from his struggling-to-consciousness state, what she hadn't understood.

For the shields had never *gone*. Once she buried her fingers in his fur and reached out to him with her heart—once they were touching—the shields had seen them as one, flowing back around Maks to protect them both.

And now, with Katie protected, with Maks protected... they no longer needed the tiger, exposed out here in the rocks...risking Sentinel secrets.

Maks shivered back to awareness, enough to see the inside of his eyelids instead of the deep recesses of a fading soul. It meant leaving the peace Katie had given him and returning to what Eduard and his creature had wrought— to a strained and broken body that, once human, would be more broken yet.

But it was time.

He reached for the human, and when he opened his eyes, he found Katie already adjusting, kneeling beside him so as to spare his body her weight.

"Now you're just showing off," Eduard said, casting an impatient glance toward the bottleneck of the approach to the outcrop and its modest clearing. "And I'm running out of time. The woman will be mine, Maks, just as your mother was mine. If those hunters come back before you relinquish her, they will die—is that what you want? One life, or many?"

As if Maks had a voice, jammed up against the rocks, blood streaming from his flank and his shoulder, the jagged pain of it battering against his ability to think, his vision teetering on the edge of gray sparkles, he struggled to draw breath, the bite of hot metal at the back of his tongue.

He used his eyes instead, as Katie looked over her shoulder at Eduard, her hand on his arm—Katie, the only reason he was conscious and breathing at all. *You can't have any of them.*

"Maks," she whispered in protest, and left it at that—it was enough. The healing would keep him alive; it wouldn't put him back into a fighting fettle.

"Everyone all right back here?"

That was the hunter, still out of sight—the big guy who had ignored the impossibility of what he'd seen to do the necessary things—fighting an impossible creature, eyeing an impossible tiger. He, too, would die at Eduard's hand if he joined them—or at the hands of the Core minion even now coming around the outcrop to join them.

"Akins was always meant to die," Eduard said. "As were you, Maks. But if you do the smart thing, Katie will survive; she is a resource to me, and I will keep her safe. If you do the smart thing, then the remaining hunters will survive, also—and I'll make sure that Katie's disappearance is blamed on Akins, as I always planned." The man shrugged, shifting the entire morning coat. "If not, then you all die. And the blame will rest on you. I can make sure of that."

Katie who had protected him…healed him…awoken him.

Katie who held his heart, every bit as much as she now clutched his hand.

Maks lifted his chin in a silent defiance, and for once he didn't feel the lack of words. He had his expression. He had his eyes. He had his intent.

And he had his shields.

He *pushed*—and he pushed hard. He gave no warning, and he gave no quarter. The shields enlarged, a shockwave of energy slapping through the clearing and smacking up against Eduard—no longer a protection, but a weapon.

Eduard staggered back, his hubris punctured by surprise—and then a second, more horrified reaction, as he slapped at his coat—first one pocket, then another, and finally understanding as the amulets detonated. He shed the coat as fast as he could even as he stumbled away, patting at himself like a man afire. The coat hung up on one arm and he flailed at it, tugging and yanking until a tearing sound heralded his release.

Katie sucked in a breath, her hand tightening around Maks's, daring to glance away from Eduard to catch Maks's gaze—to ask, wordlessly, if he was seeing what she did.

Yes.

Eduard, looking older by the moment. Eduard, stripped of workings and protections and deflating before their eyes, his posture hunching, his legs bowing slightly, his pants sagging.

He looked down at himself; his hands touched his leathery face, clawed desperately at his eyes. He made a sound more animal than any tiger, a gurgling cry of anguish—and then he fled. Not fast, not steady…but the only person chasing him was himself. In the silence that followed, a shocked curse muttered through the air—Eduard's minion, just around the lower point of the outcrop and about to make his appearance.

He changed his mind.

"Hey!" the hunter yelled, just coming into sight and

stopping in confusion—not finding the creature, not finding the tiger, not finding Akins or Eduard. He eyed them warily, taking it all in…buying time to sort it all out—or to try.

Finally he said, "Jay's hiking up to get a signal, get a rescue team in here. You guys good for now, or…well, hell, buddy, you gonna make it?"

Katie took a deep breath, her hand once more closing over Maks's—a reassurance this time. She'd be okay. He'd be okay. They could do this. They *were*.

"We'll manage," she said. "It looks worse than it is."

"Hell if it does," the man muttered. And then, a puzzled and healthy skepticism on his face, "But what—I mean, did you see—" He shook his head, apparently deciding just not to say the words. "You sure you're good?"

"Oh, yes," Katie told him. "We're good."

And Maks, sprawled on the rocks with far too much of his blood leaking out, found that he hardly cared. He looked up at her disheveled hair, her torn shirt, her tear-streaked face, her brown eyes bright with the awareness of what thrummed around and between them, and discovered that, as usual, he simply didn't have the words he needed.

And that this time, it didn't matter at all.

Chapter 22

Healer, heal thyself, Katie thought as she sat on the front porch rocker with her hands tucked up on the edge of the seat, her hand steadying a tumbler of ice water and the other hand running across the remaining swelling in her ankle.

Self-healing turned out to be a tricky thing, at that.

From her perch, she watched a tiger limping heavily around the yard—just inside the treeline, and on occasion completely obscured.

There were others here now—examining Eduard's discarded coat and the ruined amulets within it, attempting and failing to track him to the lair that Maks could describe from ancient memories but for which he'd never known a location. The entire area was absent of any scent other than that of Core workings.

Even the scent of the javelina had faded.

Katie could still smell it in her memory; she'd always

smell it in her memory. She'd always remember Maks, struggling to stay conscious once the hunters returned, his eyes gone confused...his hand reaching for hers as an anchor. She'd tried to tell him they were safe, that he could rest...

It had been a blessing when he'd finally passed out.

By then, brevis had been well on the way, healers in tow. Not Ruger, the bear healer who could have done so much for Maks, but the best they could scoop up along the way.

By then, the hunters had been packing out with their wounded, looking for a high spot that would give the rescue chopper access. The two who remained—the woman and the biggest of them—

Katie closed her eyes against the sudden sting of tears, her hand closing around her ankle as if she, too, needed an anchor.

"Please," the woman had said. "The dogs...they're suffering—they need mercy. And we heard..."

We heard what you did with the cat. We've heard the rumors. Angel of mercy.

She'd only looked at them, wary and withdrawn, her ankle puffed to twice its size and taking all the attention that Maks didn't already have. She'd shaken her head. "You have the tools to do the job," she told them, and meant it. An expert bullet, a sharp knife. The dogs were beyond fear or understanding.

It was the man who'd said it, his expression full of all the things he was asking—forgiveness for believing or participating in those rumors, forgiveness for allowing Akins to be part of them. Forgiveness for leaving her with the man, for it hadn't taken them long to understand who had shot Maks, after all, and from there to understand the game Akins had been playing.

All those things. And then he'd said, "But that would just be ending it. You can give them peace."

So she'd done it. But there was always a price.

Whiskers tickled her face, inspecting the tears; the tiger behind them gave a chuff-chuff-rattly purr, and then rubbed his head against her face. The chair rocked back; the ice water went flying. Katie flailed for balance as the chair went just...nearly...too...far—and her hands closed around a strong neck, a steady arm. She opened her eyes to Maks, and to the smile in his eyes. He brushed his knuckles across her cheek.

"Fine," she grumbled. "Be adorable. Deprive me of a perfectly good scold."

"You were thinking of the woods." He didn't have to explain how he knew. Either he'd seen it in her face or he'd felt some trickle of it. It had been hard to hide such things, since his initiation. Since *their* initiation.

"The woods," she agreed. "And other things."

Such as the vision she'd had...the one that went beyond what had happened at the clearing. Its grief tugged at her, profound and wearying...an entire people in mourning. *Her* people, prey and predator alike. That aspect of the vision still hung over her like a pall...still unresolved.

Maks sat on the top step of the porch, easing himself down with care. His bare toes stuck out in the sunshine and the rest of him in shadow. His jeans weren't snapped and his shirt wasn't buttoned, and it couldn't have been more obvious that he'd rolled out of bed—*their* bed—and into a minimum of clothes before he'd taken the tiger to prowl the perimeter.

Brevis had withdrawn from the area—back to regroup, with a new team already forming to return and cleanse the area of Core bolt-holes. Maks had only stayed in Brevis Medical long enough for them to plate his collarbone back together, stuff him full of antibiotics and healing brews and put him through a few strong, hard sessions of healing. Then he'd come back to Katie. Limping, wounded, still healing…but whole again nonetheless.

The yellow cat yawned from his corner basket, made a token conversational noise, and went back to his nap. Minus his tail, minus one leg…still king of the cabin. Katie reached down to rub a knuckle over his forehead, and joined Maks on the stairs.

"They'll want you back, you know," she said, and then leaned against him, twining her fingers through his.

"Sometimes," he agreed. He resettled his hand around hers, firm and warm and matter-of-fact. "Sometimes not."

"Maks," she said, squinting out into the bright morning sunshine. "Tell me you didn't bother to put anything on under those jeans this morning."

"Didn't," he agreed.

"Hmm," she said, a sound of both contentment and speculation. "First client's not for two hours."

His hand tightened around hers, and though he looked out on the yard, it was with a smile.

They heard the car at the same time—a car achingly familiar to Katie, and familiar enough to Maks that his initial reaction settled into a wariness—and a question.

The last time Marie had come up that driveway, it had been to fling the worst of accusations.

The hell of it was, she hadn't been totally wrong. Her Rowdy had finally eaten the wrong thing, and Katie would never fully be able to explain the truth of it.

Marie's car rocked to a stop; Maks's free arm slipped around Katie's back, his hand resting on her hip and snugging her in with only the faintest hint of pressure. An effort, that was, with the shoulder still healing, and only still a working shoulder at all because of his Sentinel nature.

"It's okay," she told him, her voice very low. It didn't matter that the hunters had sung her praises, or that her business was as it had always been, or that people greeted her with cheer in the shops and on the street. There were some things that couldn't be fixed.

She didn't get up as Marie exited the car, closing the door with a firm, matter-of-fact shove and then heading to the back hatch of the sturdy little Outback, where she rummaged briefly.

When she emerged, she had a young dog under her arm—a brindled thing with white socks and a blocky head and thin, happy tail. As she grew closer, it was easy to see that the animal had healing scrapes and far too many visible ribs, but its tail never stopped wagging.

Marie looked at them both, taking in not only Maks's presence, but his obvious claim on Katie.

"I found this guy by the side of the road," she said, in something of a determined rush. "The vet says he's fine, but…I thought if you had time…I was wondering if you'd look him over."

Katie drew a sharp breath, bit her lip on the renewed sting of tears. It was easy to feel Maks stiffen, ready to protect her, even in this small way. "It's okay," she told him, squeezing the hand she still held. "It's good."

He was slow to let go of her hand as she rose, but as she reached out for the young dog, his fingers slipped from hers, if only to trail down her calf for one final squeeze.

"I'll watch for you," he said.

And he did.

* * * * *

Sentinels Mythos/Glossary

Long ago and far away, in Roman/Gaulish days, one woman had a tumultuous life—she fell in love with a druid, by whom she had a son; the man was killed by Romans, and she was subsequently taken into the household of a Roman, who also fathered a son on her. The druid's son turned out to be a man of many talents, including the occasional ability to shapeshift, albeit at great cost. (His alter-shape was a wild boar.) The woman's younger son, who considered himself superior in all ways, had none of these earthly powers, and went hunting other ways to be impressive, acquire power. He justified his various activities by claiming he needed to protect the area from his brother, who had too much power to go unchecked...but in the end, it was his brother's family who grew into the Vigilia, now known as the Sentinels, while the younger son founded what turned into the vile Atrum Core.

Sentinels *An organization of power-linked individuals whose driving purpose is to protect and nurture the earth—as befitting their druid origins—while also keeping watch on the activities of the Atrum Core.*
Vigilia *The original Latin name for the Sentinels, discarded in recent centuries under Western influence.*
Brevis Regional *HQ for each of the Sentinel regions.*

Consul *The leader of each brevis region.*

Adjutant *The consul's executive officer.*

Aeternus contego *The strongest possible ward, tied to the life force of the one who sets it and broken only at that person's death. In Jaguar Night, Meghan Lawrence places one of these on Fabron Gausto, reflecting any workings he performs back on himself.*

Vigilia adveho *A Sentinel mental long-distance call for help.*

Monitio *A warning call.*

Nexus *The Sentinel who acts as a central point of power control—such as for communications, wards or power manipulation.*

Atrum Core *An ethnic group founded by and sired by the Roman's son, their basic goal is to acquire power in as many forms as possible, none of which is natively their own; they claim to monitor and control the "nefarious" activities of the Sentinels.*

Amulets *The process through which the Core inflicts its workings of power on others, having gathered and stored (and sometimes stolen) the power from other sources.*

Drozhar *The Atrum Core regional prince.*

Septs Prince *The Atrum Core prince of princes.*

Septs Posse *A drozhar's favored sycophants; can be relied on to do the dirty work.*

Sceleratus vis *Ancient forbidden workings based on power drawn from blood, once used by the Atrum Core.*

Workings *Workings of power, assembled and triggered via amulets.*

REQUEST YOUR FREE BOOKS!

2 FREE NOVELS FROM THE PARANORMAL ROMANCE COLLECTION PLUS 2 FREE GIFTS!

YES! Please send me 2 FREE novels from the Paranormal Romance Collection and my 2 FREE gifts (gifts are worth about $10). After receiving them, if I don't wish to receive any more books, I can return the shipping statement marked "cancel." If I don't cancel, I will receive 4 brand-new novels every month and be billed just $21.42 in the U.S. or $23.46 in Canada. That's a saving of at least 21% off the cover price of all 4 books. It's quite a bargain! Shipping and handling is just 50¢ per book in the U.S. and 75¢ per book in Canada.* I understand that accepting the 2 free books and gifts places me under no obligation to buy anything. I can always return a shipment and cancel at any time. Even if I never buy another book, the two free books and gifts are mine to keep forever.

237/337 HDN FEL2

Name _____ (PLEASE PRINT)

Address _____ Apt. #

City _____ State/Prov. _____ Zip/Postal Code

Signature (if under 18, a parent or guardian must sign)

Mail to the **Reader Service:**
IN U.S.A.: P.O. Box 1867, Buffalo, NY 14240-1867
IN CANADA: P.O. Box 609, Fort Erie, Ontario L2A 5X3

Not valid for current subscribers to the Paranormal Romance Collection
or Harlequin® Nocturne™ books.

Want to try two free books from another line?
Call 1-800-873-8635 or visit www.ReaderService.com.

* Terms and prices subject to change without notice. Prices do not include applicable taxes. Sales tax applicable in N.Y. Canadian residents will be charged applicable taxes. Offer not valid in Quebec. This offer is limited to one order per household. All orders subject to credit approval. Credit or debit balances in a customer's account(s) may be offset by any other outstanding balance owed by or to the customer. Please allow 4 to 6 weeks for delivery. Offer available while quantities last.

Your Privacy—The Reader Service is committed to protecting your privacy. Our Privacy Policy is available online at www.ReaderService.com or upon request from the Reader Service.

We make a portion of our mailing list available to reputable third parties that offer products we believe may interest you. If you prefer that we not exchange your name with third parties, or if you wish to clarify or modify your communication preferences, please visit us at www.ReaderService.com/consumerschoice or write to us at Reader Service Preference Service, P.O. Box 9062, Buffalo, NY 14269. Include your complete name and address.

PARA11

HARLEQUIN®

SYTYCW

SO YOU THINK YOU CAN WRITE

Harlequin and Mills & Boon are joining forces in a global search for new authors.

In September 2012 we're launching our biggest contest yet—with the prize of being published by the world's leader in romance fiction!

Look for more information on our website, **www.soyouthinkyoucanwrite.com**

So you think you can write? Show us!

*In the newest continuity series from Harlequin®
Romantic Suspense, the worlds of the Coltons and their
Amish neighbors collide—with dramatic results.*

*Take a sneak peek at the first book, COLTON DESTINY
by Justine Davis, available September 2012.*

"**I**'m here to try and find your sister."

"I know this. But don't assume this will automatically ensure trust from all of us."

He was antagonizing her. Purposely.

Caleb realized it with a little jolt. While it was difficult for anyone in the community to turn to outsiders for help, they had all reluctantly agreed this was beyond their scope and that they would cooperate.

Including—in fact, especially—him.

"Then I will find these girls without your help," she said, sounding fierce.

Caleb appreciated her determination. He *wanted* that kind of determination in the search for Hannah. He attempted a fresh start.

"It is difficult for us—"

"What's difficult for me is to understand why anyone wouldn't pull out all the stops to save a child whose life could be in danger."

Caleb wasn't used to being interrupted. Annie would never have dreamed of it. But this woman was clearly nothing like his sweet, retiring Annie. She was sharp, forceful and very intense.

"I grew up just a couple of miles from here," she said. "And I always had the idea the Amish loved their kids just as we did."

"Of course we do."

"And yet you'll throw roadblocks in the way of the people best equipped to find your missing children?"

Caleb studied her for a long, silent moment. "You are very angry," he said.

"Of course I am."

"Anger is an…unproductive emotion."

She stared at him in turn then. "Oh, it can be very productive. Perhaps you could use a little."

"It is not our way."

"Is it your way to stand here and argue with me when your sister is among the missing?"

Caleb gave himself an internal shake. Despite her abrasiveness—well, when compared to Annie, anyway—he could not argue with her last point. And he wasn't at all sure why he'd found himself sparring with this woman. She was an Englishwoman, and what they said or did mattered nothing to him.

Except it had to matter now. For Hannah's sake.

*Don't miss any of the books in this exciting
new miniseries from Harlequin® Romantic Suspense,
starting in September 2012 and running
through December 2012.*